A Court of Blood and Void

WAR OF THE GODS, #1

Meg Xuemei X

A Court of Blood and Void

First Edition
Silver Wheel Publishing
ISBN: 978-1726038638
Printed in the United States of America

Cover art by Andreea Vraciu
Edited by Dan McNeill

A Court of Blood and Void
(War of the Gods, #1)

They call me beautiful. They call me Monsters. Soon, they'll call me death.

As a direct descendant of the God of Death, Cassandra Saélihn is considered the most dangerous monster of all time. Her own mother locks her in a cage to protect the world from her. Cass thought this jail would be her world for a lifetime, but then four sexy, formidable warriors--a vampire lord, twin fae princes, and a demigod--find her.

They claim she's not a monster, but a powerful weapon. The Olympian gods have begun to destroy the Earth with a vengeance, and only she can stop and kill them. But Cass has a mind of her own and can't be told what to do, no matter how drawn she is to her four warrior saviors. To their dismay, the four warriors can't tame the wild, cunning, and volatile Cass. But they have a bigger problem--their growing attraction toward her.

To turn the woman they desire into the ultimate weapon and ensure Earth's survival, they'll have to conquer her body and heart, which seems even harder than winning the war against the atrocious gods. But nothing turns these alpha males on more than an impossible dare. And nothing turns Cass on more than being stalked.

TABLE OF CONTENTS

PROLOGUE

The Unseelie fae, heir to Sihde, stood atop the cliff and surveyed the scorched world. The expanse of ocean was no longer silky black glass but a dark crimson ripple of fire and blood. Behind him, just a few blackened stones and bricks remained amid the embers and ashes that had been his cabin.

The ward hadn't stopped the invaders—gods from Mount Olympus—from destroying his treasured vacation house.

Soon, this entire planet, home to immortals and mortals alike, would spin out of existence if Reysalor Iliathorr didn't find the only weapon that could kill the alien gods.

Thankfully, he'd received a vision showing him where to look for this weapon that was also his destined mate. She was hidden in a vampire court. To reach her, Reysalor would need the help of the High Lord of Night, a primordial vampire and his old rival. His twin, Pyrder, had set out to recruit another longtime foe, a ruthless demigod he would rather not see for another millennium.

The fae prince heaved a sigh, shifted into a black panther, and dashed away from his burned cabin by the reddened sea to secure a future for his people and Earth….or what was left of it.

1

I pulled at the bars of my cage, willing them to budge so I might slip between, but the iron wouldn't bend, just like yesterday, just like all the days before that. Yet every day I tried. And every day I hoped that I'd grown strong enough to finally break out of this prison.

My palms and fingers burned at the iron's touch. Blisters popped up on my skin. Iron itself couldn't harm me, but every inch of this cage was warded with the most potent, nastiest spells, designed to keep me in.

When the acid burning my palms became too much, I gave the bars one last violent shake and shrieked. "Let me out, you cunt! You can't keep me locked in here forever!"

The cage remained unaffected, as were the cold walls at the far end. It was deathly quiet here, except for my curses echoing off the walls.

I didn't slump to the hard ground. I didn't sob or beg, as I had during the first thirteen years. I paced in the cage, balling my scalded hands on my sides. My rage smoldered, yet it couldn't get me out of here.

Nothing could.

Even if I screamed myself hoarse, no one would hear me in this underground dome. My enchanted cage hung two feet above the ground to ensure that no supernatural force could sense my presence. The spells have also neutered my power, preventing it from leaving this cage.

Nevertheless, I threw up a hand and a current of air hit the bars, but it didn't rattle the metal. I sent a column of black fire to wrestle with every inch of the cage. The fire fizzled out in half a second.

My name is Cassandra Saélihn. My mother branded me as an extremely dangerous monster and locked me up in this cage when my magic manifested at the age of two, to keep the world safe from me.

"And to protect you from yourself," Jezebel had said ruefully, as if I would slit my own throat for fun.

I heard a click and stopped pacing. My head snapped toward the heavy, sealed door. It usually opened once a day, and sometimes once every few days. When days passed, anxiety drilled holes in my stomach. I dreaded that one day this door would never open again, and I'd be left to rot in here forever.

Blood rushed to my ears in anticipation as I watched the door open a crack. I prayed this time I'd see a difference person, only to find the same beautiful, innocent, and youthful face I sickened of seeing but was afraid to never see again.

Jezebel glided in regally and gracefully, carrying a tray of food and a mug of what I knew was cold tea. She took me in, her shoulders stiffening as she saw blood dripping from my palms.

She reached me in an instant, no longer pretending to be as slow as a mortal. She put the tray down on the desk a few feet outside the cage and perched on her usual seat.

"How are you today, Cassandra?" she asked gently.

"Fuck you."

She rubbed her temples, as if pitying herself for having to put up with me. "Cassandra," she sighed. "Will you ever stop hurting yourself?"

"It'll heal tomorrow."

"If you keep doing this, you'll make me sad. When I'm sad, I can't bear the sight of you, and I won't come see you for a month."

That meant I wouldn't have food for a month. She never intended to starve me, but she never let me have a full stomach, for fear I would grow too strong for her to control.

"Mother…" I hadn't begged her for a very long time. "Just let me out. I'm not a monster. You don't need to fear me. No one needs to fear me. I've never even hurt an ant."

She dropped her gaze to the ground, as if looking for ant corpses.

"Let me out of this cage, please, Mother," I said, my voice sweet and innocent. "I'll stay far away from you. I'll stay out of your sight forever, and you won't need to burden yourself with me anymore."

"That's what I'm afraid of, Cassandra," she said, her big blue eyes so full of sorrow that, instinctively, I wanted to comfort her, forgetting for a moment who she was—my eternal tormentor. "Only I can bind you. Only I can protect you. By keeping you here, no one will ever find you, use you, and harm you. Don't you understand? It's hard for me, too, but I'm doing all this for you. You have no idea how much I've sacrificed for you."

Rage surged in me. I tried to contain it, but a muscle twitching on my clenched jaw betrayed how upset I was. If I lost my temper, Jezebel would punish me.

"Every action has a consequence, Cassandra." She told me that every time she was down here. "Now cheer up, my child. Look what I brought you. An apple."

"I don't want an apple," I said, though my stomach grumbled in gnawing hunger. "Let me out for a second, and then I'll return here willingly. Just let me see the sun, the sky, and the stars for once."

My voice was full of longing, but it didn't seem to move her.

Jezebel shook her head and breathed out a long-suffering sigh. "We've been over this, Cassandra. It's not going to work. I brought you to this world, so you're my responsibility. I must keep both you and the world safe."

I looked around the frosty stone walls, the unbreakable lock on the cage's door, and the iron bars surrounding me. I would never escape this prison. I would never get away from this mad woman who was my mother.

Bitterness speared into me, filling me, and I let every vicious thought I'd ever had spur my verbal attack.

"Do you enjoy it, Mother?" I asked, my gaze lingering on the small bite on her neck near her collarbone, my lips pulling back in a sneer. "You let the bloodsucker drink from you and fuck you every night. In exchange, he lets you do whatever you want with me. Maybe you should teach me how to whore myself out. You seem to have quite the knack for it."

Her eyes widened in shock. I'd never talked to her like that before. Automatically, she moved her hand to cover the little red bite mark on her skin.

"You can't hide it, Jezebel," I said. "You reek of sex and blood. Every time you come here, I smell his stench on you."

"How can you talk to your own mother like this?" she asked, still stunned, though her voice was now laced with resentment. "Where did this vulgarity come from?" She rose from seat indignantly and tossed the tray of food at the wall. "Everything I've done, I've done it for you."

"Whatever, you delusional bitch," I said.

I was done pretending to be a good girl. I was going to rot here anyway. She would never let me out. For over a decade I'd tried every possible way to get her to unleash me and failed. Now I wanted to bleed her a little, as she'd hurt me every day.

"I never asked you to trade sex and blood so you could lock me up," I said. "You're a fucking whore. That's exactly what you are. Own it and stop pretending to be a saint. You make me sick. Every time I see you, I want to puke my guts out."

Her face paled and her dark scarlet lips trembled. She looked at me, her child-like eyes full of tears, as if I was the monster and she was my victim.

"I won't come back for a month, Cassandra," she said in a determined, quivering voice. "Until you're fully calmed down. Until you learn manners."

I barked out a mirthless laugh. "You want me to learn fucking manners when my last meal was five days ago?"

With one last, devastated glance in my direction, Jezebel turned and headed to the door.

I stopped laughing. "You stupid cunt!" I screamed after her. "I never want to see your fucking face again. Send someone else next time."

The heavy door slammed shut behind her.

I knew I wouldn't see my mother for a month.

~

I lay in bed, staring at the blank ceiling above the bars of the cage, trying not to focus on my gnawing hunger. A mortal would have died, but I was more than an immortal with a powerful monster inside me—at least, that was what my mother had told me.

I didn't know exactly what I was, even though I had unbearable, endless time on my hands to ponder that. Jezebel kept the knowledge from me. She not only kept me in this cage; she kept me ignorant.

I snapped my head toward the door when a loud noise rose from it. Usually it clicked and slid open before Jezebel glided in.

This time it was different. A bang rocked the door. Someone was kicking at it. My pulse spiked as I watched the steel door bend out of shape.

Who had such strength? I bolted up in bed. It wasn't my mother. It had to be the enemy hunters she'd tried to keep away from me all these years.

They must have found me. They had come for me.

Welcome warmth lit inside me. Anyone was better than her.

When the door tumbled down, I stood at the edge of the cage, watching with interest.

A male—not just any male, but a breathtakingly gorgeous man—stepped onto the door on the ground and charged in. An enormous black panther trotted beside him.

My gaze flicked from the male to the beast, and every dormant cell in me swirled alive as if ignited with fire.

Both the male and the beast sniffed the air, their nostrils flaring, their eyes brightening, as if they'd just caught the most surprising, exquisite scent.

And here I was, unwashed.

I grinned at them predatorily.

2

The masculine, handsome male widened his eyes, and the panther snarled at the cage then at the male beside him.

The stranger was tall and muscled. An unbuttoned white trench coat draped over his dress shirt. A lock of dark hair brushed his strong jaw. His face was cold and hard like refined marble. His piercing gray eyes shone with intelligence as they homed in on me, tracing my every movement.

His scent of faint pine and aged fine wine wafted toward me, assaulting my senses.

He was a vampire.

As soon as I identified his species, an old hatred rose in me.

Had he come for my blood?

A dark light flashed through my eyes. I knew how enticing my blood was. Jezebel's blood was nectar to a vampire, better than any mortal's or immortal's. The vampire king was so addicted to her that he'd do anything for her.

My blood was richer and sweeter than hers.

The male vampire wouldn't be able to resist the call of my blood. I could already tell by the flare of his nostrils and the intense heat in his eyes.

Come to me, boy.

If he wanted it, I could get him to free me. And then I would show him I would be more trouble than I was worth if he got his fangs near my neck.

First, I had to pretend to be meek.

The vampire's hungry look vanished in a blink, and his face became unreadable. If I hadn't had superior sight, I would have believed I'd imagined his lust.

I darted a glance at the panther. The beast hadn't taken his eyes from me. His golden irises burned with rage. He growled at the vampire, as if sending him a message. I watched them. The panther didn't seem to be the vampire's pet.

A panther thought he was equal to a vampire?

The vampire shot an irritated look at the panther before once again fixing his intense gaze on me. I stared back, aware I might never have another visitor if I missed the

opportunity. The bloodsucker was my only ticket out of
here.

Soft noises rose from outside the door.

I tilted my head to listen. The vampire and the panther
weren't alone. They had a team, waiting out of sight. They
were stealthy, but I could detect them.

They were all vampires, and none of them had
heartbeats. Jezebel wasn't among them, neither was her
vampire lover.

I wanted to know what had happened.

Another vampire horde might have taken over this lair.
That would have been a nice change. I could have missed the
sound of battle in my insulated hell hole.

A vampiress strode in with a cocky air and stood on the
other side of the sexy vampire. She crinkled her nose at my
stink, and I smirked at her.

She was a pale-skinned, green-eyed knockout. Her
blonde hair flowed down to her elegant shoulders, which
suddenly made me self-conscious of my wild, knotted hair.

The panther growled at her, disliking her presence in the
room. He'd marked this cell as his space.

The male vampire ignored the beast, his gray eyes never
leaving me.

"Jade," he addressed the vampiress without turning his head. "Your presence is not required. Clear the area. No one gets near. I need to interrogate this girl alone."

Surprise marred Jade's beautiful, cold face, and a muscle twitched on her jaw. Judging from the reaction, I'd bet money, if I had any, that he'd never dismissed her like this before.

Her icy eyes shot knives at me. That look told me all I needed to know—she regarded me as a rival and a threat.

What had I ever done to this bitch for her to be so hostile?

I gave her a taunting grin. I didn't like people looking at me like that.

"Yes, my lord," she said, and retreated as swiftly as a shadow.

I made a mental note of Jade's speed, as well as that she was his weapon, and perhaps more than that.

And this vampire dude in front of me was a lord.

He stepped closer toward my cage, primordial power rolling off him. I flashed a disarming smile at him to make him come nearer, and he did.

"Hello," I purred. "Who the fuck are you?"

He frowned at me, and then his eyes widened, as if he was struck by lightning.

His heart started beating and I had to force myself not to reel back from the surprise.

What the actual fuck?

I pricked my ears, tilted my head, and listened again. In the entire area on this level of the floor, there were only three heartbeats—his, the panther's, and mine.

Why did he suddenly have a heartbeat? I purred, and the vampire's heart started pumping.

The panther snapped his head toward the vampire lord and bared his teeth in a half-snarl. I hadn't been mistaken. The panther heard the vampire's heartbeat as well and he wasn't thrilled.

The vampire stumbled back, clutching his hand over his heart. An instant later, he realized his own reactions and quickly removed his hand from his muscled chest.

His expression became unreadable once again. He stepped toward me aggressively and stopped a foot from my cage. I didn't back down, but shock slammed me silent as heat rushed between my thighs as he entered my proximity.

His nostrils flared, as did the panther's.

Intense heat materialized in both the vampire's and the panther's eyes.

What kind of freak show is this?

Despite my fatigue from being starved, I clenched my fists on my side to stave off the liquid fire that continued to twirl around my lady bits, teasing and taunting my awakened lust. I'd never experienced anything like this. My body was out of control, and I didn't like it one iota.

"What the fuck did you do to me, vampire?" I hissed. "And why has your heart suddenly started beating? You're supposed to be undead, just like any other bloodsucker, right?"

His gray eyes narrowed, flashing with dangerous light that concealed his increased interest in me.

"I didn't expect you to have such a foul mouth and horrible manners." His voice was rich and stern; he was used to everyone obeying him. "That's exactly my question to you, girl. What did you do to end up here? And who are you?"

Despite hating vampires, despite my pent-up rage, I knew I shouldn't piss him off. I always had a temper, even as a powerless prisoner, and my fatigue wasn't helping me stay collected.

I rearranged my facial expression, hiding my scowl behind a sweet smile. "Let me out, and I'll tell you everything."

I even managed to send him a sultry look.

I had seen the flicker of intense hunger for me in his eyes. He was good at concealing it, but I was better at discovering my opponent's weakness.

Jezebel had once told me that no vampires could resist her blood, and my blood was superior to hers. She had no power—I'd never sensed an ounce of it in her. She'd complained that she was but a vessel used to bear a monster. But power coursed in me, screaming to get out every second of the day, yet the cage trapped both me and my power.

It was only natural that this vampire craved my blood.

"I'll even let you have a mouthful of my blood," I whispered. "I guarantee you it's like nothing you've ever tasted. All you need to do is open the cage."

The panther growled angrily and possessively, as if he didn't like what I had offered to the vampire.

A wave of heat and amusement flashed through the vampire lord's eyes, so fast that none but I could detect it.

"So you want to get out?" he asked.

"Who in their right mind likes being in a cage?"

"How long have you been here?"

"Too long."

"How long?" he repeated

"Since I was two years old," I said flatly.

The panther snarled, and a wince passed over the vampire's cold marble face. And again, it vanished in an instant.

Hmm. The vampire lord didn't like showing emotions.

"And you've never been out of the cage?" he asked, his voice clinical, as if he was analyzing a bug he poked around.

I was starting to lose my patience with him. He wanted answers out of me, yet he didn't seem eager to release me. I wouldn't give him anything until he set me free.

"If you want any information from me, you'll have to open the cage first."

"You'll need to answer a few more questions before I decide—"

My strategy of being sweet and enticing wasn't working. If I wasn't going to get out of here, I had nothing to lose by being myself.

I flipped him the bird. "Make me, motherfucker," I said, baring my teeth. "Why don't you come in here and get the answers?"

His face darkened with anger. I'd bet he had never suffered rudeness from anyone. I'd watched him dismiss his minions and they obeyed him as if their lives depended on it.

He was out of luck with me. I was a hell of a woman. He, and everyone else, could eat dirt if they thought they could intimidate me or make me follow any rules or social hierarchy my mother had tried to embed into my head when I was a young girl.

The panther, however, chuckled in approval at my defiance.

How could a beast even laugh? He must be extremely intelligent. I glanced fondly at the panther and controlled my urge to pat the white stripe on his nose. It was the only white on his pure, shiny black hide.

Sensing my affection, the panther edged toward me but kept his muzzle an inch away from the cage.

Smart beast.

I wasn't afraid of him, despite his formidable build. Strangely, I was so drawn to him.

I stuck my hand out between the bars, carefully not to touch the iron. I couldn't give the vampire a hint that the bar was riddled with spells. I touched the panther's snout, and he leaned his face into my hand with genuine affection.

The vampire growled at the panther. I'd thought him a rock who preferred not to display emotions.

"Reysalor, that's enough," the vampire lord said. "Quit playing. We have business here!"

The panther stuck out his tongue and gave me a rough lick before he padded back and snarled at the vampire in protest.

These two—a vampire and a beast—acted like rivals.

The vampire wasted no time stepping a half a foot toward the cage, shortening the distance between us.

I stood my ground. If he lashed out to grab my throat, I could use his hand to touch the iron bar and see if the spells worked on a vampire. If they didn't burn him, my black fire would love to get acquainted with him.

His piercing gray eyes swirled to liquid silver in an instant as they seized my gaze. The cold fire inside them tried to freeze me. Holy smokes! The fucker was using his power to enthrall me. If he achieved that, he'd make me spill my guts for free and bare my belly to beg for a scratch.

I peeked deep into his eyes, as if mesmerized. I even licked my lips to add to the effect.

"Now let's backtrack a little, girl," he demanded.

"Okay," I said meekly.

"Who are you?"

"I'm Cassandra Saélihn. How did you find me? Have you heard of me before? Did you really come for me? Who sent you?"

He frowned at me. His hypnotized subjects probably never bombarded him with questions.

"I'll ask the questions," he said firmly. "And you'll answer them truthfully."

"Yes, sir," I said cheerfully.

He gave me another stern look. "Cassandra—"

"No, I go by Cass," I said. "Call me Cass. Only my mother calls me Cassandra. I don't really like that name." I furrowed my brows. "It's too formal, too old-fashioned, and unattractive. By the way, what's your name? Does the panther have a name, too? He's adorable!"

That earned me another scowl from the vampire, though the panther grinned at me. This vampire lord was really no fun, despite that sexiness rolled off him constantly, even when he was so rigid.

"Fine, Cass," he grated. "You won't disrupt me again with long, unrelated answers. You'll get to the point."

I nodded like a good girl. "Okay, must get to the point. No longwinded answers. What's your next question?"

His lips thinned.

"Who imprisoned you?" he asked.

My playfulness vanished. "Jezebel, queen to the vampire king. Have you overthrown him and his army? Is that why you're here?" I shrugged. "That's perfectly fine with me. My enemy's enemy is my friend."

"What did I warn you about longwinded answers?" he asked.

I blinked. "Huh'?"

"Why did she imprison you?" he asked.

"Now this is getting boring," I said with a yawn, and I didn't even bother to cover my mouth. He didn't deserve my politeness. "I don't want to play anymore. Just so you know: your enthrallment experiment has failed. Do you do this a lot—bewitch naïve women? What's your success rate?"

His gray eyes widened in disbelief. Clearly, his success rate was high. Maybe he'd never failed before today.

"Why are you looking at me like that?" I said. "Got a thorn in your eyes?"

The panther rolled on the ground with barks of laughter, and the vampire cursed under his breath.

He gave up hexing me with his vampire power, his eyes wary now.

"Who are you, girl?' he asked again, his tone softening a notch.

"If you want to know, you'll have to let me out, bloodsucker," I said, stepping back, about to go lie down on my bed while he made his decision.

I was done with his game.

A wave of vertigo hit me, and my knees buckled. My hands spread in front of me, in an effort to cushion my fall, but to no avail. I hadn't realized that I'd been so weak after my confinement and starvation.

My left cheekbone hit the hard ground first.

The panther growled in urgency, and vampire shouted my name, "Cass! Cass!"

"She's starved!" I heard an unfamiliar male voice, but there was only one vampire in the room. Was the panther talking? I was hallucinating. "We need to get her out now and feed her. I shouldn't have listened to your bullshit about testing her first. If any harm comes to her, Lorcan, I'll make your life fucking hell. No, I don't even need to do that, the fucking gods will do you in better than I!"

I blacked out before I could see this new man who had spoken for me.

3

When I blinked back to consciousness, shouts, screams, and curses hurt my hypersensitive ears.

I was still down, my face planted against the cold ground. My head throbbed from the splitting pain, but mostly from hunger. I slowly peeled open an eye, taking in the partial surroundings.

Jezebel was in the room, along with her vampire husband and other vampires.

A golden crown sat atop the vampire king's head. He narrowed his eyes at me, as if I was a menace.

I struggled into a sitting position. The vertigo wasn't gone. I raised my head and grinned viciously. "Hello, Mother," I purred. "Nice of you to finally visit. What did you bring me this time? Your husband and more? How creative."

King Dario glared at me, but I winked at him. I was glad that for the first time a lot of people knew of my existence. I wasn't Jezebel's secret anymore, which meant I might finally have a chance to get out of this fucking cage.

But it was a bit humiliating having them all look at me like I was an animal in a zoo.

I ignored everyone but fixed my gaze on the vampire lord and the panther.

"Hey, Lorcan," I said. I'd gotten his name before I passed out. "Have you decided to let me out?"

"Yes, Cass," the vampire lord said. "I'm getting you out."

My heart jerked, and hope lit in my veins. Despite my nausea, I shot to my feet.

"Really?" I asked, grabbing the bars, and the iron burned into my skin. I yelped as smoke trailed up from my palms. I loosened my grip.

The panther whimpered, as if my pain hurt him.

A muscle twitched on Lorcan's jaw. "Don't touch the bars," he instructed. "Step back, Cass."

"No, High Lord!" Jezebel cried. "She can never be set free. She'll doom us all."

"Seriously, Jezebel, how can I hurt anyone like this?" I asked, spreading my arms to show others how harmless I was.

Everyone could see that I could barely stand. Maybe I was a bit more dramatic than necessary, but I couldn't let the crazy bitch convince them to keep me in the cage. I couldn't let her paint me as a monster.

Fear makes people do crazy things. Fear made my mother lock me up in here for over a decade. But who was I kidding? For fuck's sake, the room was full of vampires. They were more of monsters than I.

"If you set her loose, she'll destroy this world," Jezebel screamed, even though everyone in the room had super hearing. "She carries the mark of death. And this is for her own protection. This is the only place they can't find her."

"Who are they?" Lorcan demanded.

"The gods," Jezebel said, her eyes on him, innocent and pleading.

Lorcan regarded her coldly.

"What kind of mother locks her child in a cage for her entire life?" I hissed. Finally, I got to discredit her and make her look like a fool. "Only someone who's either crazy or a true monster."

Jezebel flinched as gasps rang through the group in the room.

The panther snarled at my mother, his amber eyes burning, as if he wanted to tear her throat out. In a flash, he moved to stand between Jezebel and my cage, guarding me.

"Back off!" King Dario hissed at the panther, who only bared his fangs, ready to attack. "Jezebel is my queen! I demand you respect her."

Lorcan gave the panther a look, but the beast refused to retreat.

"Shut up, Dario," Lorcan said, and turned to the beast. "Reysalor, I need your blood."

The panther growled threateningly at Dario one more time before padding back to Lorcan's side, his eyes not leaving the vampire king and his queen.

Sharp claws appeared and extended from Loran's hand, and with them he slashed open his palm. Dark crimson blood gushed out.

I blinked. What was he doing?

The panther tilted his head to the side, and Lorcan's claw sliced across the space between his shoulder and neck. The vampire lord spooned the beast's blood onto his palm and mixed the blood with his. Then he dipped a finger into the mixed blood and drew runes on the frame of the iron door.

No beast would expose its neck to anyone, but this beast was doing it for me.

Jezebel stared at Lorcan in horror as she realized his intent. "No!" she screamed as she charged at him.

The panther moved like a black arrow and slammed into her. The force of it threw her against the wall. She collapsed, and he snarled at her. He was obviously making a great effort not to bite her head off. For a beast, he had incredible control.

I watched him with fascination.

Three vampire guards zoomed toward the panther, claws out, to take him down.

Before I could shout a warning, Lorcan lashed out, a longsword in his free hand.

The sword rose and fell, and three heads tumbled down to the ground with a thud.

My jaw dropped. He impressed the hell out of me.

Maybe Jezebel was right about one thing—the outside world was hazardous. In a blink of an eye, I'd seen death.

A power I wasn't familiar with stirred in my belly at the sight of blood and violence. It wanted to be unleashed. It wanted to play. It craved destruction. I was a little taken aback. Maybe I did have a monster inside me. Maybe there was a reason my mother kept me completely isolated all these years.

No, there was no excuse for her behavior. I was done finding excuses for her inhuman treatment of me a long time ago.

Led by Jade, Lorcan's vampires formed a wall before their lord, their weapons drawn. As if he needed a protection after the badass moves I'd just witnessed.

"Stand down!" King Dario yelled at his guards as he moved in front of Jezebel to shield her.

His guards stepped back.

"High Lord," Dario said, bowing to his waist.

Lorcan outranked the vampire king. That was interesting.

"It was a mistake," Dario continued. "My guards reacted instinctively when they saw my queen being attacked." He eyed the panther. "Your beast needs a leash."

The panther snarled at the vampire king, ready to attack again.

"Control your pet queen first, Dario." Lorcan's voice was devoid of all emotion as he focused on drawing the runes. He'd finished working on the top frame of the iron door. "If she gets in my way again, I'll yank her heart out myself."

"She's my queen," Dario said in indignation.

"Yet she hid and locked up what's mine," Lorcan said, cold anger flashing through his merciless gray eyes. "And I'm not sure how much damage she's done to mine."

His? The word burned my mind. He was trying to bust me out of the cage, so he could transfer the ownership from my mother to him. No fucking way. I would never allow anyone to own me again. He would learn a hard lesson, but right now, I had to seem as submissive as possible.

Dario opened his mouth to protest, but shut it just as quickly.

"I would kill for a lesser offense if she weren't your queen and Cassandra's mother," Lorcan said, steely. "Now, I want everyone the hell out of here. I have work to do."

He didn't need to say it twice. The room cleared quickly.

Lorcan was the scariest monster here, except for the panther. I could live with that.

"Once it's done, it can't be undone," Jezebel whined as Dario helped her up. "They're unleashing a monster that will eat up the world. Once she's out, I can't control her anymore."

"Peachy, Mother darling," I shouted at her as her vampire king urged her out of the room. "And goodbye."

I turned my attention back to Lorcan and smiled at him in encouragement, but he wasn't looking at me, so I flashed a smile at the panther.

The beast grinned back. I would steal him when I left here.

Lorcan finished inscribing runes on three of the doorframes. He cut his palm once again for more blood, and the panther padded toward him and offered his own. With more mixed blood, Lorcan finally filled the bottom doorframe with runes.

I hadn't wanted to distract him while he was working, but now I could no longer hold back.

"How do you know all the counter spells?" I asked with a positive attitude. Now that he was going to free me instead of interrogating me, I kept my foul mouth to myself.

He ignored me, but I wasn't discouraged. "I'll be impressed if they work," I said, my voice all sugary.

I paced again, my heart pounding. I couldn't take any more disappointment.

A red light flashed along the doorframe. And the panther lunged. He opened his jaw, closed his fangs around the lock, tore it out, and spat it beside the cage in fury and disdain.

"Yes!" I shouted, pounding my palm with my fist.

I'd be out. I'd be free. Tears stung my eyes, but I forced them back. I wouldn't show my vulnerability to anyone, not even my rescuers.

Just when I was about to kick the cage door open, Lorcan seized the bars and tore the door off in one swift motion.

Holy fuck! That was the coolest move I had ever seen.

I threw him a thumbs-up. "You rock. Thank you."

I charged out of the cage and bolted.

4

The vampires formed a barrier of wall in front of me as soon as I dashed out of the underground room.

Jade sneered at me. She hadn't liked me at first sight. The way she'd stood beside Lorcan seemed territorial, yet he'd discharged her in front of me.

"I was hoping you guys would do that, you know," I said.

My hands threw up, and a strong current of air blasted out of me, sending the roadblock of vampires flying in all directions. I had practiced with my power, hiding it from my mother, because who knows what she would have done to me if she knew. Besides, one could never be faulted for being prepared for all situations.

They were lucky that I didn't want to burn them with my dark fire since I was in an incredibly good mood.

I tore through the cleared path and sprang for my freedom, only to be jerked back when I was halfway up the stone stairs.

A strong arm wrapped around my waist with an ironclad hold.

"What the—" I stopped mid-sentence, not expecting the touch to be pleasurable.

"I don't think so, Cass," Lorcan's masculine voice whispered in my ear, his cool, minty breath tickling my temple. A pleasant shiver rippled over me. "I didn't free you just to let you run away from me."

He pulled me against his hard chest, his scent of pine and wine enveloping me, enticing and seducing. I could wrap myself around it to a sound sleep. But his pounding heart against my back jolted me back from the half-trance I was in.

"Hey, you again." I glanced up at him over my shoulder, even though I stood two stairs higher than him. "I still want to know why your heart is beating but none of the other bloodsuckers' does."

The surrounding vampires heaved a breath. They glanced between their lord and me before their shock bled out of their eyes.

"Trying to distract me, are you, Cass? It won't work," he said.

I'd have run faster if I hadn't been so weak from starvation.

"You should let me go." I sighed with a half-threat.

"Why is that?" he said, taking every bit of challenge in my eyes with his own. "Didn't I just tell you that I didn't unleash you to let you run unchecked?"

I chuckled. "You think you're a comedian, I see."

I had showed him my courtesy by not using my power on him, because he'd done me a favor and set me free. But if he thought he owned me now, I wouldn't hesitate to make a statement.

"No one has ever said I'm funny, Cass," he said seriously. "I don't entertain people."

"I do," I said, and pulsed, my air current blasting out of me and slamming into him.

It passed right through him and didn't cause so much as a ripple. The vampire lord didn't move an inch.

Shit! I must be too weak to throw another blast after I had hit his vampire horde, so Lorcan could diffuse it with ease. Well, then I'd let him have a kick of my little fire.

I needed to pump fear into the vampires to stop them from pursuing me.

It was my only chance to get away.

A stream of black fire flowed from me and crept onto Lorcan's arm that clasped my waist. But still he didn't loosen his grip.

"Are you tickling me, Cass?" he asked with displeasure. "Just so you know, I'm not ticklish."

This was impossible. My power couldn't be so lame. I flicked a wrist, and a trace of dark fire flew toward a tall vampire close to me.

He howled as the fire hit his face and peeled the skin from his cheek.

I opened my mouth, dumbfounded. At the same time, I pushed more fire toward Lorcan, this time not at his arm but his chest that pressed tightly against my back.

He pulled me tighter against him until he nearly knocked the breath out of me. "Are you trying to burn me too?" he whispered in my ear.

Something clicked in my mind. The vampire lord was immune to my power, which was both unexpected and bad.

I had one last trick. I counted to three and thrust my elbow backwards toward his face. When he covered his handsome face with his hand in surprise, I'd use the air current to make myself float to the ceiling and out of his reach. Then I'd find a window and escape through it.

With my freedom at stake, I couldn't play nice and be soft.

He snapped his head back before my elbow touched him and his other hand lashed out. Before I knew it, he'd pinned me against him, both my arms locked to my front by his muscled arms. He had me in a death grip.

Why didn't my power work on him?

Rage and raw fear surged in me, and I trembled at the thought of what he would do to me. I wouldn't let anyone put me back in the cage again.

The panther rubbed his side against my thigh. The beast had been watching my interaction with Lorcan the entire time, not aiding him but not helping me, either.

Somehow his presence calmed me, and his rubbing sent another kind of shiver of pleasure all over me.

Did both the beast and the vampire turn me on?

I hadn't had any contact with anyone except my mother. That might explain this fuck-up.

I sighed. A straightforward escape hadn't worked out. It was time to change the strategy. And it appeared counterproductive to fight the vampire lord again at the moment. The last thing I wanted was to piss him off and risk being dragged back into the cage. Plus, I was exhausted and starved, and my splitting headache still pounded my skull.

I needed sustenance before any other escape attempts.

"Do you realize it's not nice to try to burn people, Cass?" Lorcan grunted.

Even in the strange circumstance, I liked the way he said my name.

"I was only teasing you, Your Lordship," I said, my body softening in his grip to let him know I'd surrendered to him. "I was trying to have a bit of fun. Don't you like a good chase?"

He snorted.

He didn't believe me. I needed to prey on his sympathetic side. I believed he had it in him. Though he was cold steel through and through, I'd seen compassion spark in his gray eyes for an instant when he'd spotted me in the cage and when I'd told him I'd been in there since I was a child.

"I just wanted to see the sky for the first time in my life," I said. "I want to know how it feels to be in the open space and have the wind on my skin. I didn't mean to bolt, but my body acted on the cravings."

Lorcan swallowed, and the panther growled.

"Is that so?" Lorcan asked softly.

"Please?" I said.

He released my waist, but offered me his hand. "Come."

Just like that? My heart fluttered.

No matter what the future held, I would soon have my first intake of fresh air.

"I'm fine." I didn't want to have my hand trapped in his.

Lorcan grabbed my hand in his and led me forward.

I didn't fight to break free of his hold. I didn't want to anger him and put myself at a disadvantage. He was dangerous. He knew how to cast counter spells to the ones that had confined me for over a decade, he'd killed a few vampire guards as if snapping a twig, and he was immune to my power.

And, his touch actually felt electrifying and pleasant.

I jogged beside him, and the panther trotted by my side, rubbing and licking my free hand every now and then.

Escorted by a vampire lord and a panther, I climbed the stairs and hopped down a few hallways, before I saw a glass door to the outside world.

My heart burst in joy as it flew in the wings of the wind.

5

Before I could kick the glass door—I had a problem with all doors after my confinement—it slid open from the middle.

Lorcan gave me a sidelong glance, probably perceiving my intention, but didn't say anything.

I strode out instead of shooting out. Quick, abrupt action would make Lorcan react. And he was too fast. He might trip me to the ground and frisk me if I pulled another stunt.

The image of being frisked by him flashed by my inner eye, and my pulse spiked. I quickly shook off the unwanted fantasy.

I was now standing outside the vast dome-like structure built as a fortress. Endless lush greens with clusters of red blossoms extended in front of me, and beyond the ridges of mountains sprawled under a faint crescent moon.

Across the mountains, pink and orange clouds met the dark green grass in the horizon, and the sun had just set.

I had dreamed about such a breathtaking view, but I had never seen anything like it in person, not until now.

The cold air was rich with flowery fragrances, and it was so fresh—like nothing I had ever smelled before.

I took a deep breath, letting the potent air into my lungs, then breathed out slowly. I repeated it several times. With my hand in Lorcan's rough, masculine one, I shared this experience of pure joy with him. He didn't let go of my hand but watched me with anticipation that was almost tender.

I sank my fingernails into his flesh. Still he didn't withdraw his hand, but merely frowned at me.

"Just to make sure this is all real, and not some fucking dream," I said. "I'm right here, breathing free air and looking at the stars."

Then I realized if I wanted to be sure it wasn't an illusion, I had to let his fingernails cut into my flesh. Pain and reality went together. "Pinch me," I ordered.

"Don't be silly, Cass," he said, waving his free hand. "This is real."

I yanked my hand from his. He was reluctant, but he let me go. I kicked a rock hard enough to hurt. Yes, this was fucking real.

With a smirk, I strolled toward the grassy land, my bare feet sinking into the soil.

Lorcan didn't stop me. He just watched, but the panther padded beside me. Where I went, he would go.

However, the vampire lord's calm didn't fool me. As soon as I bolted, he would chase and catch me. After that, he would put tight security around me, even if he didn't send me back to the cage.

I held his gaze for half a second and knew he would never let me go easily.

Gawking at me, none of the vampire minions intercepted me either, and they wouldn't unless their lord ordered it. Jade stood near Lorcan, her gaze hot on me, all hostile and steely.

I turned to the nature all around, absorbing its wild beauty. Its magic tugged at me from the deep earth, from the wind, from everywhere.

The land was calling me.

Home. A word sliced through my mind.

Yes, I answered.

In front of me, blossoms bloomed like raindrops, welcoming me, as if they'd been waiting for this day to come.

The panther stilled and tensed, sniffing for threats. Lorcan stepped toward me, and the vampire horde in the perimeter sucked in a collective breath.

I ignored them all. I was in my world. I was in my element.

My arms spreading, I threw my head back and laughed.

So this was how freedom felt.

Rain started falling, and then snowflakes drifted down, landing on my lips and caressing me.

They were all celebrating my freedom with me.

How could Jezebel think I was a monster? Would a monster bring out such fineness from nature? Tears sparkled beside my eyelids.

Thorny vines sprouted suddenly from the land, climbing on my limbs—not to harm me but to defend me. They sensed the vampires. And now they were waiting for my command. They were giving themselves up to me as my weapons.

I could escape if I wanted to. My vines would trap and stop my foes, and everything on Earth would aid me.

"Earth magic," someone murmured in awe.

"Cass?" Lorcan called, inching closer.

I snapped my head to him, my eyes menacing, not pleased to be disrupted while I was connecting to one of my power sources. Responding to my mood, the vines around me rose into the air like living snakes, hissing at the vampire lord.

"Come and play, *babe*," I said in a dark, taunting voice I hadn't known I possessed. I must have more layers than I'd thought, but none of them had had a chance to manifest while I'd been trapped in that fucking cage. "You think you can catch me this time?"

Wind whipped around me. All of nature was at my command, and the vampires were at my mercy.

Lorcan widened his gray eyes before narrowing them, probably at my calling him babe.

"Don't run, Cass," he said. "That'll be a mistake. You know I'll chase you to the ends of earth, and you don't have a map of where you're going. You don't know this realm yet."

"What is this realm then?" I asked.

"ShadesStar, one of the immortal realms," he said. "There's also mortal realm where humans reside on the other side of the veil."

I bit my inner cheek. I'd visited some mortal cities through my dreams and gained practical knowledge over the years. It was one of the abilities I'd hidden from Jezebel. But Lorcan was right. I didn't know how to reach those places.

"You'll need me to survive," he said, his voice all reason. "And right now, you're starved. You've suffered years of malnutrition. You need sustenance, and I'll provide for you."

I hadn't paid attention to my appearance, but I must have looked really bad for him to mention malnutrition. Since he brought up food, my stomach started grumbling. And with that, I became more aware of my aching, exhausted body and pounding headache.

He was making sense. I had no connection to the outside world. I had no experience in any aspect of life. I'd been raised like a beast, but I didn't intend to live like one from this point on.

I needed him before I grew strong. I could always ditch him and his horde later.

My eyes rolled slowly as I regarded him, calculating. He looked sincere—and hot—but I would be a fool to trust anyone.

"Fine," I said, letting the vines slide down my legs. "Under one condition."

"Name it, Cass."

"You won't put me back in any cage. No matter what I do and how mad you'll get at me."

I was sure that would rile him up. It was in my nature to poke people and get them all worked up.

His eyes turned stormy gray, rage inside, and the panther growled.

Deal breaker? So be it. Over my dead body would I return to my cage. But I would not go down without a fight. My body tensed in battle mode. My power coiled within me, calling the wind, the earth below, and the vines to stand ready to help me fight my way out.

"I won't cage you. Ever," Lorcan said icily, and a chill ran up my spine. "And I'll kill whoever tries to do that to you again. Their death will be slow and torturous, and they'll regret ever being born."

The panther bared his fangs, seeming to agree with Lorcan.

My throat bobbed, suddenly scratchy. "How can I trust your words?"

"My words are binding," Lorcan said. "I won't fail you, Cass. I might put my enemies in dungeons for years, but I've never done that to children." He looked straight at me. "Even a monster won't cross certain lines."

I sensed the truth in him, and what he said about the monster ticked the right box with me.

He wouldn't imprison me, but he desperately wanted something from me. He'd been so eager to get me out of the cage. He'd threatened to chase me to the ends of Earth. And I'd seen the intense hunger and heat in his eyes when he'd set eyes on me.

"Another condition," I drawled.

He arched an eyebrow. "I thought you said one condition."

"Will you agree to it or not?" I said with exasperation. My hunger was making me short-tempered.

"What is it?" he asked.

"You won't take my blood without my permission," I said. "The last thing I want, besides being back in that cage, is to end up a blood whore like my mother."

His gaze traced the veins on my neck before moving up to my lips and then locking on my eyes. "I won't drink from you without your permission, Cass. And I won't allow anyone to take your blood."

What else should I bring up? I tapped my temple. There.

"Don't ever think I'm your slave or prisoner just because you let me out of that cage," I said firmly. "I have the right to come and go freely."

He hesitated for a second, and I narrowed my eyes.

"It's non-negotiable," I said as I braced my hands on my hips, gambling that he wanted me enough to accept my terms.

The panther hissed at Lorcan, urging the vampire lord to oblige. The beast had to be a magical creature who understood our words, though he couldn't speak back. I scratched his ear, and he enthusiastically leaned into my touch.

Lorcan eyed the panther, not thrilled at his behavior. If I weren't mistaken, I could have sworn I saw a flash of jealousy in his storm-gray eyes.

"You're a free person, of course," Lorcan said. "I accepted all of your terms, but you'll also need to compromise."

My brow furrowed.

"You'll promise not to run away before you can truly take care of yourself," he said. "And you'll learn how to navigate the world under my instruction. I'll be your mentor."

That wasn't hard. Those terms actually worked to my benefit. But I frowned at the vampire lord, pretending not to be pleased with his conditions. I sent him a brooding look, and pouting, I said reluctantly, "Fine, for now. You got the better part of the bargain!"

"You need to swear it," Lorcan said.

"But I told you it was fine."

"No, you need to swear on the whole sentence, as I did," he said.

Why was a vow such a big deal? Words were easy. He wouldn't even know if I cheated him. I'd hidden things from Jezebel and lied to her all the time.

I shrugged. "I promise I won't run away unless it's necessary, and I'll allow—" I paused to regard Lorcan. "How should I address you in this serious oath you insisted on?"

"High Lord of Night," he said.

"What should I call you in a casual setting?" I asked. "High Lord of Night is long-winded and melodramatic."

"Lorcan will be fine," he said. "Finish your oath."

I heard small murmurs of surprise from his vampire guards.

He'd just put me on an equal footing with him, but I wasn't all that flattered. I didn't belong to his court. I didn't belong to him. He had no rights to lord over me. I was equal to him, and to any being. No one lorded themselves over Cass Saélihn.

"I'm getting to it," I said. "The former swear stands, and I'll also allow the High Lord of Night to be my mentor under reasonable conditions. That's it. Done."

Lorcan arched an eyebrow, but he let it slip. "Say this to seal it: I, Cassandra Saélihn, so swear."

I gave another small shrug and grinned carelessly. "I, Cassandra Saélihn, so swear."

If he believed he could trust an oath, he was a fool. But then a magical wind slammed into my chest and wiped the smirk off my face.

Fuck! My words were also binding. Why hadn't I realized it before? What would happen to me if I broke my promises?

Maybe a little panic hit me. Maybe hunger finally overcame me. I saw stars before darkness took me under.

I swayed on my knees. I wasn't sure if anyone caught me when I fell and blacked out for the second time. If no one prevented my fall, then chivalry was dead.

6

I sprawled naked on the silky bed, my left nipple in a man's sensual mouth. He suckled it with fervor. His light turquoise eyes laughed at me when I slid my lust-filled gaze over him and parted my lips. Why did he seem familiar when I'd never met him before? A tingling sensation washed over me as he grazed the tip of my breast with his teeth.

Naughty! But I didn't push him away since pleasure was making a decision for me.

A large hand cupped my right breast and fondled it with a bruising force. I snapped my attention to it. Another man, just as hot as the turquoise-eyed male, worshiped my body with his hands. He had honey-brown eyes, sun-kissed skin, and rich auburn hair in a fashionable military style.

He looked like a warrior god.

My gaze dipped to his broad shoulders, the six-pack adorning his stomach, his narrow hips, then his massive erection. I'd never seen a male's manhood before and my eyes were glued to it, utterly fascinated.

His cock jerked aggressively under the weight of my gaze, and I nearly jumped.

"Hello, Cass sweetheart," his rich, deep voice purred. "Alaric Ash Desreaux at your service."

My pulse spiked; my heart drummed.

Was I in heaven? I had two of the hottest men I had ever set eyes on cherishing my body with their hands, lips, and teeth.

"Oh," I said on a sighing moan, acknowledging him and his good service.

Liquid fire swirled between my thighs when another hand, cool and powerful, stroked my bare pussy.

Waves of pleasure washed over me at the new sensation. A third hunk?

A moan escaped from the depths of my throat as I raised my head and met Lorcan's bright, gray eyes. The High Lord of Night knelt between my thighs. He didn't look as cold and composed as usual. Heat burned though his icy exterior as he worshiped my pussy.

He brushed open my plump folds with his thumb, his gaze focusing on my flesh with ravenous hunger that made my face flame. I whimpered, stunned at my hot wetness.

As I wiggled my ass, Lorcan grabbed my legs and lifted them, positioning the crown of his hard length at my slick entrance.

I gasped at the sensation this contact brought. I wanted more. I shifted my hips, needing the delicious friction.

Before I could tell him I was a virgin, he drove into me mercilessly, his hard, thick cock stretching me, filling me until it was nearly uncomfortable.

I cried out, but the pleasure soon overwhelmed the pain, especially when the two other gorgeous males competed for my attention as they suckled and played with my breasts.

Lorcan thrust into me again, driving deeper into my molten core, and hitting every sensitive spot inside me. My toes curled and I arched my back in ecstasy.

A beastly growl ricocheted off the window. My heavy-lidded eyes fluttered open as a black panther leapt on to the bed.

I yelped. This was some weird shit. The beast couldn't be joining us!

I had let this go too far.

Just as I was about to scold the beast, the panther shifted into a beautiful man. Actually, he shifted to a fae, and he looked just like the turquoise-eyed male, though his eyes were a shade lighter. They were twins.

So, I had four males ravishing me.

Holy fuck! I moaned.

My eyes snapped open on that moan, and I was disappointed to find myself alone on a bed with clean sheets.

7

I let out a long groan. I sniffed, hoping to catch their fading, seductive scent of the four hot men in my dream, but I had no such luck. Even my familiar, unwashed scent was gone, replaced with the scent of cleanliness, jasmine, and rose.

Everything rushed back to me.

I'd been freed yesterday after being imprisoned for life.

I blinked to clear the fear of seeing the iron bars surrounding me, but when I saw I was in a furnished room with paintings of exotic landscapes on the walls, my breath evened out.

The mattress dipped on one side, and I snapped my head toward the movement and bolted up.

The black panther bared his startling white teeth in a grin before he yawned.

I'd dreamed he had shifted to a naked man who was hot as fuck just a few minutes ago. I felt my skin flush and shook the image out of my head.

"Are you kidding me, panther? We're bed buddies now?" I said, but I didn't shove him off as he settled closer to me and licked the back of my hand. "Just don't make it a habit."

I was cranky from my unfinished, unfulfilled sex dream. Lorcan's hard cock filling me and stretching me had felt so real.

Once again, I shook it out of my mind. Dwelling on an erotic image like that when my freedom and survival were still at stake was not a good way to start the day.

"Your tongue is pretty rough," I told the panther.

He sniffed, his eyes turning from turquoise to liquid gold, as if he scented my arousal.

I narrowed my eyes at him.

He grinned and licked my jaw.

"Now I'll have to wash my face," I complained, then noticed that I was wearing a blue tank top and silky undergarment.

At least I was decent in my waking hours.

I threw the blanket off me and swung my legs off the bed.

"Someone washed me and dressed me without my consent," I murmured to myself as I strode toward the window and wheeled to check the room. "Who dared!"

No one answered, of course.

I had to admit that it was good to feel clean. I pulled my waist-length hair up to my nose, inhaling the light lavender scent. Whoever had washed me had used a nice shampoo.

I pulled open the heavy curtains, only to be greeted by thick blinds obscuring the sun-proof glass panes of the window. I reached under the blinds and tugged at the window, but it refused to open, and after a few failed attempts, I gave up trying.

I'd once seen in my mother's memories that vampires couldn't stand the sun, which explained the heavy curtains, the thick blinds, and the sun-proof glass. I brushed open a space between two rows of blinds with my fingers and peered out through the crack.

On the horizon was the ridge of mountains I'd last seen, and below the window was a courtyard, guarded by the vampires. It would be difficult to escape from this room.

I released the blinds, went to the other side of the wall, and opened the closet.

It was filled with clothes—training outfits, tops, pants, shirts, and dresses, accompanied by boots, flats, and sexy high heels.

Someone had arranged things for me while I was unconscious, and this was clearly my assigned room.

However, I didn't plan to stick around for long. This place was too close to my cage and my mother. I would have nightmares every night if I stayed near either.

I took a floral dress off the hanger, moved into the bathroom, and shut the door.

The white marble bathroom was spotless and spacious with a floor-to-ceiling mirror embedded in one wall.

I approached the mirror and studied my reflection.

I hadn't had the luxury of seeing myself until today. I had never known what I looked like.

A young woman stared back at me. Her—my—left eye was a brilliant violet, and the right was golden like living fire. Bluish half-moon circles under my eyes indicated exhaustion and malnourishment—basically, starvation.

My face was creamy like porcelain, with high cheekbones, though my cheeks were a bit hollow. Nothing I couldn't fix with a few good meals.

My skin felt silky under my touch, and I traced a line from my small, straight nose to my full, pink lips. Thank the fates, I did not resemble my mother.

I ran a hand through my curly, lustrous hair, shades of blue and red weaving through the stark silver. For the first time, it didn't look like a wild nest for baby birds.

Cass Saélihn, you don't look too bad! I grinned at myself.

I'd been worried about my appearance, but now I was relieved that I didn't look like a skeleton.

I shrugged off my sleeping attire and studied my nudity—full breasts, slim waist, and shapely hips. My legs were a bit slender for my liking, but they would grow strong in no time.

I was fifteen, but I'd reached maturity at the age of nine. I wasn't human. I wasn't like any species, though Jezebel refused to tell me what I was. She'd only said that I was one of a kind and that I didn't age like the humans, vampires, or any other creature.

She probably didn't care that I had lost all my innocence and sweetness in that cage long before I'd reached adulthood. Bitch had wanted to break me and render me useless. I'd pretended to be the frail, broken doll she preferred me to be, but she'd failed epically.

My gaze returned to my red nipples.

I hoped Lorcan hadn't been the one who had washed me and clothed me. It would be beyond embarrassing if he had cleaned my unwashed body. Then my mind drifted to his large, powerful hands roaming over me, and goosebumps spread over my skin. Involuntarily, I pinched my tit and felt liquid fire pool between my thighs.

Where was this lust coming from?

I'd hated all vampires since I could walk and talk. Never would I have thought I would be turned on by thinking of the High Lord of Night, but here I was, wet and hot for him.

I'd thought it was an accident that I had been attracted to him when I'd first set eyes on him, but clearly it was no accident. I was attracted to him.

Cass, are you going to be there forever? a man's voice purred in my head.

I let out a startled yelp.

Who the fuck are you?! I demanded.

I shoved on the flowery dress before I jerked open the door. I threw my hands up in front of me, ready to toss the two kinds of magic I was familiar with—air and fire—at any threat.

I stepped out, scanning the space.

Only the panther and I occupied the room. I stood right outside the bathroom door, in a battle pose, and the beast perched lazily on my bed, his large head on his front paws.

He couldn't be the one talking in my head, could he?

The panther raised his head and looked at me, his turquoise eyes becoming molten gold again, as if he was turned on by my new look.

He wasn't even a man, but his gaze lingered on my exposed cleavage.

Strangely, I didn't even feel repulsed.

What the actual fuck was wrong with me? Maybe a monster really did lurk inside me, and she liked this panther.

I shook my head, a bit disgusted with myself, and glared at the beast in warning.

A teasing smirk danced like a leaping flame in his beautiful, predatory eyes.

Were you wondering if Lorcan bathed you? The velvet male voice sounded in my head again. *He didn't. He would have had to go through me. And I wouldn't allow him.*

"Fuck," I said. "You can talk in my head?"

I just did. He cocked his head. *The servant girls washed you, of course, under my and Lorcan's supervision.*

Could he be a man instead of a panther? Or both? I didn't know his kind, because when I dreamed, I usually wandered to the mortal world.

My eyes narrowed. "You and the vampire saw me naked?"

As naked as when you were born. The panther confirmed proudly.

My face flamed. They must have seen the layers of dirt coating my skin. I didn't want to dwell on it. It was humiliating.

"How can you even talk to me?" I asked, drilling my gaze at the panther. "You're an animal. Animals bark or howl. They don't talk."

I'm not merely an animal. The panther protested, looking offended. *I'm a magical immortal being, just like you.*

Maybe that was why he shifted in my dream?

I must have been too fucking lonely.

I eyed him moodily, biting my fingernail as I mulled over this information. "Fine, you can talk," I said in resignation.

Then an idea hit me. My eyes rolled slowly as I did a cold calculation. It wasn't such a bad thing that he could talk. He could be my errand boy as well as my bodyguard. He could spy for me and report back to me.

Amusement twinkled in his eyes, as if he could perceive my thoughts.

That made me pause. If he could talk in my mind, then he could probably read my mind.

And sometimes I had a lot of dirty thoughts.

I immediately pulled my mental shield up, shoving out anything in my mind that wasn't mine or didn't belong.

I can't really read your thoughts, though I can communicate telepathically with you, he said. *Relax, Cass baby. If you don't want people to read you, you should learn not to wear your every expression on your sleeve.*

"I do not wear my expressions on my sleeve," I said. "I don't even have a sleeve." I waved my bare arms at him. Heat grew in his now liquid-golden eyes again as they roved over my exposed shoulders and arms to my ankles.

This was some fuck up.

"Hello!" I cried out in exasperation, wanting to bring his attention back to my face.

He huffed out a laugh.

"I let my guard down around you because I thought you were only a friendly panther," I said regretfully. "I'm now correcting my mistake."

He leapt off the bed and alighted beside me, lethally graceful.

The enormous beast reached the top of my ears, even on all fours. He was formidable. Even the vampires gave him a wide berth.

I should not be pushing his buttons, though I never feared him in the first place.

He gave my nose a lick.

"Eww!" I shoved at his massive shoulder, but it was like pushing a wall of rock. I stepped back and rolled my eyes.

I'll summon the servant girls to bring your food, he said as if waiting for me to object. *I don't want you to pass out like yesterday. Lorcan had to carry you back like a sack of potatoes.*

"He carried me?" I asked.

Had he run his hands all over my body?

The panther looked at me with a scowl. *What do you think?*

I would have to get used to this beast being so expressive.

"He's High Lord of Night. And lords usually don't act like mules. He could have ordered one of his minions to do the deed, like that vampiress who's always glued to him. She doesn't like me much, though I haven't done anything to her. She gave him the goo-goo dove eyes, but when she looked at me, she seemed to think she could snap my neck like a twig."

You're observant, he said. *It'll always be either him or me taking care of you. We don't trust anyone else. In a few days, you'll meet two more of us.*

"What do you mean, two more?"

The panther padded past me to the door and hit a button on the wall with his paw.

"Reysalor, right?" I asked, remembering that Lorcan called him that.

I kept talking out loud instead of projecting my thoughts in his head to prevent him from hearing my other thoughts. Just in case. Even though he'd said he couldn't do it because of my natural shield.

I had a lot of plans I didn't want anyone to hear.

Footsteps rushed in from outside the door. I snapped my attention toward the door, my body tensing.

Reysalor pulled the door open with his front paw and stalked out first, placing himself between me and three females carrying trays of food.

"We brought Princess Saélihn food and drink," a brunette girl said, eyeing the beast with fear. She looked a bit older than the other two, probably nineteen.

Princess? Really. That was a riot. I tried not to laugh.

The other two girls were placing dishes on the round table in the middle of the sitting room. They were literally shaking from the sight of Reysalor.

I sniffed. They weren't vampires. From my experiences through my dream visits to the human realm, I knew they were all humans.

The vampires used humans as food but also as slaves. I inspected them and saw one of them had bite marks on her neck.

I scratched Reysalor behind his ear, and he licked my hand before leaning in to my touch.

"It's okay," I told the servant girls. "My panther is as harmless as a cat."

My panther? When did I mark him as mine? But I did like the idea of owning him. I liked to have something that was all mine, especially a talking animal who could terrify people.

Reysalor snorted.

"And he follows orders," I said when I saw their fear didn't lessen.

They worked as fast as they could, so they could get the hell out of here.

I turned to look at the panther sternly. "Sit, Reysalor."

Without warning, he leapt into the air.

The servants screamed but froze in place instead of fleeing.

Reysalor landed on a large white couch and perched on it, his large head resting on his front paws.

"That's your version of sitting, Reysalor?" I asked, rolling my eyes.

He grinned lazily, then trained his eyes on the three girls, watching their every move.

What could they even do to me? Throw hot soup at me?

I turned to the servants. "My panther has a serious hearing problem when it comes to orders. Just ignore him, and you'll be fine."

The youngest girl, who was probably sixteen, peeked at me from under her lashes when she thought I wasn't watching, evidently curious about me. The others gazed at the table, stubbornly not looking anywhere else.

"They say even the vampires are afraid of you, Princess," the youngest girl said. She had a round face that still held some baby fat.

"Are they really?" I asked.

"Isn't that why the queen locked you in the cage?" she asked.

My shoulders stiffened. Now everyone knew I was the girl in the cage.

The older girl in the center slapped the round-faced one's upper arm. "Shut your mouth, Frances, if you want to live longer in this place." She turned to me, her gaze dipping to the ground. "I apologize, Princess. Frances is new. She's still in training."

"I don't mind people speaking their minds, as long as they aren't malicious," I said. "And don't call me princess or any bullshit like that. I'm no princess. Call me Cass. You don't need to fear me. Queen Jezebel might have told everyone that I'm a monster, but I'm actually a nice girl. As long as you're friendly to me, I'm just as harmless as my panther."

The servant girls remained quiet. I figured they'd never heard anyone who outranked them talk to them like that. Even though I had just come from a cage, I was in the company of the High Lord of Night.

Rumor was that he came from the Court of Blood and Void, set in the center of the mortal world, and ruled over all vampires.

I smiled at the girls and gazed at the dishes on the round table. "That's a lot of food for me."

The delicious smell wafted toward me, and hunger gnawed my empty stomach. I had no idea how long I'd gone without food or water.

I waved a hand, using my air magic to pull a chair out for me. The servants gasped, as if they'd never seen magic before.

"Thanks, girls," I said, reaching for a tall glass of liquid. I needed to soothe my parched throat. "If you're hungry, you can sit down and eat too. There's enough food for everyone."

"Thank you, Prin—Cass," the oldest girl said, darting a fearful glance at the panther. "We can't. There are rules here."

"Suit yourself," I said with a shrug.

I wouldn't force sheep to be wolves. But I would never be a sheep, and no years of imprisonment, starving, or beating could force me to be one. And I would not follow any of the vampires' social hierarchy bullshit.

Wait, Cass, Reysalor called in my mind a split second before he appeared at my side.

The servants widened their eyes and staggered back as Reysalor stalked around the table, sniffing the food and drinks.

I arched an eyebrow as our eyes connected.

I have to make sure none of the refreshments are poisoned, he said.

"And you can just sniff out poison?" I asked.

That's one of my talents, he said unabashedly.

I took a long swig from my glass and moaned as the smooth liquid went down my throat and settled coolly in my stomach. Once again, Reysalor's eyes heated.

"What's this drink called?" I asked.

Before any of the servants answered, Reysalor said, *It's mulled cider.*

"Mulled cider," Frances said. "The High Lord specifically ordered it for you."

"How nice of him," I said. "I hope he knows I have no money to pay him back."

If he ordered this huge feast for me, it was unlikely anyone, especially Jezebel, had a chance to poison me. Would she try now that she couldn't control this monster?

Then I noticed Frances staring at my neck.

"No, no, no." I shook my head at her. "Are you kidding me, little one? No bloodsucker will get his fangs near my perfect skin. I'd personally pull out all of his fucking fangs." I glanced at Reysalor. "And you think I have a panther by my side for fun? He's my faithful bodyguard. He'll probably die for me."

"But he came with the vam—High Lord of Night," Frances said, subtly reminding me that I should not trust the beast.

Reysalor snarled at her, and she staggered back and pressed herself tightly against the wall.

"Reysalor, be nice," I said. "You can't just show your big teeth to anyone who disagrees with you."

Sure I can.

I drained half the glass and set it down on the table in satisfaction. Reysalor stuck his tongue out and dipped into my glass.

"Hey!" I said and knocked his head with my knuckles. "That's mine, and I'm not done."

The servants widened their eyes, unable to imagine how I had the nerve to hit the terrifying predator.

We share. We share everything, Reysalor said, smacking his lips at the taste of the cider before turning to lick my fingers as they scooped a portion of ice cream. I'd had ice cream once when I was three years old and Jezebel had been in a good mood.

As I dug into the feast, targeting the fruits first, I casually studied the sitting room. No expense had been spared in its interior design. There was even a grand piano in the corner right under a splendid chandelier.

"Who lives on the other side of door?" I asked, swinging a string of grapes in the direction of the door at the far end of the sitting room facing my bedroom door.

"High Lord of Night," the oldest girl said. "This is his suite whenever he visits."

"This High Lord is the king of all the vampire kings?" I asked, tossing a grape into my mouth.

"Sort of, right, Shan?" Frances said, eyeing the oldest girl among them. Frances was definitely the gossiping type.

Shan gave her a hard look. "We don't really know vampire politics."

Reysalor swept his tongue over a plate, taking a large steak into his mouth. The steak was practically raw, and since I was unlikely to touch it, it must have been made for him.

I'd been giddy, thinking the whole feast was for me, and forgotten that my panther needed to eat as well. He chewed loudly, irking me, but how could I demand a beast have table manners when I was flouting them with such merriment?

"Where is the king of all the vampire kings?" I asked. "I have to inform him I need my own suite. My independence is very important to me." Though I wouldn't object to someone serving me food. If the vampire lord thought he could own me or control me in any way, he was in for a world of surprises, and none of them were good.

"I think the High Lord is sleeping," Frances whispered. "Do you think we should lower our voices?"

"Hell no," I said. "Why should we act like mice when his lazy Lordship is sleeping the day away?"

Then it dawned on me. The vampires were inactive when sun came out. They spent most of the daytime sleeping and most of the nighttime drinking blood. That was their lifestyle.

Just then, the door I'd pointed to opened, and Lorcan stalked out.

He was dressed in a white button-down shirt that showed off his muscled chest and gray slacks that displayed his powerful legs. A lock of his hair brushed the corner of his gorgeous, gray eyes. It seemed he had just gotten out of bed and hadn't bothered to comb his tousled, dark hair, which only added to his indisputable sexiness.

His eyes found me.

And my mind flicked to my dream, where he'd thrust savagely into my heat. The feel of his cock stretching my—

I forced myself to dim the spark I felt and cleared my throat to shatter the image. I swept my gaze to the servant girls to break the connection to Lorcan. The girls all dropped their eyes to the ground as one, not because of my influence, but that of the vampire lord.

He carried his power like he owned the air people breathed.

But I wouldn't let him intimidate me. I raised my gaze and met his again. I chewed cheese and bread and smirked with challenge in my two-toned eyes.

"Good morning, your Lordship," I said. "The sun is high up on asses."

Reysalor heaved a laugh.

"Shouldn't you be sleeping until the sun goes down?" I asked.

"I don't require much sleep, even in daytime," Lorcan said, his eyes never leaving me. They were bright and a little surprised, as if he wasn't used to me looking fresh and smelling clean.

"Why is that?" I asked, not wanting to dwell on the embarrassing thought that my stink must have nearly choked him to death when he'd carried me to bath.

"I'm not like others of my kind," he said, strolling toward me.

"Because you have a heartbeat and they don't?" I asked, still curious about that. I'd mentioned it a couple times, but he was too evasive to give me any answer.

"More than that. How's your accommodation, Cass?"

"It isn't exactly terrible, but I'd prefer to live in the sunnier part of the dome," I said. "Even better, I want to get out of here. I don't like this creepy place. It makes my skin crawl."

This place housed my cage beneath it. I had toyed with the idea of finding a way to turn it into dust so no one could lock me up again. But even the idea of nearing it made me tremble with cold fear. I'd thought I was fearless and that nothing could scare me. But that was a lie. I had everything to lose now that I'd had a taste of freedom.

Only when I was out of here, away from Jezebel and the vampires and everyone who'd ever heard of me, would I truly be free.

I yearned for that day.

"This suite is one of the securest places," Lorcan said.

"Secure for you, of course." I glanced at him as he sat across from me.

He wouldn't eat solid food. I wondered if he'd fed last night, and whose neck he had sunk his fangs into. I felt my face shifting into a scowl at the thought, and hostility rose in me.

"And for you," he said. "I won't allow anyone to harm you, as I promised you. I can't chance moving you to another location at the moment. I know you don't fancy this place, but the fewer people know about you, the safer you'll be."

I clenched my jaw. My mother had used that same excuse to lock me up.

"Safer for whom exactly?" I sneered, tossing the remaining bread back on the plate.

The servant girls jumped, their eyes widening in fear for me, and waited for the High Lord of Night to strike me down.

Earlier, they had been terrified just whispering his name.

I might not be able to take him down since my power didn't seem to work on him, but he wouldn't get rid of me before he got whatever it was he wanted from me. He wouldn't have gone through all the trouble to bust me out of the cage just to kill me.

"Leave us," Lorcan said, not turning his head, and the girls scurried out as fast as their feet could carry them.

A guard stepped in from beyond the door, but before he could close it for their lord, an elegant hand took over and pushed the door open wider.

Jade strode in wrapped in black leather, boots, and a sword strapped on her thigh. She shut the door behind her. She didn't move any further, but remained near the door.

Lorcan raised a brow but didn't dismiss her like last time.

So, whatever he wanted to say to me, she would hear. She was more than his weapon. I didn't know how much she meant to him, but I was pissed at the idea of them having a special relationship.

I glared at Lorcan. "Are we going to have a secret meeting?"

"You'll address the Lord of Night as High Lord," Jade said in a steely voice.

"Oh yeah?" I sent her a lopsided smirk. "Why do I give a fuck who's the High Lord? I can very well call myself High Lady of Earth, and with that title, I outrank him."

She hissed, ready to lunge at me, but Reysalor snarled at her in warning, staring at her throat.

Lorcan raised a hand. "Jade!" He shot the panther a withering look.

I laughed.

"Stop being childish, Cass," Lorcan chided me. "This isn't play. I didn't go to such great lengths to rescue you for the fun games in your mind."

"What do you want from me then?" I said, my mouth suddenly dry.

No one would just let me out of the cage out of pure kindness or for the justice of the world.

"I want to be straightforward with you," he said. "I know you aren't ready, but we need to make you ready as soon as possible. We don't have much time. The world is burning. We need you to save it."

"What?" I almost spat out my drink, but I swallowed it just in time.

Reysalor edged closer to me, lending me his warmth and support. Lorcan gave him another harsh look, evidently not pleased with how cozy the panther and I were.

"You have no idea what's going on in the outside world," Lorcan said.

I sizzled with anger. Was it my fault that I had been locked up?

"The mortal civilization is collapsing," Loran said, as if it meant something to me. "Half the world is burned away. It's only a matter of time before the immortal realm will be breached. If the human terrain is destroyed, the immortal realm that's connected to it will become a shadow, and all of us on this planet will face extinction."

I hadn't seen the mortal realm burning in my dream visits, but then I hadn't had dreams for over a year. I'd been nearly broken and too weak to dream-visit any place.

"So, the world is burning," I said. "How am I supposed to save it?" I put up my hands, palms facing him, and wiggled my fingers. "Put out the fire with my small hands?"

I snatched another full glass from across the table and took a gulp of the sweet juice.

"You don't need to put out any fire," Lorcan rasped, clearly not liking my tone. "That's not your job." He heaved out a breath. "But we'll need you to kill the most powerful beings—the gods from Mount Olympus."

I couldn't help but laugh, and it was too late for me to swallow a mouthful of juice. It shot right toward the High Lord of Night, splashed onto his spotless, white shirt before he could duck.

I stared at his shirt, my eyes wide. I'd ruined it. Then my gaze moved to his face. A muscle jerked on his jaw, and his gray eyes darkened a notch.

Jade moved toward him, ready to assist in any way, even in stripping him. She would love that, wouldn't she?

I inhaled slightly as the erotic dream entered my mind again. The High Lord had looked deliciously hot when he was naked. Would he look like that in reality?

Lorcan waved her back, and she retreated, sending me a death glare.

"Oh, that was most unfortunate," I said.

Reysalor roared with laughter and rolled on the floor.

I used great effort to straighten my face into a neutral expression. I really shouldn't laugh in his face. The vampire lord was an extremely dangerous and powerful being. Pissing him off too much would do me no good. He wouldn't provide me with free meals then. And then I'd have to hunt my dinner like a wild beast. I didn't even know how to hunt.

"How am I to kill the gods?" I asked meekly. That was my best effort to appease him. He'd sounded absolutely ridiculous when he'd demanded I kill the most powerful beings. And it wasn't just one god.

If he and his vampire army couldn't kill the gods, how was I supposed to? The prick wanted to send me on a suicide mission, and he sounded like he felt entitled to do just that.

Out of the cage and marching to death? And it wouldn't be a good death for me.

Anger pulsed in me.

Jezebel had locked me up to control me. This vampire lord had set me free to use me as a tool. One way or the other, they just couldn't leave me the hell alone.

I hadn't even filled my stomach yet, and he'd already figured out a way to use me, as if putting such a burden on my shoulders was a fucking noble thing to do.

Maybe Reysalor wanted the same. I gave him a searing look. His friendliness might all be an act. At least he had the decency to look sorrowful and guilty.

"And what gives you the idea that I'm capable of slaying the gods?" I asked tightly.

"The gods have crippled the human technology," Lorcan said. "Now only magical beings can stand a chance against them. But none of the shifters, fae, vampires, demons, or mega are powerful enough to take them. You're probably the only one who can kill the gods, if our visions are right."

What visions? My mother's visions had put me in a cage and his just might kill me.

I hadn't even been able to use my power to toss him away and burn him when he'd grabbed me on the stairs.

Lorcan regarded the doubt I knew was written over my face. "We'll train you and bring out your latent power," he said in an uncompromising tone. "We'll start once you're done with your brunch."

The fucker didn't even want to give me three meals. He combined breakfast and lunch and called it brunch.

And bringing out my power? My mother had spent all her life to prevent just that.

"Tell me, why should I give a fuck if the world burns?" I said, putting my foot on the arm of the chair near me in defiance.

While I had been left to rot in the cage, the world lived on. Men and women ate, drank, laughed, and fucked. I'd heard them, watched them, and envied them whenever I dream-visited them. I craved their lives, but all I had when I opened my eyelids were a barred iron cage, the cold walls, my panicked panting, and tears burning my puffed eyes.

Maybe it was their turn to suffer a little?

Lorcan and Reysalor traded a quick glance, like two conspirators in a dirty secret.

"I hope the fire reaches this realm and burns this place to ash," I muttered.

It would leave no place for Jezebel to trap me again. If the vampires were afraid of the gods and could do nothing to stop their advance, then the gods' fire could melt my cage to a lump of metal.

Perhaps I'd join the gods instead of letting Lorcan and Reysalor use me as a weapon to kill them, which was fucking suicide anyway.

I didn't say it out aloud, but I was sure a cunning killing light flashed in my eyes, because the vampire lord's bitch was about to charge me, even though Lorcan simply regarded me coolly with slight distaste.

I glanced at the food on the table, and I no longer had the appetite.

"When the world is all burned, you'll have no place to stay, either," Lorcan said. "And the gods won't leave you alone, especially if they know who you are."

My nose wrinkled. "Who am I?"

A dangerous light glinted in his eyes. The vampire had icy fire, but beneath it I read his uncertainty. He didn't know either. But I had a hunch he'd interrogated Jezebel and her vampire king about my legacy and hadn't gotten much out of it.

She would never reveal her parentage and who my father was to anyone. She'd only told me once that I was a bastard in blood. I knew what that meant. I was unwanted.

The High Lord of Night was frustrated.

Jezebel's mind was a mess of threads, tainted by her madness. Her only good use was her blood. And she must have been a good fuck for King Dario to keep her around all this time.

I didn't know how or why, but Jezebel was even more damaged than I.

"Why don't you tell me who you are, Cass?" Lorcan taunted with a purr in his voice.

"Here's what I am," I said through gritted teeth. "I'm the wildest thing who never should have been caged. The mistake Jezebel made will be corrected. You can't control me, so don't even try. I'm ruthless and reckless. I won't obey any laws or rules—not yours or anyone's. I have no sense of morals, shame, or honor. It'll be pointless to use those damn concepts to mold and manipulate me. I carry no bond but my own freedom. And I won't allow anyone to use me as a weapon. Use me as a pawn, and I'll kill the kings and queens on both sides."

A lick of black fire twirled up my arms and into my tri-colored hair like a snake. It should have scared them, but both the vampire lord and panther stared at me, mesmerized.

"You're a survivor, Cass," Lorcan said.

"And my every survivor instinct tells me not to do your bidding," I said. "When you tore open that cage, you thought you found the treasure—a weapon you could use. Unfortunately, you got me."

You are the treasure, Reysalor said in my head.

I glanced at him. He looked sincere and gazed at me like I was the most precious thing to him. My heart fluttered, and I was turned on. I was so fucked.

"You're exactly what I've been searching and waiting for, for an eon, Cass," Lorcan said. "Even though we don't know your true heritage yet."

Hadn't they heard my fierce statement?

"If you're trying to mess with my head, it won't work," I said. "I'm not naïve."

Why don't we do this, Cass baby? Reysalor said, and Lorcan leaned forward. He could hear the beast talking to me. *You'll have the final say on whether you want to kill the gods or not. In the meantime, we'll train you and make you stronger. We have eons of experience at your disposal. Use us. Take advantage of us. When you're powerful enough, no one will ever put you away like your mother did or they'll suffer your wrath, and ours.*

That sounded fine. But too easy. The terms were all for my benefit. Reysalor might be on my side, but Lorcan didn't strike me as someone who would put other people's interests first.

My suspicious gaze traveled between the vampire and the beast.

"What do you have to lose, Cass?" Lorcan said. "Strike a deal with us. Lay down your conditions. Make your demands. I'll meet them if they're reasonable."

Right, they needed me in the future, but I needed them now. As Reysalor had said, it was up to me in the end if I wanted to kill the gods or not. I'd watch out for myself every step of the way, so they couldn't dictate my path.

"I don't like the idea of brunch," I ground out.

Lorcan arched an eyebrow.

"There must be three meals a day: breakfast, lunch, and dinner," I insisted.

"Fine," Lorcan said.

"And in between, there'll be snacks to my liking," I said, deciding to push it further.

"That can be arranged as well," Lorcan said on a sigh.

Our gazes locked. He looked at me as if I was his snack.

"No one's fangs get near my neck," I said. "If anyone thinks I'm the snack, they better be ready to have their teeth pulled out. I'll never be a blood whore."

Reysalor snarled. *I'll kill anyone before they can seek your blood.* He glared at Lorcan in warning, and Lorcan returned the glare, albeit wearily.

Two conditions settled. I ventured for more.

"I'll have a hot bath daily," I said. "Sometimes two if I'm too hot and sweaty."

"You'll have your hot bath," Lorcan said.

"I want my own, independent suite."

"That's pushing it, Cass," Lorcan said. "You'll stay in the secured room next to mine so the panther can guard you at daytime and I'll guard you at night. One of us will always be with you. We can't trust anyone here."

I opened my mouth to protest, but his statement "we can't trust anyone here" struck a chord in me.

"Fine," I said. "I'll compromise on that. You two really know how to drive a hard bargain." I pursed my lips. "I think that's it. I'll amend my terms when I think of something else."

"And I have my conditions as well," Lorcan said.

I frowned at him.

"Can't let you have all the fun," he said, but there was nothing teasing about his tone. "You'll not be lazy."

I glared at him. "That's an insult."

"You'll train as hard as you can," he continued, holding my gaze coolly. "You won't make an excuse to stay in bed. And I don't want to hear constant whining, either."

"I don't whine!"

"And you'll listen to our instructions instead of constantly defying us." His list kept going.

"Our? Us? Please define who that consists of," I cut in. "I'm not going to take everyone's stupid instructions."

"There are only two you need to listen for now: Reysalor and me," Lorcan said. "And most important, you'll promise not to run away before you come to full power."

"When will that be?" I asked. That would be the day I would truly be free.

"It'll depend on how well you listen to us and practice as instructed," Lorcan said, regarding me with a brooding and calculated look.

He made it sound like he was the star mentor everyone craved.

I snorted. My ass.

"Oh, one more thing," I said slyly. "I pick my own clothing."

"You have a closet full of them," he said. "Pick whatever you want."

"None of them are what I want," I said, shuffling my skirt. "We'll need to go shopping, and the sooner the better, so we can start the training."

That was a ruse.

I had dream-visited the shopping malls. I desperately wanted to go there in the flesh, and maybe sneak into a theater with a large bucket of salty, buttered popcorn. That would be like heaven.

From now on, I wanted to live a little, even though they demanded I train to kill the gods.

"We can't go to the mortal realm," Lorcan said. "It's not safe for you. As I said, we don't want any spies to get the wind of you. Besides, half of the mortal realm was burned."

That sounded depressing. What if the places that I'd
wanted to go to had already been leveled? It seemed the gods
were menaces. Maybe one day I would take them out if they
pissed me off enough—that is, if I could.

"We'll take you to a clothing store around here," Lorcan
sighed, as if he'd suffered enough of me. "And after that,
you'll train."

"Deal," I said with a smirk, running my fingers over
Reysalor's thick fur in victory. The motion brought a hungry,
envious look to Lorcan's eyes, as if he wanted to be the
panther. I glanced at the beast, who winked at Lorcan.

I got up so fast that the chair screeched on the floor.

"Who's going shopping with me then?" I grinned. But as
Lorcan turned to glance at Jade, I shook my head and
wiggled a finger. "No, no, no. I don't want her. She'll suck
the joy out of everything."

There was no way I was going to give the vampire bitch
a chance to strike me first.

8

I shuddered as I stepped after Lorcan into a vast training center. The place echoed the cold emptiness of the underground cell I had spent my life in.

Jade and a handful of vampire guards stood at strategic points in the room.

"I don't want to be watched while I practice," I murmured to Lorcan.

"Get used to it. They're loyal to me and will protect you with their lives."

It became clear to me that Lorcan didn't like bending his rules. For my own sake, I decided to suck up and not to fight him on a small inconvenience.

"Show us what else you got," he said, and the panther paced around me, flicking his tail.

I'd shown him my air and fire power, and neither had impressed him.

I narrowed my eyes. "Only because you're immune to my power, for some fucked-up reason."

He darted a casual glance at Reysalor. "Try it on the beast, then."

Reysalor growled at him, but when the panther turned to me, he was grinning.

"Do you mind?" I asked the panther.

Be my guest, Cass baby, he said, putting on a brave face.

"I'll be gentle, at least in the beginning, I promise," I said.

Without warning, I tossed a stream of icy air at him, but it didn't move him even an inch. I pushed more power at him, and the air slammed into him. A desk layered with training weapons far behind the beast flew backwards and crashed against the wall, but the panther remained still. My air simply ruffled his fur in a gentle caress.

I blinked.

It was like a cold shower, Cass baby.

How about a little spark? I asked, and black fire rolled on his shiny back. It danced on his fur instead of burning him.

A nice, hot massage, babe. Reysalor grinned at me.

My power was useless. My crazy mother had locked me up for no reason. What a waste!

I clenched my fists in frustration. Jade and a vampire guard beside her snickered. I threw up a hand, and my air crushed into Jade and tossed her to the ceiling. While her companion's jaw dropped, my dark fire crept up on him, melting his red tie, and incinerating half of his hair.

He screamed, and I withdrew my fire. The vampire restrained himself from cursing me, out of fear of his master, but hatred ignited his eyes.

"It seems my power can't touch the two of you, but no one else is immune to it." I turned back to glare at Lorcan and Reysalor. "Why the fuck is that?"

They shared a look, but both remained quiet.

There was a crash behind me as Brook dropped from the ceiling with an archetypal vampire hiss, and to my delight, Lorcan didn't even look at her.

"Can your fire burn a house down?" Lorcan asked after a beat.

I grinned. "Which house do you want me to burn down? I can try it on the bloodsucker king and his queen's chambers. Just say the word."

Lorcan ignored my snide comments. "Your air and fire can kill mortals and immortals alike," he said. "But they might not do much to the gods. All the Olympian gods have elemental power—like fire, water, lightning, and storm.

Elemental power won't bring them down. There should be
something else in you, something more."

He thought I had a killer power I was holding back.

I started to snort but my mind raced. If I had that kind of
power, would I have been tossed into the cage? I'd have
killed Jezebel for making my life hell. But how would I know
if I had a power like that when I'd been in the cage since I
was a toddler? And that cage had been made to repress my
power.

I couldn't let Lorcan know about my depth. He might
have released me from that cage, might be training me, but
that didn't mean that I trusted him.

I couldn't trust anyone. Not when everyone wanted a
piece of me.

"You're the wise instructor," I said. "Why don't you tell
me?"

The vampire and the panther shared another glance, and
I realized what they were doing.

They were communicating telepathically without me. I
sent my mental power toward Reysalor, intent on
eavesdropping, but he shut me out with ease. I tried to latch
on to his mind again, but all I saw were mental walls all
around. Damn it, the panther's mental shield was fantastic.
How could a beast have that kind of powerful magic?

His earlier words rang through my mind: *I'm not merely a beast.*

"Are you two just going to discuss me while I'm right here?" I asked, my hands braced on my hips. "That's rude, don't you think? And you guys are trying to teach me manners?"

"Last time you showed earth power out of blue," Lorcan said. "Can you do it again?"

I clenched my jaw, my eyes trained on the floor in concentration. *Come on, Earth, Cass here. Show me the cool power again.*

Nothing happened.

"C'mon!" I closed my eyes, concentrating, and willing the power to flow to me. "It's fucking show time!"

Nothing.

Take her outdoors. Maybe Cass needs to connect to the earth for the power to manifest, Reysalor said.

We moved out of the suffocating dome, and I stood in the exact spot I'd made the blossoms bloom, the wind twirl, and the snow fall.

This was the second night I'd been free. The sun had gone down, and the moon had risen. I stepped out of my sneakers, my toes sinking into the damp soil under the grass.

Potent magic ran deep beneath the land, singing a long-forgotten song.

Rise to me, I summoned it.

I felt a ripple under my feet, and then nothing.

Now you're embarrassing me, I told the land. *The vampire is going to think I'm a phony.*

The magic slid away, traveling somewhere else. The grass didn't welcome me like last time, and the ivy vines didn't rise to defend me, either.

They refused to do my bidding.

"No dice," I said, training my eyes darkly on Lorcan and Reysalor. "But I don't think it's me. It's you dudes. Earth doesn't like your kind, so it's refusing to show me the trick again."

"It isn't a trick," Lorcan said. "Your power has been repressed for too long. I'm not surprised that it's blocked after the initial spark. We'll train again tomorrow."

She might need a rite of passage, Reysalor said.

The hair on the back of my neck stood up. I did not like the sound of that. Anything involving a ritual couldn't be good. Jezebel had used a ritual to keep me locked up.

I wouldn't let it happen, I vowed, fear and anger bubbling inside me.

If I was stuck with them, I'd be screwed.

9

Lorcan refused to let me pick my own outfit for the court party tonight.

We both stood half-inside the walk-in closet, him on the left, hand on a hanger with a long, green gown draping from it. I shuffled through the new clothes I had selected earlier in the store.

"One of my conditions was that I pick out my own clothing," I said. "And you agreed to it."

"You will pick your daily outfit but not the attire for special occasions," he said as patiently as he could, as if he knew better.

"What's so special about tonight? It's just a vampire party with a bunch of bloodsuckers milling around, talking stupid politics, and doing creepy things." I gave a mock shudder. "I hope they don't feed in front of me. I won't be nice if they do."

"You won't call anyone 'bloodsucker' to their faces," Lorcan said sternly. "Try not to offend everyone and put yourself in harm's way. You'll learn to be diplomatic under my guidance. You'll learn how to interact properly with people."

I wasn't sure if vampires qualified as people, but I bit my tongue. I wasn't in the mood for another long lecture from him.

"Tonight's party will be serving that purpose," he continued. "You'll stay in a corner to observe. Be inconspicuous instead of standing out. In the end, you'll gradually merge into the society."

I arched an eyebrow. "Why would I merge into the society? What's in it for me?"

"For your future survival."

"Your way won't work. I'm not a sheep. I'm not a follower. I don't play by anyone's rules. And I don't care if I get along with anyone or not. Society can kiss my ass." I spat. "Especially vampire society."

The veins on Lorcan's temples started to jump. "Must you defy me at every turn, Cass? What did I say about listening to my instructions in our bargain?"

Menacing power rolled off him, and I backed a few inches away from him.

"I was just saying you can't make me pretend to be someone I'm not," I said.

Reysalor perched on the bed, his big head resting on his front paws, half-napping, half-listening to us. His occasional puff showed that he remained interested in my argument with Lorcan. I was hoping he'd jump to my defense, but the sly panther decided not to take a side.

He wasn't forced to go to tonight's event. He had more privileges than I had, and he was a beast! Lorcan never made him to do anything he didn't like, and treated him as an equal.

Intelligent or not, he was still a panther. I should rank above him, right?

"The party is training, and you promised to listen to me!" Lorcan's voice rose in pitch when he saw me clenching my jaw. "If you go back on your word, you'll force my hand."

I nearly sneered. What could he do now that I was out of the cage?

His stare grew more menacing. "I'll have to reconsider our deal. I'll have to reduce three meals a day to two meals a day. Or even one meal a day without snacks!"

It wasn't worth fighting him. He wasn't worth it.

"Fine, I'll wear that ugly, heavy green dress you picked," I said, as if I'd just done him a favor. "But I'll drink all the wine I want at the party."

He eyed me warily. "I don't know if alcohol will affect you or not. For safety's sake, you'll drink one glass. You'll stay in a corner, observe how others act and react, and take notes while sipping the wine slowly. The wine can be your prop."

I rolled my eyes. That was ridiculous.

"Then I'll need at least three or maybe four glasses of wine," I said. I was giving him room to bargain. "The night will be long, and I'm a big girl, you know."

"No more than one glass. And don't protest again," he rasped as he handed me the gown. "You exhaust me like no one else."

Right, others might fear him and do whatever he ordered them to do, but no one bossed Cass Saélihn around. I'd promised myself that a long time ago in the cage. I'd vowed that once I was free, I'd be completely free.

I wouldn't even allow death to take away my freedom.

"As you say, sir," I said, and my two fingers brushed my temples in a mocking salute.

His eyes narrowed for a second, then gave me a once-over. "And for the drinking, I have to ask: How old are you actually, Cass?"

"Fifteen," I said with a small shrug.

The room froze, silence engulfing us.

Even the panther raised his huge black head from his paw and stiffened, as if it was the worst news he'd ever heard.

"I was in the cage for thirteen years," I added.

"So, you—you're still a child?" Lorcan said. He almost staggered back as if I'd slapped him.

I giggled, pointing at his utterly shocked expression, which was priceless from the formidable High Lord of Night. "Look at your face, Lorcan."

His throat bobbed as he swallowed hard. "You're kidding, right, Cass?" His face turned serious. "This isn't a joking matter."

"I'm fifteen," I said. "If you don't believe me, go ask my dear mother."

The silence seemed to stretch between us. Lorcan and Reysalor traded looks of utter dismay.

"For a fifteen-year-old, you seem—" he paused to ponder, seeking words, "—taller than a regular —"

I wasn't tall. I was only five foot three, which was considered small. All of the vampires I'd seen were much taller than me. Even the human servants were taller.

He meant I had a full bosom but seemed too reserved to say the words.

I smirked at him. "You mean I have big boobs?"

He sighed. "You're not what I expected."

I sneered. "That statement alone is full of logical errors. You'd never heard of or met me before. How did you know what to expect?"

The panther coughed.

My brows furrowed. They'd heard of me before? From what source? I'd been completely isolated until now. My mother had even kept me a secret from the vampires in her court—except for King Dario, of course, since he'd allowed her to put me in the cage. And she called him our protector. The bitch was insane.

"Cass," Lorcan started again, then stopped, lost for words again.

I decided to cut him some slack. If I saw me as child, he would never look at me with heat and appreciation again. People would call him a child molester, and he would back off. And I liked him viewing me as a woman, as I was. At least, I could take more advantage of him if he regarded me as a useful and attractive adult female.

"Look," I said, my hands cupping my breasts to show him how womanly I was. His gaze dipped to my creamy cleavage before jerking up abruptly. "I might be fifteen, but I reached maturity at the age of nine. I didn't mature like the humans, vampires, shifters, fae, or any other creatures. I have my own timeline. Quit judging me by your puny standards. If you absolutely need a number, I'm equivalent to twenty-three in human years."

He didn't seem to be offended by my lecture. Instead, his eyes lit up with unconcealed delight. He covered it up the next second and coughed, just like Reysalor had a few seconds ago.

The panther let out a breath of relief, his ocean blue eyes swirling to slight amber.

I waved the gown in front of Lorcan. "I'm going to change now. Can I have some privacy, High Lord?"

Lorcan looked annoyed, but he retreated nevertheless. Reysalor grinned at me.

"You too, Reysalor," I said. "Out!"

It's not like I haven't seen you naked. He had the nerve to protest.

A Court of Blood and Void

Lorcan halted at the doorway and glared at Reysalor. The panther rolled his eyes, then lazily arched his back, stretching his formidable form before he leapt off the bed and followed Lorcan out.

I probably had to draw a firm line with the panther. I had to prohibit him from sleeping on my bed, considering that damned dream I had with Lorcan, him, and two other gorgeous dudes.

My stomach fluttered at the mere memory of the dream. It was the hottest dream I had ever had. I could still feel Lorcan's big cock filling me and the humming pleasure the two other men bestowed upon me. I blinked back to the present. I was supposed to be getting ready, not dwelling on my erotic dream, which was a bit perverted, I had to admit, considering that I had fantasized about the panther.

Shaking my head, I put on the gown and strode to the bathroom to take a look at myself.

I wasn't pleased.

The high-necked gown draped to the floor, covering almost every inch of my creamy skin and swallowing my curves. The deep green didn't bring out the color of my unique eyes, and it made me look silly.

I hissed.

The High Lord of Night wanted me to appear as plain and boring as possible, so no one would pay attention to me while I cowered in the corner, a wallflower.

I wanted to look stunning because I was sure my mother would be at the party. I wanted to outshine her and let the image of a new, free me slap her in the face.

But I'd argued with Lorcan for an entire morning due to our very different world views, and he'd worn me out. I didn't want to get into another heated debate with him and have him snarl at me. He might make good on his earlier threat and take some of my meals away.

Sulking, I pulled open the door and ventured out, a scowl on my face.

The panther and vampire stopped in the middle of their mental discussion and turned to me.

Reysalor grinned at me. *Cass baby, you look good.*

I huffed. The beast had no sense of fashion.

"What's that for?" Lorcan asked, arching an eyebrow at my expression, then shut me up before I could voice my opinion. "Well, actually I don't need to know. Let's leave for the party. My subjects are waiting."

~

I bunched the material of the gown in my hands so I wouldn't trip over the hem as I hurried along beside Lorcan on my much shorter legs.

The High Lord of Night wasn't going to accommodate me by slowing his pace, and I didn't want him to view me as a whining trainee.

I managed my sprint beside him, passing one long hallway after another, then a couple of chapels. I took in everything and memorized every turn and exit.

This was the vampire palace. If it wasn't for my grudge against their species, I'd be more appreciative of their luxury decorations—marble tiles, authentic paintings on the walls, and pillars curved like sculptures.

A horde of vampire guards ahead blocked my view, and another horde behind us made me jumpy. Why did Lorcan need guards if he was the most powerful vampire roaming the realms?

He wouldn't appreciate me deriding his security details, so I couldn't even ask him.

Light piano music floated to me from a grand hall. Before I could follow Lorcan into it, his guards split into three groups. One pressed into the hall and spread out like fleeting shadows, and the second group flanked Lorcan. Suddenly, I wasn't among his rank.

Jade and another vampire gestured for me to follow them, and led me to a corner—my destined post.

I watched Lorcan in the center of the hall. Males bowed to him and females curtseyed. Evidently, he was the most important figure in the party. It hit me then as I watched the women fawn over him. He didn't want to be seen with me by his side. Did he consider me an embarrassment?

I hadn't thought I would care, but the hurt was sudden and stabbing and made my head swim for a second.

"You're not in his league and will never be," Jade said beside me, her voice icy and vicious. "Remember your place, and you won't be in for a world of hurt, little girl."

It had seemed that I had a way with the High Lord of Night, until this moment, when he effortlessly tossed me aside and returned to his own high circle, his limelight, to be worshipped.

"Stay here and be the quiet, little mouse the High Lord told you to be," Jade ordered. "Until we come to collect you."

She stalked away, leaving me alone in a forgotten corner.

A sudden bleakness rippled over me—the same bleakness I'd felt back when I was younger, when I had first been locked in my cage and my mother left me alone for weeks on end.

Unwanted.

Used and discarded.

Lorcan hadn't even bothered to give me instructions when he'd brushed me aside.

To be fair, Lorcan hadn't exactly used me. He hadn't had the chance yet, but he planned to.

His freeing me from the cage, providing for me, training me, and now taking me to the party to make me feel so small all served one purpose—to make me an assassin for him.

In the end, whether I was ready or not, he would send me out to kill the gods—the most powerful, brutal beings in existence, according to everyone.

He was going to throw me to the wolves.

I snickered. Lorcan had forgotten one thing.

I wasn't naïve.

I, Cass Saélihn, wasn't a fool.

I had my own plans.

I would use him first. And when I had more practical knowledge of the world and could stand firm on my own feet, I would kick the sucker to the curb.

If I was to be a weapon, I'd be a weapon for myself.

The High Lord of Night had my path mapped out for me—from cage to death. But I had my own grand design—from cage to true freedom, to a life I had been deprived of.

The music was exquisite, the scent of wine was heavy in the air, and the laughter from the beautiful females surrounding Lorcan was flirtatious. The way they ogled him sickened me. They were all probably competing to be the lucky one he'd invite into his bed tonight.

The image of Lorcan licking my pussy and then thrusting his massive shaft into me flashed through my mind again. I nearly moaned at the feeling it evoked in me, but I shoved that image aside with violence.

What exactly did the flirty fucker want me to learn tonight? How to flirt or what? I vaguely recalled him mentioning that I might need to infiltrate some parties the gods would attend. Did he want me to learn how to flirt with the gods and then stab them in the back?

That was a dumb plan. And wearing in this heavy gown and playing the wallflower weren't going to advance my training. It all just made me sulky.

My rebellious gaze wheeled across the room. My superior hearing caught mundane conversations. Oh, dear fuck! I drummed my fingers on the wall behind me. I was bored out of my mind.

Instead of learning—there wasn't a fucking thing to learn anyway—I kept my stare on Lorcan.

He laughed with the ladies, listened to them, and nodded in assent every now and then. He hadn't been that agreeable toward me since I'd set eyes on him. I hadn't even heard his laugh until now. Mostly, he'd frowned and sighed at me.

When one of the servant boys passed me, a few drinks left on his tray, I lunged and snatched a shot.

He gave me a slanted look he wouldn't have dared give one of the vampires. Even servants looked down on me because I was alone in the forgotten corner. The servant seemed confident that I wasn't important.

Other than Lorcan's elite vampire guards and the three girl servants assigned to me, no one in this court had met me anyway. Since he held the drinks, I decided to be friendly to him.

"What's this drink called, dude?"

"Pincer vodka," he said. "It's very strong." He gave me another once-over and frowned. "No one has ever called me a dude. Are you sure you want to—"

I poured the vodka down my throat.

Fierce fire lit a path to my stomach, knocking the breath out of my lungs for a moment. The fire numbed and quenched my rage a bit.

Let the vampire lord laugh himself to death with the elegant ladies. I couldn't care less about him and his fucking high class vampire world.

Not once had he spared a glance at me. The fucker had already forgotten I even existed.

Yet I noticed in a room full of vampires, he was the only one with a heartbeat.

And if I wasn't completely mistaken, he hadn't had a heartbeat when he had first stumbled into the room that held my cage.

While I bit my lip, pondering the odd phenomenon of his heartbeat, his groupie escorted him out of the hall.

I'd picked up a few things from Jezebel's mind when she'd come to visit me in my cage in her drunken state. Vampire parties all had one thing in common: group feedings and sex orgies.

So, he was going to feed and fuck, and I had to cower in the corner like a cockroach?

No fucking way!

Just as I was about to chase after him, Jezebel stepped into my line of sight.

As an immortal, she looked the same age as me. Unlike me, she didn't have two-toned eyes. Her big, beautiful eyes were so clear and blue that anyone would think she was the

most innocent, pure being they'd ever met. But I knew better.
Her virtuous appeal only masked her madness and cruelty.

She wore a silvery, lace evening gown with diamond
beading. She wasn't curvy, though she was elegant. She fit
right in with the thin vampiresses, despite not being one of
them. Her glamorous air made her queenly.

I glanced around, seeking Lorcan, but he was long gone,
and there was a chance that he would not return for the rest
of the night.

Sighing, I flicked my gaze back to Jezebel. She'd asked
to see me, but Lorcan had denied her. Even her vampire king
couldn't persuade the High Lord of Night on that matter. As
always, my mother was a cunning cunt, and chose the
vampire lord's absence to approach me.

"Hello, Mother darling," I purred, though my every
nerve bristled. "Come to see how I look without bars in front
of me? How awfully sweet of you."

The servant boy who lingered nearby widened his eyes.
Bowing deeply to the vampire king and his queen like their
other subjects, the boy stole a nervous glance at me, then
scurried away. No smart humans wanted to catch the
vampires' attention, especially not their king's.

Jezebel gazed at me, a teardrop rolling down her cheek.

"Please." I wrinkled my nose in disgust. "Quit the act. For the first time in my life, I don't look like a filthy animal. I get three meals a day with as many snacks as I want. I get to have a warm bath whenever I want, and I can go out as often as I please."

With Lorcan or Reysalor escorting me, of course, but she didn't need to know that.

"Cassandra, my daughter," she said. "All I did, I did it for you. It breaks my heart to see you suffer, but your safety is everything to me. And now, you're not safe. They'll be coming for you, sooner than you expect."

"I expect nothing," I said. "But I'll burn any gremlins coming my way, so you should think twice before you summon them."

A column of black fire formed and twirled on each of my palms and then connected like a trace of lightning. I stretched them back and forth like an accordion.

"Or maybe you want a taste of my monster fire first, so you can warn your minions how fun I can be," I said. "I couldn't release this fire of mine in that cage on you. How many nasty spells did you have to use to keep me in there? Where did you get them?" I waved a hand impatiently. "Looks like you aren't inclined to answer. Fine, I don't even want to know your dirty secret. I'm free now, so if any of your bitches come near me again, they will get a full dose of my fire, and more. And that goes for you and king, too. Understand?"

Jezebel staggered back as if I'd slapped her. "How could you assume the worst of your own mother?"

I snorted, letting the fire fade from my palms. "Oh, please. Don't make me throw up my lunch. I'd prefer to keep it down, seeing as I haven't had dinner yet."

King Dario, clad in a magnificent purple robe, stepped behind his queen in a flash, grabbing her shoulder to stabilize her. She pressed her cheek into his chest for comfort.

I knew all vampires moved fast, but their king was even faster, though he didn't possess Lorcan's speed.

I should have expected his move, but my emotions were so raw at seeing my mother. I was in the enemy's territory; I should have been more alert.

"You'll show respect to my queen, your mother, when you talk to her," Dario said, his dark brown eyes flashing in righteous fury.

Vampires obeyed a very strict hierarchy, and their punishment for violators was severe.

I tilted my head, taunting him. "Why the fuck is that?"

A ring of crimson formed in Dario's eyes.

"You're my subject, as is everyone else here," he said. "I could kill you with one strike for a lesser offense. If it weren't for my queen—"

I cut him off. "Let me enlighten you, bloodsucker! Lorcan is not my lord, you aren't my king, and that stupid cunt is definitely no mother of mine. As of this moment, I denounce her. No mother would ever lock her own child in a cage when the child did nothing wrong!"

The hall fell into shocked silence. All vampires had super hearing, though probably not as good as mine. But it didn't matter. I was sure even all the humans had heard me.

Heads turned to us, yet Lorcan was still nowhere around.

The fucker must be in the middle of the blood and sex orgy and he'd left me to fend off these vermin. I caught the sight of Jade, my guard for the night, blending in with a shadow at a far corner. She wouldn't come to my aid, nor would she go fetch Lorcan. She wanted to see the vampire king finish me off.

"I must teach you to learn your place," Dario snarled, and moved, bullet fast.

I'd expected it.

Before his hand grabbed my throat, a blast of air slammed into him, sending him flying at least twenty yards away.

Jezebel's hands flew to her face, covering her trembling lips.

A squad of vampire rushed toward me, and I sent blasts of air in each direction. They flew back at the impact, crashing into the tables and walls. Glasses broke and drinks spilled.

I stalked toward Dario. He struggled up and zoomed toward me again, but my dark fire lashed out and strung him up. I could shape my fire into any form I wanted.

I kept the fire icy low. I wanted some fun before I turned up the heat.

"Kill the offender!" Dario shouted.

"Dude, you need to chill out," I said sweetly. "You're jumpy."

My net of fire heaved him up and down, showing just how jumpy he was.

He opened his mouth to curse me again, but I could manipulate air faster than he could speak. Chunks of ice materialized near his mouth and forced themselves into his mouth and down his throat.

I grinned. That was a new trick. Perhaps I needed more assholes to challenge me on a regular basis; it certainly seemed to bring out new power in me. Wasn't that what

Lorcan wanted anyway? Now, I could conjure ice as well as fire and wind.

Jezebel had repeatedly said the power in me was a monster in disguise, and I was more than giddy to set it free, just to see the pathetic, terrified look on her face.

Dario's eyes widened in fear and I watched him intently. So, vampires knew fear, too.

"They should never have let you out," Jezebel whimpered.

Damn, she moved faster than any vampire could. The bitch snuck up on me while I was having a little fun with her husband.

"I'm sorry, Cassandra, but you're my responsibility," she said, and with that, she threw a string of spells at me.

I widened my eyes and dodged, but she was too close to me.

An unseen force hit me straight in the chest, and acid ate at my skin.

I hadn't known that she had more of the dark spells. I'd assumed she'd used them all to wire my cage. And with Lorcan—my supposed protector—gone, she'd found another opening to sabotage me.

How could I have been so arrogant and stupid as to think I was safe from her?

The burn increased in a nanosecond. Fear pounded in my skull, worse than the pain. She was going to take me and lock me in another cage, and I'd never see the light of day again.

I lunged at her before I went down, the heel of my palm smacking her in the nose. The sound of her cartilage fracturing would have been satisfying if I didn't feel like an invisible cage closed in on me.

My eyes rolled to the back in feverish panic as I fell on my back.

"Lorcan! Reysalor!" I bellowed.

10

I heard a roar in response.

The walls of the vampires around me collapsed. Lorcan and his elite guards tossed the onlookers away. One vampire who hadn't scattered fast enough lost his head to a quick swipe of a sword.

And now Lorcan's guards formed a protective ring around their lord and me, their backs toward us. Why hadn't they come to my aid when Jezebel attacked me?

I howled as the unbearable pain seized my body and I convulsed on the marble floor like a broken, motorized doll. But before my head could hit the floor again, I was in Lorcan's arms.

"Cass, you're safe now." He cradled me. "I'm here."

My teeth clattered as I struggled to speak past the pain gnawing at me. "Safe, my ass! You left me!"

"I was called away to inspect a valuable dagger I wanted to get for you," he said, his voice laced with regret as another scream tore through me.

It felt like tiny insects were gathering on my belly, digging into my flesh and eating it. Shrieking, I tore at my midriff until the gown ripped away from my body, revealing my front.

Lorcan muttered a curse under his breath. "How the fuck did this happen?"

With the little strength left in me, I raised my head and looked down at my stomach.

A crimson pentagram was etched on my belly, a strange, menacing rune atop each of its points. They burned my skin, and the fire traveled from the five points to the three daggers imprinted in the center of the pentagram.

Dark energy burned through, only to start all over again once the circle was complete.

Nothing could be more excruciating than this pain I was enduring.

"Cass! Cassandra!" Lorcan shouted over my howling, forcing my attention back to him. "How can we stop this? Who did this to you?"

"Jezebel… The cunt threw the spells at me," I panted. "She used them to bind my power. Make her reverse it. Yank her fucking black heart out if that's what takes."

I was both surprised and impressed that I was still coherent with this unholy pain attacking my body. If I were a lesser being, I'd have been dead already.

"Secure the room," Lorcan ordered. "Bring Jezebel to me. In chains."

"My lord, please reconsider your treatment of my queen," King Dario pleaded. "Cassandra offended my queen and me. We were only trying to discipline our subject."

"When did I assign Cass as your subject?" Lorcan asked.

"She's my queen's daughter."

"Don't you know the girl is under my absolute protection?" Lorcan asked in an icy voice that made everyone cringe. His power rolled off like silent, violent thunder, and the tang of fear was thick in the hall. Even the vampire king shuddered. "Even so, your queen thought it was a good idea to harm the only asset I have who can save our race?"

Of course, he didn't want his little knife to be disposed of before he could use it.

I screamed as another surge of pain radiated from my belly and shot to my skull. It was more than I could take.

Someone, other than my mother, knew all about me and my weakness. Was it a god? He or she knew how to customize the spells to bind me, cage me, and harm me. If I got out of this, I would find the threat and eliminate it.

"Look at the girl," Dario said, contempt dripping from his words. "How can she be useful to our race? She's nothing but a rabid creature."

I could picture how rabid and demented I looked. My damp hair stuck to my sweaty forehead, my two-toned eyes darted wildly side to side, like a wounded, cornered beast, and my body trembled and kept thrashing.

"Dario, if she dies, I'll kill every being in your court, including you and your queen," Lorcan said softly.

The vampire king flinched, tensed in fear.

Two of Lorcan's elite guards pushed Jezebel forward, then shoved her into a kneeling position.

Dario hissed. "Be careful with my queen." He turned to Lorcan. "My lord, please. My queen might have been a little harsh with her methods of disciplining her daughter, but my queen hasn't been well lately. Her stress has increased exponentially since you freed Cassandra. She shouldn't be held responsible—"

"Take Dario to the dungeon," Lorcan ordered his guards. "Anyone approaching him without my permission will be executed on the spot."

A guard zoomed in, disarmed him in a blink of an eye, and dragged him away.

"High Lord, please—" Dario's begging was cut off abruptly. Lorcan's guards must have knocked him out.

The hall quieted. It seemed at some point the guards had driven the crowd out of the room. Now there was only Lorcan, his guards, a chained Jezebel, and me.

Jezebel gazed at me with tremendous sadness.

"Hand over the counter spell," Lorcan said, "and I might let you live."

"There's no antidote, my lord," Jezebel said. "All I've done was to protect her and everyone else. You don't know anything about my daughter. She's a monster. The worst you can imagine. She has no morals and no inhibitions. If I don't bind her, she'll be too powerful one day. And even you'll be her prey and victim."

Lorcan gently laid my head on the floor and moved away from me. In an instant, he was in front of Jezebel. He grabbed her throat and lifted her from the ground, chains and all.

He snarled, his eyes burning with rage. A burst of power peeled off him and rammed into her. Jezebel gasped but gazed back at him with pity.

"As powerful as you are," she said, "she's already wrapped you around her little finger. That's how seductive and dangerous she is."

"You'll reveal every ounce of truth about Cassandra Saélihn," Lorcan commanded, using his immense power to compel her. "First, you'll undo the hex. Give up the counter spell and release her from your vile grip."

He dropped her to the ground like she was a bag of garbage.

Obedience coated her eyes. He could compel her but not me. I almost cheered.

"We can't get rid of the spells, my lord," she said. "I didn't make them. I stole them. The spells were designed solely to bind her before she was born. I was supposed to be one of the most powerful beings walking the earth, but my daughter siphoned my power and rendered me weak at her birth. I was the product of careful genetic calculation and manipulation. My true and only purpose was to be the vessel to bear Cassandra Saélihn, so she could be the final instrument to destroy the world. When I learned the scheme, I fled with my daughter."

"Where did you get the spells?" Lorcan asked.

She shook her head. "Some powerful force messed with my mind. Someone took away the crucial memories when I was pregnant with Cassandra and left me with bits and pieces in shadows. I strung them together and knew that my daughter was the destroyer of the worlds, and it's always been my duty to stop her." She raised her head, tears flowing down her pale face and dark scarlet lips. "She should never have been unleashed. I've done my part binding her again, and no one can unbind her now."

I bit down on my lip to stifle the scream of pain, and blood seeped into my mouth and down my chin.

"You piece of shit!" I hissed. "Why didn't you just kill me when I was an infant and be done with it? Why did you have to make me suffer?"

Color bleached further from Jezebel's face until it was paler than white paper. "I tried. I tried to drown you. I put you in the fire. And I threw you from high buildings, but you always regenerated. It broke my heart to do so, but I had to save the worlds."

Ouch. I shouldn't have asked.

Lorcan kicked Jezebel in the face with his shiny leather shoe. "How dare you do that to any child?"

Jezebel fell backward, her head hitting the ground with a thud. "Don't you get it? She isn't as innocent as she looks. Wherever she goes, destruction and death will follow. She'll be the death of us all, including you, the most powerful vampire—"

Before I could blink, Lorcan was on her, his fangs protruding and sinking into her neck.

Dario would do anything for Jezebel because of her blood—the most exquisite taste in the world. She had no power, but her blood held intoxicating and irresistible magic.

Despite my pain, concern for Lorcan speared into my heart. I didn't want him to get addicted to her. She would have control over him if that happened.

The High Lord of Night swallowed half of Jezebel's blood and spat out the rest in utter disdain.

"Get her the fuck out of my sight," he said, blood tainting his sensual lips before he wiped it off with the back of his hand.

I howled as the burning runes sank to my insides, searing me.

Lorcan was at my side again, holding me in his arms. "Cass, we'll find the cure."

"Kill me," I bellowed. "I can't take this." I'd rather take a coward's way out than suffer this pain for eternity.

But Lorcan wouldn't kill me, not until I had fulfilled my part in his plan—kill the gods or be killed.

A beastly roar rumbled through the hall.

My panther had arrived. I choked. If he'd come to the party at the start, I wouldn't have been abandoned. Reysalor would have stayed with me and guarded me.

He tore through the vampires who tried to block him, jaws open wide, snarling in rage.

"Let him pass," Lorcan ordered.

Reysalor moved to my side and lowered himself. *Who did this to her?* His voice echoed through my mind.

Lorcan looked at Reysalor, before he gazed back down at me. Pain was raw in his stormy gray eyes.

You failed her! You fucking failed her! the panther roared at Lorcan. *Why did you even let her out of your fucking sight? What could be more important than her?*

Lorcan's eyes also flashed with rage, yet he didn't reply. Regret ate at him.

I screamed and thrashed. The burning pain had spread throughout my body and multiplied.

A bright light burst in the air, and where the panther had been, a broad-shouldered, golden-red haired man stood—a beautiful fae warrior. He crouched beside me, his turquoise eyes gazing at me with worry, rage, and agony. He looked exactly like the man the panther had shifted to in my dream.

Reysalor was a fae shifter, and he'd kept it from me!

The fae stared at the burning runes on my belly. "Can you use the runes that diffused the spells on the cage to remove these?" he asked Lorcan worriedly.

Lorcan shook his head. "They'll hurt her. When I received the vision of those spells, the instruction was they could only be used to open the cage. As soon as I inscribed them, they were erased from my mind."

"What vision?" I demanded as unceasing pain wracked me.

Lorcan sighed, and helplessness pained his gray eyes.

I had wondered how he'd obtained those counter spells. A bigger power in play, and it seemed we were all pawns.

"You've tasted the bitch queen's blood," Reysalor said. "You know her dark secrets now. Just get the counter spell from her fucking mind!"

"Jezebel doesn't have it," Lorcan said. "Her mind is muddled, all shadows and fragments, except for a determination to protect the world from her own daughter. The spells were her backup plan. If Cass survives the next forty-eight hours, her pain will lessen, but the spells won't leave her. They'll continue to bind her power."

I let out ragged breath. My power roared beneath me, unable to break free of the dark spells. I was caged yet again, but this time in my own body. When I pushed my power and rammed at the inner prison, the burning on my flesh only increased.

I trembled at the onslaught of agony.

Without my power, I was useless to the vampire lord and the fae. They should just leave me here and save themselves the trouble.

Reysalor gently pushed my damp hair back from my forehead. Lorcan watched him. He didn't like the fae touching me, but he didn't stop him, either.

"We'll take care of you, Cass," Reysalor said, his eyes filling with pain as if he felt my torment.

His words made me feel like I was more than just a tool to him.

"We need to get her back to our suite and figure something out," Lorcan said. "Let me carry her back."

"I'll carry her," Reysalor insisted.

Reysalor carefully scooped me up into his arms, and the pain seemed to lessen a little in his embrace. My head lolled onto his arm.

Reysalor tried to run as smoothly as he could, but it didn't matter. Pain riddled me. I drew a few shaky breaths to gather strength.

"You're a fae, Reys," I croaked. "I want you to change back to the panther."

I didn't get an answer, because right after my protest, I passed out.

When pain awoke me, I heard the voices before I could peel open my eyelids.

"She's burning up," Reysalor said in a low voice. "If this keeps going, she won't survive."

"She'll need to drink my blood," Lorcan said.

No! I thought in horror.

But I couldn't object. I was still struggling to come back to the world, and my voice seemed to have left me.

"She isn't a human," Reysalor said. "Can she take a vampire's blood? We don't know what she is. I've never met anyone like her."

"She's one of a kind," Lorcan said. "Jezebel's blood revealed no heritage to me, not even her own. She isn't any species I'm acquainted with, either. But I tasted potent old dragon blood in Jezebel."

"Dragons don't exist anymore," Reysalor said. "They all left with the Dragon God."

"Jezebel kept accusing Cass of being the spawn of Death," Lorcan said uncertainly.

"You mean there's a chance our Cass is the daughter of Hades, the Death God?"

My heart stuttered. Did Reysalor just call me his, theirs?

"Jezebel is a loose cannon," Reysalor continued. "Nothing she said can be proved."

"We have a lot of digging to do," Lorcan said. "You've seen Cass carry dark fire, even though she hasn't fully developed it yet. Hades also wields dark fire in the underworld."

"The demigod knows more about the gods than anyone," Reysalor said. "He might have a counter spell for Cass, or something that can help her. My twin has set out to search for him, but I haven't heard from Pyrder yet."

The dream I had with the four males swirled back to me. Reysalor's twin and the demigod had suckled on my nipples. When my fascinated gaze had dipped to his massive manhood, the demigod's honey-brown eyes had laughed at me.

I fluttered my eyes open. "The demigod Alaric Desreaux?"

Lorcan and Reysalor both leaned toward me, tension and anticipation etched on their handsome faces. My eyes flicked away from them for a second to take in where I was.

They had set me down on the large couch in Lorcan's sitting room.

Lorcan and Reysalor were the only ones with me. They hadn't even bothered to call the healers, because no healer could help me.

I sensed many guards outside the door.

"How do you know about Alaric?" Lorcan asked.

Reysalor glanced at him in annoyance. "Cass baby, we'll get the cure for you." He brushed a kiss on my forehead, which made me feel better.

"I dreamed about him," I said. "He told me his name. He has sun-kissed skin and auburn hair. He smells good."

Lorcan and Reysalor traded a look. The vampire lord seemed to swallow a growl, and a dark light flashed through Reysalor's turquoise eyes.

"What did he do in your dream?" Reysalor asked, his voice velvety and enticing.

I gave him a sly smile, which quickly morphed into a grimace as pain speared into me. "He was giving me a foot massage, and I approved of his good service."

Reysalor and Lorcan traded another perturbed look.

"Not in a million years would Alaric give anyone a foot massage," Lorcan declared.

Reysalor ignored him. "Did you dream about anyone else, Cass baby?" he asked hopefully.

The fire traveled along the runes bordering the pentagram on my skin again, and the symbol of three daggers in the center of the pentagram turned to phantom blades, stabbing and twisting into my abdomen.

I howled.

It would only stop after it finished the circle. The spell fire would give me a few minutes of interlude, then start again. I'd figured out its pattern, but there was nothing I could do about it.

"One of us needs to find Alaric as soon as possible," Lorcan muttered. "Since Pyrder hasn't succeeded. it's best if I go."

"I'll guard Cass," Reysalor said. "Be swift."

Lorcan nodded. "My guards are at your command."

Lorcan looked at me with longing before he stalked to the door. Then he ground to a halt and returned to me.

"We still need to try this," he said. "My blood is purer and superior to any other vampire's. Even if it can't get rid of the spells, it'll give you energy to fight the pain."

"No!" I hissed through gritted teeth. "I don't want to be like your kind."

"It takes a lot to turn," Lorcan said roughly, though I heard the concern under his voice. "And I doubt any vampire can ever turn you."

"No!" I insisted, blowing out a breath to stop myself from screaming in pain. "I don't want anyone's blood, least of all yours. I'm not a blood whore."

"Cass baby," Reysalor said. "What about letting Lorcan be your blood whore?"

That was the worst idea I'd ever heard. Even Lorcan growled. But Reysalor ignored him. "The High Lord's blood is the most potent among vampires. He doesn't give it easily. I believe it'll help you. He's the first and only natural-born vampire."

I blinked. "Is that why he smells different from the rest?"

Lorcan arched an eyebrow.

"The other bloodsuckers smell like they have been made or turned," I said. "They were altered, their original scent a shadow clinging to their unnatural essence. But Lorcan has a fresh, earthy scent, as if he's part of nature."

Surprise warmed Lorcan's face for a short moment.

"Then you shouldn't worry about my blood tainting you," he said drily.

His claws protruded and he sliced open his wrist. Blood gushed out in rivulets. He pressed his wrist to my mouth. "Drink," he commanded.

I pressed my lips together, but the asshole cupped my cheeks hard with his other hand, forcing my mouth to open. I couldn't fight him. I glared at him with all the menace I could muster, and in his eyes, I saw the manic glint of my own irises reflecting back at me.

The vampire would pay for this.

"You'll be fine, Cass baby," Reysalor said. "Lorcan and I will never harm you. We can never harm you."

Baby, my ass! Silver-tongued devil!

I cursed under my breath. Ever since Reysalor had shifted from beast to fae, I no longer trusted him. And this forcing me to take blood just made it worse.

The first drop of Lorcan's blood hit my tongue. It didn't taste metallic, rustic, or rotten as I'd imagined it. It was rich, sweet, and smooth. It tasted like ancient wine with special spices—cinnamon and something else I couldn't discern.

My eyes widened as a stream of blood flowed down my throat, cooling the burning along the way. Then a shockwave of pure ecstasy pumped into my veins, washing over my agony.

I closed my lips over Lorcan's wrist and sucked hard, my tongue lapping over the cut.

Lorcan's gray eyes glowed silver, intense desire burning through them. The image of him burying his face between my thighs flashed before my heavy eyelids.

The tender flesh between my thighs ached, and my pussy was slick with urgent need. I clenched my thighs to relieve the pulsing, but to no avail.

Both Lorcan and Reysalor sniffed, their nostrils flaring, their eyes brightening in lust. Lorcan clenched his teeth for control, his heart beating wildly.

My arousal didn't even embarrass me. Anything was better than feeling knifed without a break.

I kept drinking, the pounding pleasure from Lorcan's blood a pure energy. I'd never let him go. I could drain him dry.

Lorcan pulled his wrist from my clinging lips, and I darted my tongue out to lap up any stray droplets on my lips.

"That's enough for now, Cass," he said harshly, yet his masculine voice was full of heat. "Too much of my blood won't do you good."

My chest rose and fell as I panted. I should have been ashamed at my weakness, but pleasure still pulsed through my veins.

I'd vowed to never exchange blood with a vampire, and I'd just broken my vow by drinking from one, and not just from any vampire, but from the High Lord of Night, who ruled them all.

My lips parted in shameful want, and I wondered if his blood glistened on my skin.

Lorcan stared at me, his eyes hooded, burning with hunger and desire. He moved his thumb along the ridge of my bottom lip, and another kind of pleasure shot toward my heated core.

Lorcan leaned over me, and I opened my mouth in anticipation of his kiss, but instead he brushed a kiss over my burning cheek.

"I'll return for you," he said, and in a flash he was gone.

11

I woke up nestled against a warm body in the middle of the night, my head resting in the hollow of his broad shoulder, my hand splayed on his hard chest.

The smell of the forest, of pure, powerful man enveloped me, giving me a sense of safety and satisfaction. Reysalor. He was naked form the waist up, his trousers hanging low on his pelvis.

He murmured something in his sleep and pulled me closer to him.

Had he held me like that the entire night? If he had, I wouldn't complain. My skin craved touch and connection. No one had ever held me like that. I sighed contentedly and licked my lips, reminded of the taste of Lorcan's blood.

Lorcan's blood had neutralized the spell fire. The pain was merely a dull echo now. The cursed runes on my skin had gone from leaping fire to ash-colored marks. But my power was still bound.

Without it I felt vulnerable. I didn't like depending on anyone, not even Reysalor. And I had no trust in Lorcan's guards. Jade had done nothing to help me when Jezebel attacked me.

Reysalor had told me before I fell to slumber that Jade had fled. Lorcan's vampires were still hunting her. The High Lord of Night didn't take any form of betrayal lightly. Even I shuddered for Jade's fate.

Dario and Jezebel were both locked in the dungeon under heavy guard, awaiting Lorcan's verdict upon his return.

"All those who want to hurt you have been kept away," Reysalor had promised. "I won't let anyone touch you again."

I inched closer to him, my legs pressing against the hard muscles of his thigh, and basked in his body heat. His touch was like a healing balm. Strangely, both Lorcan and Reysalor were like soothing medicine while my own mother felt like a burning poison.

Dreamless sleep took me to its sweet nest with Reysalor beside me.

I woke up again to knuckles brushing my cheek fondly. My lashes fluttered as I stared up at a pair of turquoise eyes that sparkled with laughter.

His touch was so pleasurable I never wanted it to end. However, I had an attitude to maintain and I didn't want to lose it. I wouldn't be Cass Saélihn without my power and attitude. And now I was only half of what I was, caged by the spells seared into my flesh.

I let his touch linger a few more seconds before I swatted at his hand.

"What are you doing on my bed, Reysalor?" I demanded.

"Sleeping," he said with a smile. "You're soft and warm and you smell good."

"You need to get out of my bed," I said.

I didn't want him to, but I had to be a badass so no one would take advantage of me. People had a habit of taking a mile if you gave them an inch.

"I will, later," he said. "I like being in bed with you."

My heart fluttered at his confession.

"Now that you aren't a panther anymore, we need to establish rules and boundaries," I said, though I wasn't certain if I wanted a barrier between us.

I huffed in displeasure as I remembered that he'd hidden his true form from me. He'd almost made a fool out of me.

"I'm still a panther," he said. "I can shift back if you want me to."

"You can stay fae for now," I said. His sexiness was getting to me.

He grinned.

"Even in your panther form, there are still rules," I emphasized.

I wouldn't let him charm me out of my principles and integrity.

A smile ghosted his sensual lips. How it would feel to have those lips on my skin, tracing hot, sensual kisses, slowly all the way—?

I swallowed.

Quit going there.

He would smell my arousal if I didn't rid my mind of that image.

"Cass baby," he purred. "But you hate rules."

"Not my own rules."

"You'll have to list all of them on a piece of paper, so I don't make mistakes."

I sneered. Like I had time to do that.

"Now, you'll come clean and explain to me who the heck you are," I said. "And don't bother lying. I can tell it a mile away and I don't take kindly to it."

He sighed. "I haven't really lied to you. I told you I was more than a beast when we first talked, mind to mind. There was a reason I kept my panther form when I first came to the vampire court. Vampires don't like outsiders. They're a paranoid lot and there's no love lost between their race and mine. We've been fighting for dominance in the realm for as long as I remember."

I didn't blame him for not getting along with the bloodsuckers. I'd hated vampires since I was young. I'd despised my mother for being a vampire's whore more than anything. Yet I couldn't explain why I was so drawn toward Lorcan. My body reacted to his presence as strongly as it did to Reysalor.

Whenever they trained a heated look in my direction, the apex between my thighs immediately turned hot and slick.

I narrowed my eyes. "Is your name even Reysalor?"

"Everyone knows me as Reysalor Iliathorr, but only a handful of people know my full name."

"Does Lorcan know your full name?"

"He should be the last ones—he and the demigod—to know my true full name."

So, he and Lorcan and the demigod were actually rivals. And I'd dreamed all four of them shared a bed with me.

I peeked into his beautiful blue eyes. Who had the privilege of knowing this man's deepest secret?

"Who are those handful of people?" I demanded.

"My parents and my twin." His eyes flashed with a challenge, as if he wanted me to ask him his full name.

"Why is your full name such a secret? I don't see why it's such a big deal!"

"Oh, it's a big deal," he smirked. "Those who know a fae's full name hold power over him. I have a lot to teach you about this world and the mortal world. I don't intend for anyone to take advantage of you."

"What if you take advantage of me?"

He flicked my nose. "Cass baby, I'd never take advantage of you." The way he rolled my name on his tongue made my toes curl.

He pulled me closer to him, my breasts against his hard chest. Thankfully, I wasn't naked, though I wouldn't mind being naked with him at all. My face flamed at a naughty thought.

I was clad in only a sports bra and shorts. Reysalor must have wanted to make sure he could check the runes on my belly when he'd chosen this outfit for me.

I pulled away from him. "Who dressed me?"

"I did," he said.

I glared at him. "How dare you?"

"You were too exhausted to stay conscious, and your gown was in shreds."

I scoffed. "You could have asked the servant girls to dress me."

"Not a chance. I don't trust anyone. And I don't want anyone else touching you." He had the audacity to flash me a grin. "It's not like I haven't seen you naked before. If you think it's unfair, I can show you my nudity."

His hands moved to the waistline of his trousers, ready to pull them off.

"Stop!" I called.

"Why?" He looked at me with confusion. "I thought you wanted to get even."

"Forget about it," I said with exasperation.

Reysalor was the most incorrigible being I'd ever met. Lorcan was seriously annoying, too.

"Are you sure?" he asked, his big blue eyes gazing at me.

"I'm certain," I bit out. "Anyway, you need to tell me more about your background—who you really are and where you come from. Omit nothing. I'm not going to share a bed with anyone I barely know anything about."

"So you'll share a bed with me if I tell you everything?"

"It's my ass on the line! I might have a lot of unknown enemies."

His face suddenly was devoid of all playfulness. "Is the pain all gone, Cass?"

My irritation shifted inside me. Reysalor had only been trying to distract me from my pain.

"It's still there, but it's dull and throbbing now, not the sharp burn like before," I said. "Nothing I can't handle."

He rolled me over, examining the runes on my belly, then carefully ran his fingers over them. I shivered, but not because of the pain. His touch cooled my skin and heated it at the same time.

"We'll remove the spells," he said. "When Lorcan and the others return, we'll allow no nastiness to mar your perfect skin."

"Who are the others?"

"Alaric and Pyrder, my twin."

Four men. Just like in my dream.

What did that mean? Would I share a bed with all four of them? Would I have a relationship with all of them? Just one was enough to give me a headache. No, not really. Reysalor was sweet. Lorcan wasn't sweet, but he had his merits.

As I thought of him, my heart clenched at his absence. I shook my head at the longing.

"So this Alaric is good with spells?" I asked.

"When it comes to spells and summoning," Reysalor said, "he's incomparable."

"That's good to know. Tell me more about the four of you. Start with yourself, and don't omit any of your weaknesses."

"My weakness now is you, Cass."

My heart fluttered, my stomach dipped.

"We can talk after your shower. Over brunch."

I bristled. Brunch again. Did they still not realize I did not want my meals combined? After all that time of only eating once a day, I couldn't shake the fear that I would have to go back to that.

"And we'll have lunch after the brunch," he added on a laugh.

"That's the most sensible thing you've said," I stated as I rolled off the bed and headed toward the bath chamber.

Reysalor's gaze trailed after me, heat licking up my thighs. I almost asked him to shift into his panther form. There was no pressure between the panther and me, but the sexual tension between the hot fae male and me lay heavy in the air.

I jumped into the shower and washed myself as fast as possible. I was hungry. I hadn't eaten since yesterday's lunch, and Jezebel's nasty spell had eaten a lot of my energy. It was still sapping my power, but at a much slower rate.

I strode out of the bathroom and shrugged on a flowery dress. My tri-colored hair fell in curls down to my waist. I was sure Reysalor would appreciate my refreshed look and the faint scent of coconut on my skin from my new shampoo.

A full feast occupying almost the entire round table in the sitting room caught my attention before I flicked a gaze at Reysalor. He'd showered. The dude was even quicker than me.

My eyes roved over the muscled chest I'd used as a pillow for the entire night. He wore a gray T-shirt with black pattern, a pair of washed-out jeans, and white sports shoes. When I dream-visited the mortal realm, I saw human men wear the similar attire in casual settings.

Reysalor must have traveled to the human realm a lot. Did he have a mortal lover? The possibility tasted sour and bilious on my tongue.

I glared at him, his sexiness now irritating me, even as he stalked toward me with a teasing smile on his beautiful face.

He lifted me and pressed me along his length, which was all hard muscle. I clasped my hands behind his neck.

"Let me down, Reysalor," I murmured. "It's different between us now. You never should have shifted to this form!"

"I'm still me," he protested. "No matter what form I take."

He carried me to the table and set me down on a chair while the servant girls, Shan and Frances, put drinks before me.

"Now you eat, Cass baby," Reysalor said.

My gaze darted between a few glasses, as I decided on my first drink.

Frances brought a mug in front of me. "We made this herbal tea especially for you, Cass. It calms the nerves. I heard what happened last night."

News and gossip spread fast in the vampire court, even among the servants.

Before I could take a sip, Reysalor took my glass and sniffed it.

I rolled my eyes.

"You're excused," Reysalor told Frances and Shan. "I'll summon you when we're done."

The girls moved toward the door. They were less scared of Reysalor when he wasn't in his panther form. In fact, they stared doe-eyed at the fae and seemed to have little crushes on him.

"Bye," I said.

They turned to smile at me before heading out. Through the half-opened door, I glimpsed a few guards outside as they stole a glance at me.

The security was tight.

As I devoured my food, Reysalor kept me entertained and informed, just as he'd promised.

"So, you're an Unseelie fae, heir to Sihde, the Spring Isles," I said, looking at him from beneath my lashes as I sipped the rest of my tea.

I was quite full, and my stomach was content, which was rare. And the tea made me mellow and sleepy.

Reysalor arched an eyebrow at my comment, which only made him look sexier.

"What does the fae realm look like?" I asked, willing my fluttering heart to calm.

"Beautiful and dangerous beyond measure," he said.

"All beautiful things are dangerous, aren't they?"

He smiled lopsidedly. "Like you, Cass baby."

I smiled back predatorily, though I liked it that he thought me beautiful.

"Maybe I should go live with you, Reys?" I asked. "I don't like the vampire court."

I hated any place associated with Jezebel.

"It would be my honor, Cass Saélihn," he said softly, his eyes sparkling. "And I'll do anything in my power to make you safe and happy in my realm."

I sat straighter on my chair. "Why don't we leave now?" I whispered. "We can ditch all the vampires. We don't need them."

But as I said those words, the mere idea of leaving Lorcan shot a sharp pain to my chest.

It worried me. I despised vampires. Why did I feel so attached to the bloodsucker lord?

I pressed a hand on my heart, hoping it would ease the ache.

"Are you okay, Cass?" Reysalor asked, his blue eyes full of worry. "Has the pain started up again?" He was at my side before I could reply, stroking my arms.

"It's nothing," I said. "I think I ate too much."

He laughed and flicked my nose. "Take it easy, will you?" His bedroom eyes flashed darkly. "I'll never let you go hungry. You'll always be taken care of."

"So, are we going to Sihde?" I asked in a low, uncertain voice.

And again, pain rose at the prospect of leaving Lorcan behind.

"We're not ready to go to my fae realm yet, Cass," he said on a sigh. "Lorcan and I have discussed this. It isn't safe to move you to another realm just yet. The fewer people who know about you, the safer you are. We need to remove the binding spells on you, train you, and equip you in every possible way. Only then will you be ready for everything." At my brooding look, he added, "The dark fae court is vicious, more wicked and manipulative than the vampire court. Even as princes, my brother and I have to constantly fend off all sorts of backstabbing. You'll need to at least understand the basics of the fae court before I can take you there. I won't throw you to the wolves."

"I'm the lethal knife you and Lorcan need to hone," I said.

Everything they'd done for me was but a means to an end, and here I was, warming up to him like a fool just because he'd held me all through the night.

"Cass, you know it's more than that," he said, but he wasn't denying that I was their weapon.

I smiled. "I'm sure." I snatched the red wine, my fingers tapping the stem of the tall glass before I drained the liquid.

12

I formed a plan.

Reysalor, the one I'd thought was sweet and caring, also wanted to use me. No matter how valuable I was to them, I would not allow them to treat me like a weapon. I knew that when Lorcan returned, he and Reysalor would focus on sharpening their knife—me—so I could be ready to kill the gods, or die trying.

I'd toyed with the idea of using the vampire lord and the fae. I'd thought of taking off after Lorcan managed to remove this hex from me, but there was a possibility that he would add something to the counter spell to ensure that I stayed in his service.

I couldn't afford to underestimate how capable both Lorcan and Reysalor were.

If I wanted to disappear, I had to do it now while Lorcan was away and before anyone could sabotage my freedom again. I had no money and no experience, but I was tough and cunning. I could adapt to my surroundings. I would survive. First, I needed to get out of vampire territory, then out of the immortal realm altogether.

I'd spent most of my childhood dream-visiting the mortal realm and had knowledge of it. It'd be easier to disappear into the human world. Plus, the mortals fascinated me. They had such a short lifespan, but they burned fiercely during that blink of time.

When Frances returned to collect the dishes, I carted her to my bedroom. Reysalor tried to follow us, but I blocked him at the doorway.

"What's that about?" Reysalor asked suspiciously.

"I need some female necessities. I don't want you or any man to hear about it," I said. "I'm a girl. I'm shy. I need my privacy."

Reysalor shrugged, and then blinked. "Is it the time of the month? I thought—"

"Yeah, I'm a full-grown woman," I hissed, folding my arms on my chest.

He stared at me, as if trying to figure out another intriguing puzzle. I slammed the door shut in his handsome face.

"Cass baby?" he called outside the door.

I rolled my eyes.

Frances covered her mouth to stop a giggle from escaping.

"You're so badass, Cass," she whispered. "No one dares to talk that way to the High Lord and the fae prince, and you boss them around like they're your servants."

I blinked. "I don't order them around like they're servants. I wouldn't do that to anyone. I only ask them to bring me food when it's time to eat. Hunger makes me cranky."

"They'll kill anyone for the slightest offense," Frances said. "But they treat you like the royalty you are. No one attacking the king is ever left alive, but they threw the king and queen into the dungeon for you."

I sneered. "I'm useful to them."

My words reminded me why I'd brought Frances here.

"It's more than that," she whispered. "They look at you like you're the most delicious dessert in the universe."

I smirked. "The panther might think I'm his next snack, and the vampire lord regards me as his midnight drink, as if that would happen."

Frances snickered.

"Come," I said. "We don't have much time. Reysalor is very controlling. If we stay here any longer, he'll blow the door down."

I locked the door, whisked the girl into the bathroom, and shut the second door.

"Why all this secrecy?" she asked, but her eyes sparkled.

I turned on the shower.

Fae had superior hearing. But with the shower on and two closed doors, Reysalor couldn't hear our whispers, even if he pressed his ear against the wall.

"I like the sleeping tea very much, Frances," I said. "Could you bring me more tomorrow at breakfast? I need it to be heavily dosed, at least twenty times stronger than what I had today."

"It'll knock you out!"

"That's what I need. Reysalor is a sadist. He wants to turn me into a super soldier. Tomorrow, he plans to make me do a thousand sit-ups to start with."

"A thousand?" she cried.

"Shush. As I said, he's a sadist," I said. "I'm still weak after the bitch queen's attack. I need to knock myself out after breakfast, so he can't make me train."

Frances nodded in sympathy, then leaned closer. "Why did your mother treat you so bad?"

I stifled the cunning smile that wanted to stretch my lips. I'd judged the girl right. She thrived on gossip.

"That's a story for another day," I said. "If we don't get back to the sitting room soon, Reysalor will lose his shit. He's a bad panther."

"He's also a very handsome fae prince," Frances said with a dreamy look.

I squeezed her hand as I expected a friend might do. "Will you help me and bring that tea tomorrow?"

She bit on her lip, as if contemplating her next words. "I have something better if you want. The vampires have a sleep elixir that's even stronger. I know where to get it."

I gave her a thumbs-up. "This needs to stay between us. Not even Shan can know about it."

She nodded, pleased that I trusted only her.

Reysalor banged the outside door. "Cass baby, you okay in there?"

I rolled my eyes again. "See, I told you. We've only been in here for a minute or two. He's insufferable. I must set him straight."

"I'll take that kind of insufferable any day," she said wistfully. "I like when a man dominates me."

"You're helpless, girlfriend," I said, and opened the bathroom door.

She giggled.

"Cass," Reysalor asked outside the bedroom door. "Can you answer me? I need to know you're all right."

I wrenched the door open and glared at him while Frances sent him an adoring glance before she left the room.

13

The next morning after I breakfast, Frances came back alone and brought a bottle of wine.

"Sorry, Cass," she said. "We forgot to serve you the wine, so I brought the whole bottle. This is one of their best."

That was our code.

Reysalor slanted me a look. "Cass baby, I don't like it that you drink every morning. It's a bad habit."

"Says who?" I asked. "The mortals? You know I'm not one of them. You know alcohol has no effect on me. And I don't take kindly to you scowling at me!"

"I'm not scowling at you. I'm merely concerned. If you think alcohol has no effect on you, you're in for a surprise once you try the fae brew."

I pursed my lips. "But you refuse to take me to the fae realm."

"We'll live in Sihde as long as you want once the realm is safe," Reysalor said.

He and Lorcan would dangle that bait in front of me when they demanded I kill the gods in the near future—that much I was certain of.

"Whatever," I murmured as I picked up the glass of wine Frances had poured for me.

"Wait," Reysalor said. "I'll taste it first."

I handed him the glass and nodded at Frances. "You can go. See you at lunch."

She gave me a knowing smile as she retreated.

Reysalor took a sip of the wine from my glass.

"It tastes strong," he said, his brows creasing. "And it has an herbal aftertaste."

"It's a fruit wine, genius," I said, bluffing.

I couldn't chance him figuring out and ruining my plan, so I stood from my chair and strutted toward him, settling myself on his lap and grinding my ass into his crotch.

"Cass?"

He had held me in his sleep the whole night, and now he had an issue with this?

I clasped my hands behind his neck. "Yes, Reys?"

He immediately put down the glass, his hands wrapping around me. He didn't have a problem with me straddling him, after all.

"You okay, baby?" he asked uncertainly, but his arms remained wrapped around me.

"Never better, Reys," I said, batting my eyelashes at him. "I had a dream about you the other night. I also dreamed about the demigod Alaric."

"What was the dream about?" he asked, his body tensing beneath me.

"Let me show you," I whispered, and I crushed my lips to his.

He became very still, but the pounding of his powerful heart was so loud I almost mistook it for my own racing heart.

"…know what you're doing, Cass?" he murmured against my lips

I pulled my lips half an inch away from his, my body protesting at the sudden loss of contact. It wanted the fae male.

I traced his bottom lip back and forth with my tongue, my breath growing shallower with every stroke. "I'm not a child, Reys," I murmured, and placed my lips on his again.

His skin heated under my touch, mirroring the heat that spread through my body. With a little coaxing, he kissed me back, moving us from gentle to hard, from uncertainty to fierce.

His control slipped away.

Reysalor wanted me. He'd wanted me the first time he'd laid his eyes upon me, even though I had looked like a filthy savage in the cage. I knew that instinctively.

Right now, I was simply acting on my instincts.

This was my first kiss, and it was much more pleasant than any kiss I'd ever imagined. His delicious warmth and that intoxicating woodsy scent wrapped around me. All my thoughts left me, the world around me disappeared. The only thing that existed was him, and the feel of him against me.

I kissed him raw, though I lacked skill in this department.

Reysalor took over. The tip of his tongue swept over my lips, then urged me to part them. I opened my mouth on a gasp and thrust my tongue roughly to meet his. He guided me with patience, seduction, and fire, until I learned the dance.

His tongue thrust deeper, mating mine with carnal fire.

A jolt of pleasure hit my nerve ends, and heat rushed in my bloodstream.

A low moan escaped my throat.

Liquid fire pooled between my thighs, soaking my panties. His massive erection pricked beneath me.

My breath came out in shallow pants as pure need for him took over my body. I rocked my hips against his arousal, my fingers twining in his hair. I wanted his cock inside me right now, more than anything in the world. Fiery lust coursed in my veins, and only he could cool it down before it consumed me.

He tore his lips from mine.

"No," I whimpered. "Don't stop."

This might be the last time I had a chance to have him. I wanted to keep his memory with me, even though his ultimate plan was for me to be his lethal weapon.

"Cass baby," he groaned. "We need to stop, or I won't be able to stop."

"Don't you want me?"

"I want you more than anything in the world," he said, his turquoise eyes turned pure, burning golden. "I've wanted to claim you and make you mine from the moment I set eyes on you. But I also have to honor my pact with the others— the four of us."

The dream of the four men sharing me flashed across my mind, but right now I didn't care for any of them. All I wanted was Reysalor, and I wanted his cock buried inside me.

"Just let me have a little taste, Reys. We won't go further than that," I murmured as my fingers worked the fly of his jeans and pulled out his cock. I looked down between our bodies, and gasped at how hard, silky, and beautiful it was.

Heat burned in his golden eyes as he watched me stare fascinated at his massive erection. He pulled me closer and took my mouth.

He placed a hand in my thick curls and his other dipped into my dress and cupped my right breast.

Lust and pleasure surged in me, rocking my senses.

He tweaked my nipple, rolling it between his thumb and forefinger. I pulled my lips from him, my thumb spreading the bead of moisture on his tip over his cock.

Reysalor groaned, and he abandoned my breast, his hand making its way down between my thighs and into my panties. He gathered the moisture pooled between my swollen lips and stroked my clit.

I arched my back as a moan left my lips.

I lifted my hips. I was ready, but he denied me the pleasure of his cock, instead inserting a finger into my tight entrance.

"More," I gasped.

"Just a little then, Cass baby," he said roughly. "I'll only fuck you and claim you when we're ready."

"Whatever you want, Reys," I panted.

He pulled out his finger, gripped the length of his cock, and aimed the thick crown between my plump folds. I eagerly glided down an inch, and we both gasped at the incredible pleasure at the shallow joining.

He thrust up, and then he was two inches or so inside me. I winced at the girth until my body relaxed into him and the pain became pleasurable. I tried to push down, needing him to fill me completely, but he held firm on my hips.

"We should go no further," he said huskily, lust slurring his voice. "We'll just taste each other a little."

He gripped my hips and moved me on the two inches of his length. We went slowly first, then he moved faster and harder.

We both panted, our breath mingling as we fucked each other shallowly.

This carnal pleasure topped anything I'd ever experienced.

I wanted more of him. My hands dug into his shoulders, and before he could react or stop me, I plunged down all the way to his base, my shapely ass slamming into his balls.

Pain pierced me as he tore through the barrier—he was too large for me, and my depth was narrow. But then waves of pleasure washed over the ache.

Reys let out a rasping breath at our full contact. Reluctance and unbridled lust warred in his liquid golden eyes that burned with beautiful fae fire.

Before he could pull out of me, I said, "It feels so good, Reys. Just a little bit more."

"I'll have to take you hard and claim you properly another day," he said. "Soon."

"Fine, just give me a few seconds," I said as I rocked my hips, sending a different, more pleasing sensation through me.

Even though the pleasure was all-consuming, my plan still lingered in the back of my mind. I had to act now.

I grabbed the glass of wine with the sleep elixir in it, took a mouthful, and pressed my lips against Reysalor's. When he opened his mouth for me, I poured the liquid into it.

Our tongues tangled as he swallowed the drugged wine.

I took another swig. After the third time, the glass was nearly empty.

His tongue twirling around mine slowed down, as if it grew heavy.

I withdrew my tongue, and cupped his face.

I rocked on his hard cock, need and lust still lashing at my molten core. It was a pity I wouldn't be able to finish this.

His eyelids drifted shut. "There's something wrong, Cass baby," he slurred. "It's either the kiss or the wine."

"You're tired, Reys," I whispered. "Take a nap. You need it." I brushed a kiss over his lips.

With a struggle, he peeled open his eyes and blinked at me. Then rage formed in them as he realized what I had done.

"Cass, did you intentionally drug—"

His hand lashed out. I thought he was going to strangle me, but he didn't. His fae power roared over me, but it was too late.

The potent elixir was in his bloodstream, and the wine made it flow faster.

"Don't, Cass. I need to protect—" His head lolled onto his shoulder as sleep dragged him under.

His cock was still granite hard inside me.

By sheer will, I pulled off him, leaving my body screaming in frustration.

Sighing, I arranged his cock as best I could back into his trousers, then grabbed a blanket to cover him. I shed my dress as I moved to the closet and grabbed some hunting clothes and boots. Once dressed, I grabbed one of Reysalor's daggers and hid it under my leather jacket.

I went to the bathroom to rinse my mouth and brush my tongue, lest any remnants of the sleeping elixir affect me.

When I was done, I went to Reysalor and gave him a warm, sensual kiss in farewell.

"I have to do this on my own, Reys," I murmured. "Otherwise I'll always have a target on my back, or I'll forever have to do your or Lorcan's bidding. I'll never be free if I stay."

I turned on my heel, opened the door, and slid out, making sure to shut it noiselessly behind me.

14

I flashed a vicious grin at the four guards outside the door and strode toward the other end of the hallway, as if I owned the building.

I'd chosen this hour to depart because vampires were most languid during daytime, and right now most of them slumbered in their shaded quarters.

Once I got out of here, the vampires wouldn't be too much of a threat to me.

"Stop!" a guard called after me, then chased me when he saw I had no intention of halting.

Panic rose to my throat, but I didn't rush my steps. I couldn't let them see how worried I was. Vampires are predators. As soon as you run, you become prey, and they hunt you down.

"Where are you going, Miss Saélihn?" the guard asked, his hand grabbing my biceps, trying to make me stop.

If I had my power, he would have lost his hand. But Jezebel's spell prevented me from accessing it. My only hope was that her spells would eventually wear off.

I elbowed the guard.

"How dare you lay a finger on me?" I said with barely contained rage. "And who the fuck are you to question me?"

He stepped back, a grimace clouding his pretty face.

He'd seen my bad attitude toward Lorcan and my assault on the vampire king, so he knew I wouldn't be civil if a lowly guard crossed me.

"You're supposed to stay in your room, Miss Saélihn, for your safety," he stuttered. The poor thing looked exhausted. Of course, this was his usual sleeping time.

I let a manic light glint in my eyes. "Are you fucking threatening me?"

"No, Miss Saélihn, I wouldn't," he said meekly. "We're your guards. It's our duty to keep you safe."

"I'm going for a walk," I ground out, turning on my heels and keeping my pace. "This whole place is like a fucking cage."

"Shouldn't Prince Reysalor accompany you?" he inquired.

I wheeled on him with a taunting grin. "You want to challenge His Highness Reysalor and question his decision to let me have fresh air?"

It sounded ridiculous to call Reys "His Highness." His haunting kiss still burned on my lips. I'd seduced him, and his control had slipped. I wanted to cry out at the sudden stab of pain at leaving him behind, but I clenched my jaw to conceal it. I didn't even know him or Lorcan that well, and yet it pained me to be away from them. This strange, strong attachment was doing me no good.

The guard looked uncertain. "But he's always with you."

I shrugged nonchalantly and kept walking.

He sighed and followed me, and then two other guards trailed after us.

Great. Just fucking great. I couldn't even fool them into letting me take a walk on my own.

"Prince Reysalor agreed to let me enjoy the view outside alone," I said, my voice full of menace. "Do you lot really want to piss him off?"

He didn't halt. "I'm sorry, Miss Saélihn, with respect. We have to do our job to safeguard you, or the High Lord will have our heads."

I could see the guard was grappling with a dilemma. Lorcan had never issued an order that I couldn't leave the dome unescorted, since he'd assumed Reysalor would keep me in line. He'd never expected that I would try to escape.

I'd vowed to him that I wouldn't run away before I was ready, but under the circumstances, I had to go. I didn't trust that Lorcan would put my interests first. When he brought the help and released the spells that bound my power, nothing would stop him from adding his own spells to keep me on a short leash.

The lord of all vampires would never let his most lethal weapon be uncontrolled.

If I didn't flee now, I would never escape the path he'd set for me. I couldn't afford to be weak—mentally, physically, or emotionally—if I wanted my freedom.

Just as I pondered how to ditch the vampire guards, another vampire spoke up behind me, "Let Miss Cassandra Saélihn enjoy the fresh air undisturbed. I've just checked with Prince Reysalor, and that's his order."

Why was this guard lying to help me out? I looked over my shoulder at him, narrowing my eyes when I realized he was one of Jade's friends. He'd sneered at me when my power hadn't worked on Lorcan or Reysalor in the training hall, and I'd lashed out at him with my black fire. I smirked when I saw that he was wearing a wig now.

He hated me, so I truly had no idea why he was helping me. I shrugged. I needed to hurry before Reysalor woke up.

"I'll tag her in the distance," he said. "And I'll bring her back later."

As if he could.

"I'm not sure, Gasper," the guard who had first stopped me said. "We should all go with her and protect her."

"Why don't you and I tag along instead of having everyone follow Miss Saélihn?" Gasper said. "You know how it'll turn out for us when the wild thing bites."

I almost snorted, but I didn't slow my pace.

The plan worked for me. I could ditch the two of them. The vampires were fast, but they hadn't seen my speed yet. Jezebel's spells inhibited my aggressive power, but they couldn't limit my natural ability—my eyesight, hearing, and speed.

"Trust me, Fagan," Gasper said. "I'm much older than you. I've handled hundreds of the High Lord's women."

That stung. If I didn't have to hurry, I'd slap him for the gossiping bitch he was.

"She isn't like any of them," Fagan said, lowering his voice. "His High Lord treats her differently and gives her leverage, despite her manners."

"He might think she's interesting right now, but in the end, it's all the same for him. He never keeps anyone after a couple of months."

The information of Lorcan's past women grated on my nerves.

"I'm not Lorcan's bitch, dicks," I half-shouted.

I strode past an archway and headed to a side door at the end of a chapel. Light bled into the room and thrill shot through me. My freedom lay just outside that door.

Guards usually milled about all over the place, but it was quiet today, too quiet. But I chalked that up to the hour.

I kicked the door. It cracked but still hung on. I gave it another boot, and the door tumbled down. I needed to leave this place with attitude, so no one would suspect that I was fleeing.

The gossiping behind me subdued, and I could picture the guards trading an alarmed look. When I stepped on the heavy wooden door and went outside, the guards didn't follow me immediately.

I took a lungful of air. The scent of fresh grass, morning dew, and faint blossoms wafted toward me, calling me to venture further into the nature.

The sunlight was dim and weak. It seemed always dim and weak in ShadesStar. It must have been the deciding factor when Dario had picked this terrain as his lair. It was too bad. I had been hoping for strong sunbeam to bake the vampires' asses.

A trace of magic from the soil tugged at me as I trod on the infinite fields of lush grass, but when I called it, the magic slid away. The earth sensed the binding spells inside me and wanted nothing to do with them.

All the more reason to get the hell out of here, before more spells came my way.

Strangely, the guards were scarce outside the dome as well, even in such a weak sunlight.

I bolted toward northwest toward the mountains.

Reysalor hadn't tried to keep me ignorant when I asked him about the geography of the immortal realm. The vampire domain was called ShadesStar. Over the mountain was Moonshine, the shifters' territory. On the west across the shining sea was the fae realm of Sihde, the Spring Isles.

Between the three immortal realms was a triangular area, where a leyline to the mortal realm rested. That was where I raced to.

The vampire guards shouted behind me and gave a chase.

They zoomed in toward me and I zoomed out of their range.

Bloodsuckers.

I laughed. They hadn't expected me to be this fast. What could I say? I was full of surprises.

The only two who could equal me were occupied now—one out looking for the demigod, and the other napping.

I laughed again at my shrewdness, and joy filled me. I was almost free.

Faster than an arrow, I ran past a cluster of pink bushes in a blur. The knee-high grass was untended on this fraction of the field, but it didn't slow me down. Thorns poked through the vines, but I swept past them undeterred. I was clad all in leather—boots, pants, and jacket—and it shielded me from any thorns.

"Stop, Miss Saélihn! Please stop!" Fagan's pathetic begging faded with the wind.

I reached rocky terrain, never once slowing my pace.

Once I entered the mortal realm, I'd blend into the crowd, become one of their faces, and vanish without a trace. I would live off the grid. I would make sure no one found me. My freedom would be mine to keep.

I would have to change my appearance, though. I would have to dye my hair, or at least get it all in one color. Right now, I was too noticeable. I would have to conceal my eyes somehow as well, but I would ponder that as soon as I reached one of the three cities I'd dream-visited: New York, Portland, or Sydney. Mostly Sydney. I would have to toss a coin to decide, and I would have to steal a coin from somewhere to do that.

I slowed as I spotted shadowy specks ahead.

Vampires.

An entire horde swarmed toward me.

I sharpened my focus and noticed more of them pouring out from an underground tunnel to the surface.

Half of the dome was built under the ground, and the vampire army had taken a shortcut to cut me off. In no time at all, more than thirty goons surrounded me.

"Fuck you all," I spat. "I'm not going back."

"Who said we want you back?" a familiar cold voice asked.

King Dario stepped through the opening. Jade fell in step to his left, her longsword drawn.

Reysalor had said that Jade had fled and Lorcan's guards had been hunting her. It was obvious that they hadn't been hunting her seriously enough if she'd managed to free the vampire king from the dungeon.

Jade tilted her blonde head. "You thought the guards would let you out so easily without a reason?"

No wonder her friend Gasper had urged the other guards to let me out, so this bunch could hunt me. And I'd thought that vampire rat was trying to gain my favor by kissing my ass.

It had been a fucking set-up.

They didn't want to capture me. They wanted me dead.

Without my power, I doubted I could even take down two of them.

My heart beat an erratic rhythm, and Jade's upper lip curled in a sneer.

They could all hear my frenetic heartbeat.

"I thought bloodsuckers don't like the daylight." I managed to say it casually, stalling them, but in my head I screamed Reysalor's name. I'd once called for him in the vampire's hall, and he'd come for me, a bit late though. Now the chance of him reaching me in time was remote, since I'd drugged him into a deep slumber.

Dario flashed a black sapphire ring on his finger. "Daylight doesn't affect us much when we have the day ring, and the sun is less intense here than in other realms. It's pity you've never been properly schooled."

Whose fault was that? But I couldn't challenge him now. I was weak. And alone.

"Who made the rings?" I asked, noticing that the vampires all had black rings on their fingers. I needed to keep the conversation going while I tried to come up with a plan. "A witch? Do you have a witch on your payroll? She must be expensive if she can make day rings for bloodsuckers. Perhaps I should meet her since she's so useful."

"I'm afraid you won't get that chance. Today, we'll kill you," Jade said, stepping one foot closer to me and flashing her blade. "It's nothing personal. But I have to protect my interests and those of my sister, who is the mistress of the Court of Blood and Void."

"I thought the court belongs to Lorcan," I said.

Jade hissed in rage at my blaspheming her High Lord by using his first name. I gave her a shrug.

"Mistress, huh? Like a concubine?" I was both mad and curious that Lorcan had a concubine.

She ignored my question.

"Listen," I said, putting up my hands defensively. "I'm not a threat to you. I was planning to disappear into the mortal realm. Just let me go, and you'll never hear from me again."

"The High Lord will search for you to the ends of Earth," Jade said. "It's best we end you, so he can't follow, and life will go back to the way it was."

"Before you, no one could enthrall the High Lord of Night." Dario's voice dripped with distaste. "He's never acted like this before. He was highly intelligent and never thought with his dick. But the moment you came onto the scene, he put you in the center of the universe. He put you above the court and everyone else. You've been out of the cage for less than a week, and you've already caused havoc and turned everything upside down. You disturbed the balance. You have no regard or respect for any traditions, and he doesn't even care. He even threw me, the *King* of ShadesStar, into the dungeon for you, and chained my beloved queen."

"Once you're dead, the spell you put on our lord will drop," Jade said. "And the High Lord will return to his true self and lead us to the glorious days ahead, with me by his side."

There was assent to her words in every vampire's eyes. They were truly under the impression that I had bewitched Lorcan, and that they were doing him a loyal service by eliminating me. I had no way to persuade these delusional assassins.

Fagan's voice came from outside the circle. "What is this? It's a coup! You can't do that! Let her go. She's important to the High Lord."

That was the wrong thing to say. Now they wouldn't let him live, either. I felt sorry for the guard.

"I told you not to follow, Fagan," Gasper said.

The sound of blade cutting into flesh made me flinch. Fagan gagged and slumped to the ground, eternally dead.

None of the vampires batted an eye.

"We don't know what kind of monster you are, Cassandra," Dario continued. "But my queen was wise to lock you up in the cage. She's heartbroken knowing you can't be saved."

The mere mention of the cage made my blood boil, but I contained my rage.

"We'll all have a taste of your blood," Jade said, her teeth glinting even in the dull sunlight. "Then we'll see for ourselves why the High Lord is so taken with you."

Thirst blazed in the vampire horde's eyes. They all wanted to drink from me.

"No!" Jezebel shrieked somewhere.

Mother dearest had arrived, or perhaps she had been there all along. I'd been so distracted by the assassins that I hadn't sensed her presence.

Would she save me? Would she try to whisk me to another cage?

"Do not drink her blood," Jezebel said. "You promised me, my king."

Dario's eyes softened. "Worry no more, my queen."

"Just end my daughter quickly," Jezebel said, moving forward and standing beside her husband. "Don't make her suffer."

I smiled at her like a hungry wolf.

"I'm sorry, Cassandra," she said. Sadness shone in her blue eyes. "High Lord Lorcan and the fae prince have no idea that you are destined to be the death of the world. Lorcan thinks you'll kill the Olympian gods for him, but you're one of them. A glimpse of one of my memories showed me that you're the worst of them. It breaks my heart, but I must sacrifice my own child for the good of the world."

"Shut your face, you cunt," I said.

"You'll respect my queen, you unruly little bitch, or I'll silence you!" Dario snarled, his eyes turning crimson.

He was determined to kill this unruly little bitch, but at least he hadn't called me *stepdaughter*. That would have given me the creeps.

A beast's feral roar thundered across the land.

"Reys!" As I screamed his name, I turned and charged the vampires closest to my panther, piercing my dagger into a vampire's heart.

15

I had no battle training, but I had the speed of rampant fire that no vampire could catch.

I yanked out the dagger from the vampire before he fell, then kicked down another, so I could charge out of the small opening toward Reysalor.

The panther raced toward me like a black shadow.

He slammed into a vampire, who was about to sink his claws into my flesh, and tore the bloodsucker's throat out. Reysalor shifted, not to fae, but to something in between. A hybrid form.

His fae eyes burned through his panther head, glowing golden fire. He stood over eight feet high, his long muscled legs those of a fae. His right arm ended in sharp claws, but his left muscled arm was fae-like and a flaming sword appeared in his grip.

Reysalor swung the sword in a wide arc. The blade sizzled as it touched the vampire's neck, burning through the flesh as the steel removed the bloodsucker's head from his body.

I cheered him on, delighted.

Dario yelled, "Kill the fae, then the girl!"

"Run, Cass," Reysalor shouted. "Run toward the mountains. Go to the shifters' realm!"

He had once told me vampires and shifters were ancient foes and would always be, even though the two races weren't at war right now.

Reysalor rammed into the vampires' rank like a force of nature. He leapt high in the air, and when his sword of fire rained down its wrath, vampires fell around him.

But the vampires were also formidable predators and there were legions of them. They rushed toward Reysalor in sheer numbers and with monstrous strength.

"Go, Cass! What are you waiting for?" Reysalor roared as he thrust his blade into a long-haired vampire.

I wasn't going to leave him behind, even though my safety had led to this battle in the first place. He was too hot, wicked, and loyal for me to leave him now.

I roared, waving my dagger like a mad woman and thrusting it toward the bastards who tried to sneak up on

Reys, but Jade lunged and cut in front of me with a cold, cruel smile.

Seven vampires closed in on me while the rest battled Reysalor.

I shouted a warning as Dario dashed toward Reys from his blind side. The vampire king slashed his claws across Reys's back and tore a patch of fur and flesh out. Reysalor roared in pain, and my blood bubbled with fear and rage. I wanted to go to him, to rip Dario's head off his shoulders. But I couldn't before I handled the vampires surrounding me.

I had no fighting technique, and all the vampires were trained warriors, especially Jade, who had captained Lorcan's elite guards. Thanks to my mother binding my power, all I could rely on was my speed and my cunning.

I spun as fast as I could, and swung my dagger toward the vampires. I bled several of them, but none fell or withdrew, which didn't bode well for me.

From Reysalor's side, the cries of combat increased. He had over a dozen vampires on him, his fur and skin tainted with blood.

Just as my heart ached for Reys's injuries, Dario, the most-skilled vampire fighter, slashed open another gush on the panther warrior's side. The fucker had some big cuts from Reys, too. A deep gash on his neck pleased me.

It was a pity Reys hadn't been able to finish the job. There were too many vampires attacking him. One on one, Reys probably would have taken the vampire king down already.

Reysalor swung his sword toward Dario again, intent on beheading his foe, but Dario's broadsword rose just as fast to meet the flaming sword.

It seemed that Reysalor's fire sword couldn't break Dario's black steel. The dickhead king's sword was probably warded with spells, considering how his crazy wife had stashed spells.

Reys fought toward me, but the vampires swarmed him, stopping him from reaching me.

I kept spinning like a blur. As soon as I found an opening, I stabbed a vampire's chest. I had aimed for Jade, as I was most eager to take her out, but she deflected every single one of my moves with her longsword.

The impact of our blades crossing almost threw me onto the tip of another vampire's sword. I had the speed, but Jade was extremely skilled. Without my powers, I doubted I had a chance of damaging her.

As I dragged my dagger out of another vampire, my motion slowed a flick, and that second cost me. Jade drove her sword toward me. I ducked, but I couldn't dodge fast enough. Her longsword missed my heart and buried into the flesh below my shoulder blade.

I cried out as pain exploded in me.

"Cass!" Reysalor roared my name.

His fear and panic for me cost him. I saw him go down, the vampires pinning him to the ground.

Jade laughed and dragged out her sword, and blood shot out from my wound.

I staggered back.

The vampires around me sniffed, their eyes turning completely crimson. My blood was even more irresistible to vampires than my mother's, rigged with richness and magic.

They closed in on me in a frenzy. Every single one of them wanted my blood.

"No!" Jezebel screamed. "Just finish her. Don't take her blood! Once you cut her head off, you'll need to distribute her body parts to all corners of Earth, otherwise she'll just regenerate."

I gasped, both from the pain of my wound and the shock of my mother's words. Why did she still surprise me?

A claw slashed my leather pants open and left a gush on my thigh. Then another claw sliced across my other leg. They were now toying with me since my protector was no longer a threat— Dario had him pinned under his heavy boot.

My pants were in tatters in a matter of seconds.

Jade hit me again, slamming her fist into my face so hard I fell backward. My head crashed against a rock protruding from the grassy field.

I barely had time to draw a breath before the vampires were upon me, pinning me down and disarming me.

As Jade leaned closer with her usual leer, I spat at her, my own blood rich on my tongue. Everything in me raged at the malevolent spells that bound the power coursing in my veins.

"Cass!" Reysalor roared my name in infernal fury as he struggled to break the vampires' hold on him. "Let her go. You can kill me. She's but an innocent girl."

The king sneered. "You'll all die, but I'll let her watch you die first."

"Reys!" I screamed back.

Something snapped in me. I couldn't let them kill him. I'd never experienced warmth and laughter until Reysalor came into my life. He and Lorcan had freed me, and Reys had given me more than just carnal pleasure. He'd given me friendship and more.

I no longer cared whether he wanted to use me as his weapon or not. He was willing to lay down his life for me. He'd wanted me to leave him and escape to the shifter realm.

My fists pounded on the earth. I knew I had an affinity to it, and it was all that could save us now. At my roaring call, the magic hidden deeply in the soil rose to me.

"Take my blood as my sacrifice!" I shouted, my voice filling the air. "Aid me. Rise in me. Merge with me. Free my binds!"

The ground rumbled, and rocks rose all around me.

"She's going to free herself of the spells!" Jezebel shrieked. "Take her now before it's too late!"

"Die, Cassandra Saélihn," Jade hissed, raising her blade high and plunging it toward my heart.

"Don't you touch her!" Reysalor roared, throwing off the vampires, even with a dagger half-buried in his chest.

Just as he pulled the dagger out of his body and tossed it toward Jade, my power blasted out. My hand broke free of the restraint, grabbed the female vampire's blade, and stopped it from plummeting further. Another two inches and it would have punctured my chest.

Jade widened her eyes in disbelief as black fire streamed from my hand and melted her blade. Her body flew backward, Reysalor's flaming sword piercing right through her rib cage.

I snapped my fingers and my fire engulfed her.

Jade screamed as the dark fire burned her inch to inch, licking the blood that dripped from Reysalor's blade in her chest. It had pierced one of her organs, though not her heart.

My air current sent the vampires around us flying into the air, their shocked expressions dying on their faces. Before Dario could zoom toward Jezebel and take her to safety, my wind grabbed him.

"Going somewhere, stepfather?" I laughed drily.

The vampire king jerked back and forth like a marionette as he struggled to break free from my magical hold.

"Let him go, Cassandra! He's your king!" Jezebel shrieked.

I sent a blast of wind to slap her pretty face, and my black fire danced on her thick hair. She was going bald.

"You monster!" she screamed.

"I came from your womb, Mother dear."

I let my icy current enter Dario's chest and grab his heart like an iron hand, only to find that his heart didn't beat. Why was I even surprised? The only vampire with a heartbeat was Lorcan, and he wasn't here.

Reysalor picked up his flaming sword and gave it a wide swing. The blade glided through Dario's neck.

The rest of the vampires fled like flying shadows, yet my wind and fire were faster. They hit Gasper first.

While my air tore the vampires apart and my fire burned them to ashes, I wheeled toward Jezebel with a diabolic smirk, two columns of black fire twirling on my palms, traveling along my arms, hissing, raging, and desiring more destruction.

"Hello, *Mother*," I said. "Are you proud of your little monster?"

Pain flickered over her face. Her ability to feel pain made my skin crawl.

Reysalor stalked toward her, the sword dripping with the vampire king's blood.

"You're the worst creature ever spawned," he said to her. "You don't deserve to be a mother. No mother could do to her child what you did to Cass. You don't deserve to live, and I'll rid Earth of your filth."

She turned to Reys, her eyes widening as if his words wronged her.

I wouldn't stop Reys from terminating her—as long as we both lived, she'd always be my worst enemy and would never cease to find a way to either cage me or kill me. But I didn't want to watch him decapitate her.

Just before I closed my eyes, Jezebel threw her head back, her arms spreading, and shouted a string of ancient words.

Power—not hers—ripped the air, and black wind rose around us.

Reysalor swung his sword, but Jezebel vanished with the wind before the sword could bite into her flesh.

"What the fuck?" he yelled in displeasure.

I sighed, resigned. She would return once she'd found a way to do worse to me. I would have to wait for that day.

Reysalor scanned the corpses, ashes, and burned landscape. When he perceived no further threat, he muttered an ancient word, and his flaming sword disappeared.

He shifted fully to the gorgeous fae I'd seduced earlier and moved toward me in two long strides, pulling me into his arms.

I rested my head against his broad chest, wrapping my arms around his firm waist. We were alive. We'd vanquished my enemies. And I'd gotten my power back.

His body heat seeped into me, caressing and comforting me.

I waited for him to scold me for drugging him and then running away, but he didn't. I was only glad that he was powerful enough to conquer the effects of the sleep elixir and reach me in time. Reysalor tightened his grip on me before releasing me, then he examined me, even though he'd been hurt worse than me.

My wounds were mostly healed already.

Since the earth power had aided me and purged the spells that bound me, my healing had sped up. To my relief, Reys was also healing fast.

He regarded me, a thousand words in his turquoise eyes that were like the bluest sea in my dream. I could tell that he had already forgiven me because I was in one piece.

I smiled at him. "Where did you get that wicked sword of fire, Reys?" I asked. "Think you can make me one?"

He sighed. "Don't run from me again."

Uh-oh, there he went. Now he was going to lecture me and ruin my victorious mood.

"The next time you do that, it'll be the death of me, my little Cass," he whispered.

16

"Reys," I said with a clenched jaw as I looked in the direction of the vampire dome. "I won't go back."

"I'm not asking you to go back."

My eyes must have sparkled, and a smile tugged up my lips. "Really?"

"ShadesStar isn't safe for you anymore," he said. "We don't know who's in league with the rogue vampires."

"You're so wise." I gave him a broader smile. "Where are we going then? Should we go to the mortal realm?"

"The mortal realm isn't safe, either. We'll go to the edge between the mortal and immortal realm."

"Is there such a place?"

"We'll leave for the Academy," he said, his eyes crinkling at the corners.

"You mean a school?"

I had always wanted to go to school, where I could make friends and study. It wasn't like my mother had seen any need to homeschool me. Everything I knew came from my dream-visits to the mortal realm. It was one of my gifts Jezebel had never found out about and thus couldn't take from me.

"It's called The Gifted Academy."

I bounced up and down on the rocky terrain in excitement. "How do we get to that awesome place?"

It had to be awesome, right? It was a school!

"You have me, Cass baby," he said.

I grinned ear to ear. This was my lucky break. I would have a fresh start. There really was first time for everything.

First fresh air. First sight of the night sky. First school. First kiss. And first boyfriend.

I slanted a gaze at him. Would Reysalor be my boyfriend? His eyes shifted between turquoise and golden, burning with desire. My heart fluttered.

"What are you smirking at?" he asked, tousling my curly hair.

"We need to bring Frances and Shan," I said. "I can't leave them behind. The vampire lair isn't safe for them."

The girls were nice to me, and I wouldn't forget a debt.

He frowned. "Frances and Shan?" Then it dawned on him, and his face turned to stormy clouds. "The ones who got you the sleep elixir?"

"They weren't in on it," I said. "They didn't know. We need to get them and bring them to safety with us."

"I'll have them collected for you, but not now, not before Lorcan returns and cleans his house."

I fell into step with him as we headed northwest, my original direction.

"Are we still going to get in touch with Lorcan?" I asked hesitantly.

Pain throbbed in my chest at the prospect of never seeing Lorcan again, but then—

Reysalor sent me a sidelong glance, never once breaking his stride.

"What's that about?" he asked.

"What if he brings back another spell that can harm me?" I asked. "A spell that will bind me to his will and enslave me?"

He stopped in his tracks, his gaze roaming my face, studying every line and missing nothing.

"Is that why you ran away, Cass?"

The vein in my temple jumped. "I don't trust easily. Don't ask me to."

"You can learn to trust us, Cass. But we'll have to earn it first, right?"

"Well." I gave a small shrug.

"He'll never do that to you," he said matter-of-factly. "Nor will I allow him or anyone to do that to you."

There was no lie in his words, just simple truth.

"Lorcan—none of us—will ever hurt you or try to control you beyond reason," he said.

"Which means you'll try to control me within reason?"

He smiled and kissed my cheek, causing my pulse to spike. I wanted more. I gazed up at him through my lashes. I want him to devour my mouth.

"A certain degree of control is healthy," he said. "We'd want you to keep us on our toes as well."

"I can keep you on your big toes?"

He brushed his lips across the tip of my nose before stepping back and shifting to his panther form.

Come on, Cass baby, he said in my head. *We gotta run. The day isn't waiting.*

"The day isn't going anywhere, either."

He laughed lightly in my head, and the sensuality echoed in the chamber of my skull.

We raced northwest together.

Once he saw I could easily keep up with him, he pulled out his top speed. I ran beside him and we soon passed the rocky terrain and whisked through the meadow.

Everything around us became a blur as I raced beside the panther, feeling utterly free for the first time in my life.

I threw my head back and roared with joy.

Reysalor suddenly shifted back to fae, flung me over his shoulder, and sprinted with me laughing. He murmured a string of ancient fae words, and golden mist appeared in front of us. He didn't slow down, but shot into the mist.

I was spinning within a band of stars.

When the world returned to me, lush green, purple, and blue zoomed toward me, until Reys and I stopped in front of a two-story mansion enclosed in an overflowing garden and forest.

"Will you let me down?" I asked. "I have legs, you know."

"And they're shapely and beautiful." Reys put me down with a grin.

I swayed on my feet, my legs wobbly. I wasn't sure if it was because of his sexy grin or something else. I was a little annoyed at both him and myself. I was Cass Saélihn. I shouldn't falter or stumble.

"You'd better tell me what this place is," I said.

Five figures—four men and one woman—in gray armor zoomed toward us. They all carried swords and crossbows and they looked badass.

"Incoming!" I shouted at Reysalor, even though it was unnecessary. He'd spotted them before they'd emerged.

I immediately adapted a battle stance, my hands out in front, ready to throw shit.

"Don't attack them, little Cass." Reysalor laughed at my pose, his arm wrapping around my waist. "They're my men."

"Don't call me little," I hissed. "Especially in front of others. I have an image to uphold."

He arched a brow, laughter deep in his light turquoise eyes. "And what image is that?"

He thought I was trying to amuse him? I should probably stomp on his toes and wipe that smug look from his face.

He pulled me closer, as if staking a claim, his heat melting me. But as I'd said, I had an image to uphold. I broke free of his grip with a bit of a struggle, my face a little flushed. I took a couple of steps away and schooled my face into a stern expression. I braced my hands on my hips and looked up at the five fae before us, waiting for them to report.

The five warriors with different shades of blonde hair all towered over me—though I stood on the top step by the front door—which wasn't cool.

"Prince Reysalor." They bowed.

"Three of our scouts have returned," a warrior with scars on his face said. He seemed to be the leader of the ones before us. "The gods have been quietly lately. No one has spotted your twin."

I scowled at them. They flicked a glance at me, a nearly identical, shocked expression flitting over each face. They subdued it quickly. I could tell they were trying not to sniff at me, but their nostrils still flared subtly.

I'd heard that supernatural beings could detect subtle scents mortals couldn't. Could they smell their prince's scent on me? We'd fooled around just a few hours ago. Even so, I didn't want to let anyone think I was Reysalor's bitch. He was a prince, the heir to the crown in Sihde. Women probably flocked to him, and people, especially his household, would assume I was one of his groupies.

"Thank you, Hector," Reysalor said. "We need to find my twin as soon as possible."

Hector nodded solemnly.

The door swung open, and an older man, dressed like a house manager instead of a warrior, appeared at the foyer. He also bowed to Reys. "Your Highness."

"Who are you?" I asked the older man, needing to take some control of the situation. "You'd better tell me whose house is this."

Reysalor smiled. "It's my house at the edge of the mortal and immortal realm, near the Academy."

I landed a punch on his biceps with a grin. "No kidding, Reys. You kept your promise. We're going to visit the school." I actually wanted to be in a school. It was one of my unfulfilled dreams.

Reysalor flashed me a doting look, and I entered the house, passing the older man like a rush of wind.

"Lady Cassandra Saélihn is *mine*," Reysalor said to his men. I wheeled around to face him, ready to counter him. "My honored guest," he said in a half-hearted correction. "You can call her Cass. Don't tell her any house rules; she'll break every one of them."

"That's not true," I said. "I have manners. I just don't bother with them because I'm powerful and dangerous."

Reysalor chuckled and a few of his men joined him, believing I might be a comedian. They saw only my size. But at least they didn't snicker like the vampires.

"Hector, Rainer, Victor, Luke, and Ambrosia are my elite guards," Reysalor said, walking beside me as I sauntered into the vast living room where a full glass wall faced the garden of lush greens and purples.

I liked windows. They reduced my claustrophobia.

"The entire house is warded," Ambrosia, the female fae warrior, said behind me.

I turned to her with a sharp grin, my teeth showing. "I'm not worried. By the way, do all fae have blonde hair? Is it genetic or some kind of fashion statement?"

"It just a coincidence with us five," Ambrosia said, eyeing my hair of platinum, blue, and sunset red. She frowned, probably thinking I'd dyed it. "Humans often can't tell the difference between us."

"Oh, I can tell," I said. "You all have blonde hair, but each one is a different shade." I pointed at the warrior who was slightly bulkier than the others. "That dude's hair is called dirty blond."

He glared at me. I guess fae didn't like being associated with the word dirty.

The other warriors laughed and Hector patted the glaring warrior's shoulder. "We've got a new name for you: Dirty-blond Luke."

"We're warriors, the best of the best," Luke said. "Why are we even discussing hair? We've never discussed it before." He shook his head. "Humans."

He didn't like me, which suited me just fine, for I'd just found my punching bag.

Hector sniffed the air. "She isn't a human."

Now they all sniffed at me. I didn't appreciate that.

"What are you?" another warrior with curious green eyes asked.

I wish I knew.

"Your scent isn't like any species I've encountered," the green-eyed warrior persisted.

"What's it to you?" I asked. "Why should I give you free information? What can you offer me in return?"

He blinked, as if he couldn't understand why I wouldn't answer him.

Reysalor chuckled. "I see you've all gotten acquainted. Cass baby, cut them some slack, will you? They'll be around a lot. Their loyalty is unquestionable. Boone, who so kindly opened the door for us, is the head of the staff in my household."

"Welcome, Lady Cass." Boone bowed, his eyes bright and intelligent and his manner humble. "It's an honor. If you need anything—"

"Do you have food and something strong to drink? I didn't finish my breakfast today." My face flushed a little at the reason, but I quickly recovered. "And I fought a good, hard battle on an empty stomach. By the way, don't call me lady. Call me Cass."

The warriors darted a glance at their prince then at my bloody and tattered clothing.

"Yes, Cass," Boone said with a smile. "We're prepared. I'll have the servants bring refreshments to the dining room." He gave me a quick glance. "If you'd prefer to have a bath first, I'll have the servant girls ready the tub."

I nodded in approval. This was the way to treat a special guest, not just empty words of "It's an honor, blah, blah, blah." As long as he fed me well and didn't try any funny business, I'd get along with him well.

"Fine, I can compromise," I said, as if I was doing him a favor. Attitude was everything. "But the water must be hot and the soap must smell amazing. I don't like doing anything half-assed. If you insist on lighting candles in the bath chamber, putting on music, and bringing me a glass of wine, I won't object."

Boone stared at me, as if making a mental note of everything I said. So I offered him more instructions. "On second thought, I'm not picky, but the wine should arrive with naturally-grown grapes, cheeses, and crackers."

He blinked and nodded.

"What kind of cheese do you have, Boone?" I asked.

"Uh," he said, evidently not finished taking notes. My mind worked faster than his. "I'll have to check with the chef."

"You do that," I said. "Tell him goat cheese is the best, and I'd like it cut into small cubes. That's all."

I strode toward the spacious corridor but halted after two steps. "Oh Boone, I forgot to mention one more thing." I looked over my shoulder and spotted his eyes flashing in amusement. He must have sorted out my orders. "No carrots. I hate them."

Most of my meals from Jezebel had had carrots, and now they were prison food to me.

I resumed my stride. "This house is so big. Can someone show me the bath chamber?"

Reysalor was at my side before the words had even left my mouth, his arm sneaking around my waist, "Let me show you," and led me toward a broad swirl of stairs.

I had a feeling Reysalor wasn't pure in his intent. The prospect of getting in the bath with him was enticing, but I needed to establish my status here, and I didn't want to be seen as Reysalor's plaything.

"This is my bath," I said firmly, standing my ground. "I don't share."

"I'm sad and disappointed to hear that, my little Cass," he said. "You'll have to learn to share one day. It's all about sharing."

I turned to glare at him.

He laughed. "I'll give you a tour of the house while the servants prepare your glorious bath."

We climbed the stairs to the second floor.

"That's the library," he said, waving a hand to the left.

The open library took nearly half of the floor with shelf after shelf of books. My heart sank a little. I didn't know how to read, but I couldn't let Reys or anyone know that. It was a weakness, and I was done being weak. So I was more than cooperative when he led me up the stairs to the rooftop garden.

Blossoms the colors of the rainbow dangled from the exotic trees.

But what truly caught my eye was the colossal courtyard in the distance. A group of students were running laps around the perimeter. In the center of the square, groups had gathered, some practicing sparring, some listening to an older man in the center of the ring and hanging onto his every word, and some deploying magic with one another.

No one looked in our direction.

As if reading my mind, Reysalor said, "They can't see us. We're concealed by my twin's and my magic. The whole house is glamoured."

"What else you can do other than shifting and glamouring?" I wanted to know.

"You'll have to find out for yourself, Cass." Reys winked at me. "I'd like a little mystery between us."

I rolled my eyes. "You know, I could see the house just fine when I first arrived, so your glamour isn't as mysterious as you think."

"Because you're mine," he said. "I didn't even need to lower the ward when you passed the threshold. It recognized you."

"I'm not yours," I cried in outrage. "I'm no one's. I'll never be anyone's. I won't be in any kind of cage."

"I'll never cage you, my Cass," he said softly, yet power rode his every word. "Over my dead body will I ever let anyone do that to you again."

I swallowed, tears pricking my eyes. No one had ever said such nice things to me and meant them. And I knew Reys would keep his word. I snuggled closer to him.

He draped an arm around my shoulders.

"What about I'm yours?" He chuckled.

Unlike Lorcan, who was always serious, scary, and hard ass, Reys laughed easily when he wasn't furious and fierce and killing. As my thoughts flickered to Lorcan, my heart tugged in pain. Why did I even miss him? Would he be able to find us? The house was glamoured, and Reys hadn't even left him a note to tell him where we were going.

"You aren't mine, either," I said. "You're a fae prince, the heir to the throne. And you're rich!"

"My riches can be yours," he said, the amused laughter in his voice. "You used to call me your panther. You claimed me as yours."

"I prefer you in your panther form. You're never annoying then."

"You can't enjoy me in some ways if I spend all my time as a panther."

I flushed, pretending I hadn't heard him as I turned my gaze back to the courtyard.

His chest shook as he tried to contain his laughter.

My eyes were drawn to a magical group. One girl threw a ball of fire and a boy conjured a stream of water to put it out. Then someone sent dirt and leaves into the air. Each of them seemed to have only one kind of magic.

My pulse raced in excitement. That was my kind of crowd. I wanted to join them. But could I? I stared at them with envy. I'd missed out on my childhood and teen years. I could never have what they had.

Reysalor must have seen the shadow pass over my face. While I watched them, he was watching me.

"Come, little Cass, time for your bath," he said, kissing me on the cheek.

I growled at him, but I followed him down the stairs. I was looking forward to a bath, and then some food.

17

The bath was exactly what I'd requested: hot water, lit candles, a glass of wine, a plate of fruit and cheese. I sipped at my wine and enjoyed the snacks. At some point, I must have dozed off.

A knock sounded on the door.

I slipped into the water and jerked awake. I peeled open an eye and wiped the bubbles off my face.

"Cass, you okay there?" Reysalor asked outside the door.

I was annoyed that he disturbed my nap, so I refused to answer him, but I didn't expect him to push the door open.

He strode in wearing a clean shirt and trousers. Everything about him screamed sex. He smelled so damn delicious. Had he used a better soap than I? Probably. He was the prince, so he must have gotten the better treatment. I

didn't like class separation or species discrimination. I'd
have a word with Boone soon.

My gaze tore from Reys's powerful legs to his face.

"Some privacy?" I asked.

"You've been in the bath for over an hour. I was getting
worried when it was too quiet in here."

"My usual style is quiet. I was taking a nap."

"Nap time is over, baby," he said. "Let's get some solid
food in your stomach."

That sounded good, too. I inhaled and the mouth-
watering smell of stew wafted into the bath chamber.

"Fine," I said as my stomach growled. "I'm getting out
now. You need to leave."

He grabbed a large green towel from the rack and
unfolded it. "It's not like I've never seen you naked. Now,
come on. Time to get you nice and dry."

My heart fluttered, the image of our joined flesh
replaying before my eyes.

I wasn't going to be shy and demure. I bolted up, water
pouring from my body. The soapy bubbles still coated my
breasts.

Reysalor wrapped the soft towel around me, patting me
dry. When he wiped the bubbles from my tits, his eyes grew
so heated that my pulse started galloping. He looked like he

wanted to pluck my nipples into his mouth. I would let him suckle my left nipple first, then right, and then….

My already wet pussy grew slicker with want. My tongue darted out of my mouth, wetting my lips. My breasts grew heavier with every look he gave me.

My gaze flicked to the counter. I would let him set my ass there, and he could get between my thighs and fuck me. I had never had an orgasm in my life and I craved one after having a taste of what it might feel like earlier today.

"Reys," I murmured, my hands falling on his shoulders, ready for him to pick me up and fuck me on the counter.

He swallowed audibly. "I've dried your front," he said, his voice nearly harsh. "Now turn around."

Liar. He hadn't dried my pussy. He'd simply swept the towel over my legs, though his gaze had darted to the flesh between my thighs.

I didn't expose his lie, though. I was curious to see what he would do next, even though my skin burned with carnal need. I turned as he'd commanded.

He started to dry my hair, then my shoulders and back. The towel slowly moved toward my butt. I parted my legs, bent forward a little, and bared my pussy for him.

If he'd prefer to fuck me from behind, I'd take it.

He stiffened behind me. A swath of the towel got between my thighs, rubbing back and forth with his large warm palm beneath it. I swayed my hips a little.

"Don't move, Cass," Reys said huskily and roughly. "If you move again, I'll have to fuck you."

A smile curved my lips and I swayed more to challenge him. I couldn't wait for him to thrust his cock into me. I needed more than he had given me this morning. I remembered the feel of his manhood filling me and stretching my narrow passage. I loved the weight and hardness of it inside me.

I expected him to brush open my plump folds and nudge the thick head of his dick at my slick entrance, but instead he withdrew the towel and ceased his rubbing.

Then he spanked me.

I yelped in surprise. What the hell?

"Nice girls get fucked," he said. "Naughty girls get spanked."

I wheeled toward him, ready to give him a piece of my mind.

He wrapped the towel around my body and scooped me into his arms.

"What the fuck are you doing?" I demanded.

His turquoise eyes, once again molten gold, mirrored my urgent lust and frustration.

I thought he desired me. The hurt of rejection turned to anger, and I struggled to get out of his arms, but he only gripped me and pressed me against his chest.

"I want to take you right here, right now more than anything, Cass," he said. "I want to bury my cock deep inside you and forget that the world is burning. But I can't. We'll have to wait until I can claim you properly."

"Does a simple, quick fuck need some fucking ritual?" I asked.

"With you, it'll never be a simple, quick fuck, my Cass," he said, choking out a strangled laugh that held no humor. "I'm not the only player in the game. I have competition— four other competitors. I swore a blood oath. I have to honor the pact. You'll meet them soon, and then you'll decide."

The dream of me entangled with four males under the sheet, including Reys and Lorcan, swirled back, heating my lower belly.

My heart stuttered. How could I be with all four of them? Reys said I was the one who'd decide. Must I choose one? My mind was made up. I chose Reys. But then Lorcan's piercing gray eyes seemed to peek into my soul, and there was great need in them for me. My heart soared. I wanted him, too. I hated vampires, but I wanted their High Lord.

I stopped writhing in Reys's arms as he carried me out of the bath chamber.

"I want to court you first, Cass," he said. "Give me a chance to give this to you."

I gazed into his eyes, and the tenderness and heat inside them warmed me. He wasn't rejecting me. He wanted to treat me like I was valuable to him instead of just using my body. Being courted seemed more enticing than just having sex.

But my need for him raged on. I might have to tame this carnal beast inside me.

"I'll compromise and let you court me," I said. "Under one condition."

His eyes sparkled with amusement. "I'm listening."

We were heading up the stairs now, and I wrapped my arms tighter around his neck.

"Actually, under three conditions," I amended, deciding not to limit myself.

"I'll accept only one condition this time," he said. "I can't always be on the losing side."

I glared at him, and he brushed a kiss over my lips. Just like that, I lost my train of thought.

When I recollected myself, we were in an upstairs hallway.

"Where are you taking me, Reys?"

"To your room," he said. "After you're properly dressed, we'll dine."

"But I don't have any clothing here."

"While you were taking a long bath, Boone sent his assistants out and got you the basics. They're all in the closet."

"That was fast."

"There are stores inside the Academy."

My eyes sparkled. The school really piqued my interest.

"Who are all the people showing off in the courtyard?"

"They're our future elite army who will fight the gods," Reysalor said, watching me closely. I kept my expression neutral, showing not the smallest hint of emotion. "They're mostly supernatural beings: shifters, vampires, mages, fae, witches, valkyries, and the brightest humans who have a grasp of war strategies and human technology."

My heart jumped. He and Lorcan had asked me to be their weapon to go against the gods, and they'd been training me. I wasn't the only one they had recruited—they'd assembled an army. But Lorcan had said I was the only hope to save the realms, and to kill the gods. If that was the truth, why did they need an army?

"The gods of Olympus have their own minions, ones who betrayed their own races to seek safety under the alien gods," Reysalor said in scorn. "The war between us and them is coming."

I'd missed out on all the excitement while I'd been stuck in that damn cage. I was so glad that Lorcan and Reysalor had let me out. Or else I'd be rotting in there as the world ended. I shivered at that fate.

Reysalor must have spotted the dark glint in my eyes, because his gaze on me intensified.

"It's not pretty in the mortal world," he said quietly. "The immortals are hiding from the gods. Our ward and glamour still shield us, but when the gods tear down all human cities, annihilation will come to our realm."

I had no realm, no land, and no home.

"So, the Academy is a military school?" I asked, changing the subject.

"Yes, but only for the gifted."

I would fit in well with the gifted. But why hadn't Lorcan and Reysalor taken me to the Academy instead of training me themselves?

Did they intend to isolate me because they only wanted me to be an assassin and not one of the soldiers in their army? The more I thought about that, the further my heart sank.

Even if they got me into the Academy, it would never be for my benefit.

I wouldn't have fun there. I would be trained for the sole purpose of becoming a weapon.

On second thought, I probably wouldn't be accepted in the Academy. I didn't even know how to spell my own name.

I bit my lip and my eyes dimmed as reality rushed in.

Even out of the cage, I didn't know where my place was in the world.

I might never belong anywhere.

But I was Cass Saélihn, a survivor. I wouldn't let the unknown future shadow any moment of my day. Whatever came, I'd deal with it.

"I hope they got my size right," I said. "I'm not picky, but I must maintain a certain style of fashion."

Reysalor leaned against the wall near the door. "And what style is that?"

I rose from the bed and let the towel drop to the floor as I strode to the closet. I put an extra sway in my hips as I walked, baring myself to the fae prince. My scant pubic hair remained moist, and my pussy still pulsed with the need to be filled.

Though I liked the idea of being courted, my body was on fire.

Reys watched my every move, licking his lips, his eyes darkening with thick desire. He'd resisted me in the bath chamber, and now with the scent of my heady arousal in the air, it'd be hell for him to fight his own carnal need.

I was right in front of him, ready and ripe and available for him to take.

I palmed my pussy and rubbed a finger through my folds.

"I ache, Reys," I whimpered.

He let out a curse and stalked toward me. "I won't claim you. I won't fuck you the way I want, but I can pleasure you and make you come."

I clasped my hands behind his neck as he scooped me into his arms, pressing my heavy breasts hard to his chest. I wanted skin on skin. I wanted every touch I could get.

Fire coursed through me.

Reys slanted his mouth over mine, his tongue thrusting through my parted lips. Our tongues tangled in a mating dance, and a low moan left my throat.

He lowered me to the bed, his mouth never leaving mine, his tongue fucking mine with wild abandon. A low growl rumbled from his chest. His beast wanted to play.

His large, powerful hand added weight on my breast, fondling it. Pleasure rippled across my skin as he pinched my nipple, the sensation taking me halfway to heaven.

How could a man's touch be so good?

His one hand cupped my head, tangling into my hair, while his other hand abandoned my breast, trailing an achingly slow path down to my pussy. He skimmed over the soft curls, his fingers dipping and sliding. His thumb circled my sensitive nub, teasingly in the beginning, then quickened and rubbed it hard.

I cried out as pleasure pulsed through me. As he continued his torturous assault on my clit, he eased a finger, then another into me, stroking my center. I moaned, my walls clamping down on his fingers. Reys pulled out, then thrust back in.

"Babe, your pussy is so tight." He pulled away from kissing me and groaned roughly. "I can't wait until I can fuck your little pussy with my cock."

"You don't need to wait." I writhed against his hand. "Fuck me now. I want your cock. It felt so good last time you were inside me."

He growled, his beast unable to resist my pull.

"Your cock is so big and rock hard," I breathed out. "It stretched and filled me to the brim. I want to feel it again."

"Soon, I'll give you my cock, little Cass. I'll fuck your little curvy body in every way I can until you beg me to stop, then beg me for more."

He fucked me hard and fast with his fingers.

Pressure and pleasure built up, sending me to the brink, but then he stopped and withdrew his fingers.

"No, Reys! I need—" I protested, but I swallowed the rest of my words when his tongue lapped at my swollen clit, flicking mercilessly over the peak of my nub.

My legs jerked as tiny electric shocks moved across my skin, and I lowered my hands to his head, gripping his hair.

I gasped. I hadn't known a man's tongue could bring such delight. Reys opened my legs wider, and his mouth enveloped my entire pussy. He licked and suckled before his tongue separated my plump folds and thrust into my heated channel.

"Your pussy tastes like honeysuckle." He raised his head for a second to gaze into my eyes before thrusting his tongue into my heated channel again.

He thrust repeatedly and twirled his tongue inside me, his thumb and forefinger pinching my clit. When his tongue delivered another sequence of hard, merciless thrusts, the liquid fire in me leapt high and exploded into lava.

I arched my back and cried out as the first orgasm pulled me under.

The waves rocked me and rippled over me for a long time. After it all faded, Reys licked me for a few more seconds before laying me flat in the center of the bed, his panther rising to the surface through his golden eyes.

I knew he wanted to fuck me more than anything, but he still controlled his beast. He kissed me on the lips, both gently and hard, before withdrawing from bed.

"Wait until the day I can truly fuck you, my little Cass," he said. "Get dressed. Come down and dine with me."

He left the room and closed the door behind him.

I smiled to myself, basking in the afterglow of my orgasm.

I couldn't wait for him to fuck me. I couldn't wait to get his cock inside me, penetrating me, and screwing me senseless.

I wanted his touch again, but I would have to be patient and let him court me first, though I had no fucking idea how a man courted a woman.

18

It turned out that Reysalor had an excellent chef. While I stuffed my face, I dragged more intel out of Reysalor. He was cooperative, an attitude which must be part of the courting.

Before I finished the lunch—I'd soon have an afternoon tea and dessert, guaranteed by Boone, who also confirmed that he'd make chicken Panini with dried figs and tomatoes inside again—I had the Academy's layout.

Geography was important to me. I had to know all the exits in case I needed an escape. I knew Reys would protect me, but I wasn't going to put all my eggs in one basket.

The Academy lay at the edge of the mortal and immortal realms. Its land fell into the crack of time and space, according to one of the five warriors who joined Reys and me. Reysalor said that they'd always be around me and their job was to protect me, so I didn't object to them sharing my food.

However, I piled the food high on three of my plates before I started eating.

The warriors shook their heads at me and chuckled.

"You sure all that food can fit into that tiny body of yours?" Dirty-blond Luke asked, eyeing my plates with interest.

Ambrosia snickered. She was nearly as tall as the men, and they were all well over six feet. I wasn't thrilled about being short, but life was never fair.

I moved the plates closer to me. "I can eat all of this. I may not be built like a horse as you five are, but I am not tiny."

There, I delivered my insults.

And I wasn't ashamed of eating more than I could take. Anyone who had been starved for their entire life would do exactly what I was doing.

"We're built like warriors, the best of the best, not horses," said Rainer, the quieter one among the five. He didn't have a sense of humor.

"I don't see the difference," I insisted.

"Cass baby," Reys said. "You don't need to hoard food. I'll always feed you. Even if I don't get to eat, you'll eat."

The warriors darted glances between their prince and me, as if they weren't used to him calling anyone baby. *Baby* was better than little. I didn't take kindly to being called little.

"So, explain this to me—" I stopped my mid-sentence. I shouldn't ask them to explain time and space tech stuff. I wouldn't understand it and they'd all see my weakness.

Never expose your back to anyone. Never show your vulnerability.

"So, the Academy is the most protected place on Earth." I changed direction and summarized what they had told me. "It's concealed from unwanted eyes. There are two leylines that lead to this place: one from the immortal realm, and one from human territory. And if we walk through the veil that separates the two realms, we'll appear right under the Brooklyn Bridge in New York."

"You can't just walk through the veil," snorted Victor, another of the five guards, the one with a pair of curious green eyes. "Only seven council members can open the leyline and only those they grant access to can enter it and leave Academy."

Which meant it wouldn't be easy if I had to flee again. "Who are the seven council members?"

"His Highness is one of the councils," Ambrosia said. "You should've known. He brought you here."

I wrinkled my nose at her. "I know he's one of the powerful ones. I need to know who the other six are."

"Why?" Luke asked.

"Why? How could you ask me why?" I said. "Use your brain. I don't know about you, but I'm not comfortable with just anyone in charge of such important matter." I drained the coconut juice and put the empty glass down. "Let's go, Reys. I want to take a look at this leyline to the mortal realm."

"It's on the other side of the Academy," Reys said lazily. He sank deeper into the chair, clearly not planning to move anytime soon.

"That's even better," I said. "You can give me a tour. I need to burn some fat, not that I have any, but just in case."

I kicked the chair back to show I meant business.

"We can run around the garden to burn calories," Reysalor said. "I don't want anyone who isn't in my trusted inner circle to see you yet."

That was why he brought me here instead of to the fae realm across the shining sea. He planned to confine me to his estate, when I'd thought I'd have exhilarating freedom.

Anger flashed through me. "Then this is another cage. Only this time you want to lock me up in your house to have better control over me."

"Cass," he growled in warning. "I never want to control you."

"Then prove it," I said. "Didn't you promise me that you wouldn't let anyone cage me again?" My voice was thick with emotion. "Don't you know you're the one who's doing it with all these limitations all around me? Why don't you just send me back to the cage? It's no different than being locked in your glass house."

It was very different, but I refused to admit that to Reys while I tried to work on him.

"What cage?" Boone asked.

In my excitement I hadn't noticed him standing at the entryway.

"It's a long story," Reysalor muttered darkly.

I waved a hand at him. I didn't want him to tell anyone about my humiliating past.

"You asked me not to run away," I said, sounding even more indignant. "I can do that for you. All I want is some freedom."

A muscle jerked on Reysalor's jaw. It looked like I was stressing him out. Apparently no one talked to him that way, but hadn't I warned him that I followed no one's rules?

And I didn't give a fuck whether he was a prince or a servant.

"All I want is to keep you safe, Cass," he said. "You don't know how treacherous and violent the outside world is. It's full of unexpected perils."

I spat. "That's exactly what Jezebel said to me when she put me in that cage."

A terrible, dark light flashed in the fae prince's burning eyes.

"Don't underestimate me, Reys," I said, my tone softening a notch. "I'm not afraid of danger, but I can't be caged."

I laid a hand on the wooden table, black fire twirling beneath my palm, leaping through the space between my fingers. The five warriors all leaned back in their seats, a wary look in their eyes. When I removed my hand, the part of the table I had touched dissolved into ash. Boone had a pained expression on his face. That dining table must be expensive.

"You see, I can be a badass, too," I said. "Don't you want me to be your lethal weapon?"

"Cass, you know it's more than that," Reysalor said.

"I'm sure it is," I said with a predatory smile. "But if you keep me in the glass house, I'll never become the assassin you and Lorcan want me to be. Your little knife will be too blunt to cut into anything or anyone when the time comes."

"We need to train you first and make sure you're ready before we set you upon the world," Reysalor said.

Men were full of contradictions, weren't they?

"Do not measure me as you measure humans or other immortal races," I said. "You can't train me in a box."

"One day you'll be the death of me, Cass," Reysalor said. "It's not the right time to introduce you to the Academy. You should remain anonymous for now." He ran a hand over his golden-red hair in frustration. "Would it appease you if we went for a walk in the mortal realm?"

I grinned. "Reys, I know you're always on my side."

He rose from his chair. In an instant he was beside me, twining his fingers with mine that still sparked with black fire. Boone and the warriors stared at our linked hands, shocked to silence.

"Stay away from Cass's fire," Reys said. "It burns all others."

Except him and Lorcan.

"What are we waiting for, Reys?" I snapped my fingers. "Let's go for a stroll."

"Do you have some specific place in mind?" Reys asked, arching a brow.

Right, no one snapped fingers at the fae prince, but I was excited.

"Yes," I said cheerfully. "Misery Twist in New York. I want to try their famous cocktails. Devil's Love is their house special."

"How did you learn about that club?" Reys asked, his expression unreadable.

"I told you that I dream-visited the mortal realm, didn't I? It's one of my more useful abilities, you know. I had nothing else to do in the cage."

I'd been robbed of any chance at an education. Dream-visiting had taught me about the world and kept me sane in my prison.

"No, you didn't tell me about that gift of yours. I see, our little Cass still has layers of secrets." He regarded me thoughtfully, and I regretted volunteering the information. "I was wondering about all this passionate talk of freedom. In truth, you just want to go to a nightclub to get a cocktail." At my anxious look, he sighed. "I'll take you to Misery Twist, but I have some conditions."

Why must there be conditions every time? I bit my lip. "I thought we just ended the bargain. You agreed to take me there, and I graciously accepted it."

He shook his head. "Oh no, I haven't even laid out the terms."

"We can do that later," I said.

"Probably," Reys said. "But first you'll promise to follow a couple of rules for your safety. Then we'll get ready and leave in an hour."

I would do anything to visit the places I'd dream-visited. Freedom to venture into the world and live a little was worth everything.

"Half an hour," I said.

Reysalor narrowed his eyes, and I smiled meekly at him.

Reys had a soft spot for me.

"Fine, an hour," I said, putting up my hands to show that I was compromising. "I'm as ready as if I was born for it. All I need is to put on a pair of boots and grab a dagger." I spun around to head upstairs to my room, but then I turned back to him. "On second thought, Reys, may I borrow your flaming sword?"

240 A Court of Blood and Void

19

The five warriors wanted to come along to guard their prince and me, but I knew they wanted a free drink. I was fine with that since I wasn't the one buying.

Reysalor wore a navy-blue t-shirt and dark designer jeans. The fae prince looked hot as fuck, and I had to put effort into slowing my pulse down.

The four male guards put on sweats and slacks that fit in the mortal world. Ambrosia wore a tight black top and leather pants.

Their clothing concealed their weapons well. If I hadn't known they were armed, I never would have guessed it.

Initially, I had put on a sexy dress that exposed most of my breasts and barely covered my ass—I'd seen girls dressing like that in my dream-visits—but Reysalor intervened again.

"Do you want a drink, or do you want an army of men swarming you?" he had asked, not actually wanting my answer. "The first rule is: Don't bring attention to yourself. Your scent is already irresistible. With an outfit like that, you'll probably get us all killed. I don't know what Boone's assistants were thinking when they got you dresses like that."

The buzzkill then made me wear a plain blouse and a pair of jeans, though the jeans did hug my ass nicely.

Reys was controlling and didn't want me to stand out, but I decided not to fight him on the small things, since my main goal was to go out and have fun. If I had to sacrifice looking sexy for a taste of freedom, so be it. But I salvaged some of my sexiness by fixing my hair a little and blow drying it. I also highlighted my eyes with a light eye shadow.

Reysalor's approving look was worth everything. "You're a natural beauty, Cass. You don't need makeup like the mortals."

Reysalor was never stingy with compliments, unlike Lorcan.

Where was the High Lord of Night now? Had he acquired the spells I no longer needed? He wouldn't try to bind me. Reysalor had given me his word.

My heart twisted at the thought of vampire lord, but I tried to push him to the edge of my mind. Tonight would be

Cass Saélihn Night. I planned to dance a lot, drink more, and party till dawn.

The seven of us gathered in the center of the forest-garden outside the mansion.

Boone waved at us at the doorway. "There'll be a large chocolate mousse cake ready for you when you return, little Cass."

"With cherries on the top?" I asked.

He winked. "With many cherries on the top."

"The cake is only for me, right?" I glanced at Reys and the warriors.

Ambrosia rolled her eyes, and the others shook their heads in disbelief.

I needed to stake my claim now before they thought they could take what was not theirs.

"I'll guard it for you faithfully," Boone said.

I smiled at him. "I'll remind Reys to give you a raise." It was Reys's money anyway. And if I could remember by the end of the night, I would also remind Reys to bring back a bottle of liquor for Boone.

Boone chuckled. He'd grown on me—I was the only one who truly appreciated the superb meals he prepared for us.

Reysalor wrapped an arm around my waist as if afraid of losing me. The five warriors formed a ring around us, towering over me, which was not to my liking. They each placed a hand on either Reys's shoulder or mine.

"What's that for?" I grunted. "Why is everyone touching me? I don't like surprises."

Reysalor smirked. "You love surprises more than anything, little Cass."

That was true.

"But I need an explanation—" The rest of the words stuck in my throat as I was lifted in the air, spinning in the wild wind around me.

The blossoms and trees blurred into a kaleidoscope of dancing colors.

It stopped as suddenly as it started, and I landed behind a fence of high bushes, with the Academy courtyard and school buildings over the fence, and Reys's mansion on the far end.

"What the hell was that?" I demanded.

Reysalor and all his warriors laughed as I tried to get my bearings. They must have done that a hundred times. They hadn't even given me any warning.

"I can shift in the mortal realm," Reys said. "The Academy is at the edge of two realms, but technically, it's in the terrain of the mortal realm."

"You can't shift in the immortal realm, even though you're a fae heir?" I asked.

"No one can shift in the immortal realm," Ambrosia said, always quick to shoot out opinions.

I sneered. "Someone shifted right in front of your prince and me in the immortal realm this morning. Right, Reys?"

Before Reysalor could finish off Jezebel after we'd eliminated all the vampires, she'd vanished into the air. I hadn't told him it wasn't her power. She'd had help.

Reysalor's expression darkened. "We'll figure out how that was possible."

"Who is she?" Hector asked.

"An enemy," Reys said. "We'll get to it later."

He regarded me with concern and pulled me closer. I was grateful that he didn't tell them she was my mother. I didn't want anyone who didn't know Jezebel to associate her with me.

I had no problem leaving her behind and starting a new life, possibly with Reys.

"Ready to party, little Cass?" Luke said.

I narrowed my eyes. "Call me little again, I'll let my little fire toast your big monkey ass."

The others chortled, including Reys. They weren't taking me seriously. I'd need to set an example to have them fear me. Reys was too easygoing. While his warriors all respected him and showed him their loyalty, they also joked with him.

No one joked with Lorcan. The vampires all feared their High Lord and I preferred his management style. No vampires had called me little, but a lot of them had tried to kill me. On second thought, I wasn't exactly sure whose style was better.

Luke charged into the wall of bushes and disappeared without a trace, his teasing laughter lingering in the air.

Who would imagine a fence of tall bushes standing between the mortal and immortal realms? It was quite clever. Now I knew where to look, I narrowed my eyes on the shimmering veil instead of the plants.

"You can see through the glamour?" Hector asked incredulously.

"Of course," I said, spreading my arm. "It's right there. What's not to see?"

"Can you see His Highness's mansion from here?" Hector asked.

I pointed. "Right there. A bit far, though. You guys need to trim the purple wisteria on the rooftop."

"Damn," Rainer said, giving me a weird look. "She's short, but she can be useful."

He dove through the shimmer and vanished before I could send my black fire after his ass.

My attention fixed on the veil connecting the two worlds. My pulse pounded, and my heart filled with excitement. Just as I was about to throw myself toward the bushes, a strong hand grabbed me from behind.

What now?

"You go where I go, Cass. And you don't go alone," Reys said, sliding his arm around me and pulling me through the veil.

There was no resistance from the leyline. It was as easy as stepping through a door. The bushes and Academy vanished in a blink, and a half-burned city across the river greeted me.

20

It was night in the mortal realm. I stood on an abandoned deck under a long, broad bridge, with Reys by my side, overlooking the scarce artificial lights glittering under the dark sky.

Most of the skyscrapers along the gray river were cut down to a third of their former height and many slanted. Sparks of fire and plumes of smoke spilled from the blackened, broken windows. The city that never slept was no longer the glistening gem of my memories.

"What the fuck!" I said.

"That's the aftermath of the gods' fire and lightning," Reys said. "New York is in relatively good shape. Half of the continents are now rubble. Most of the UK, Europe, and Asia are gone. The gods leave part of the human technology running after showing the mortals how useless their weapons are against them. Only Australia stands intact, for now, because a demigod rules there. The gods want the world to keep in mind how easily they can destroy the civilization the humans built over two millennia."

Something stirred in me, then rage and sorrow rose and coursed in me, as if I regarded the cities and the planet as mine—my territory and my possession—and some terrible beings had trespassed and set what was mine on fire.

Where did this odd, intense possessiveness come from? I didn't own the land. I had no claim on it or anything.

A spectrum of magic, different than its kin in the immortal realm, rose from earth and tugged at me, as if it wanted me to own it, as if it was my birthright.

"Did you feel something, Prince?" Hector asked quietly, and stood behind us in a guarding position.

Reysalor watched me with interest. "Magic has risen and appears in the mortal land."

I didn't want them to look into it, and I had more urgent questions.

"The mortals just surrendered?" I asked.

"Most of them," Hector said. "The few who refused to bow to the alien gods joined us." He snarled. "We're the only ones who stand a chance fighting back, and we'll fight them until the last one of us stands."

That was why Reys and the other council members had hidden an army of magic students in the Gifted Academy.

And he thought I could kill the gods and save the world. So, he and Lorcan had sought me out. Who had misled him with the absurd idea that I could be a superhero? I didn't want the burden. I might have fire and air power, but from the destruction of the city before me, even an idiot could see that the gods' powers were way beyond mine.

My mother had locked me up to prevent the world from being destroyed, but the world had been burning this entire time.

"The gods know that we're preparing an army to go to war with them," Reys said. "They've been trying to find the leylines to the immortal realm. It's only a matter of time before they breach our last defenses. In physics, our realm is linked to the humans'. When their world is destroyed, the immortal realm will collapse."

I tore my eyes from the sore sight of the broken city across the river. I'd dream-visited the marvelous streets of New York City for several years since I was child—for some reason my dream-visits had stopped after I reached adulthood, making my life a hell. This scene was hardly what I'd expected.

Fury surged in me. I didn't know how to handle the sudden, unbearable heaviness that pressed into my chest, choking me. I'd had enough sadness in my lifetime. All I wanted was some lightness and fun.

I needed a drink. Desperately.

"Did you bring me here for a drink or what?" I snapped at Reysalor.

If Reysalor thought he could manipulate me with this grotesque sight and have me vow to kill the gods, he wasn't just delusional. He was cruel. And I would have been wrong to think that he actually cared about me. Whoever had left this mark on New York City would squash me like an ant if I ever stood in front of them. My air and fire magic and bad attitude would only amuse them while they picked at their teeth before snuffing the life out of me.

"For the cocktail, of course," Reys said softly. There was a hint of melancholy in his voice that I hadn't heard before. "We should get going. We've stayed long enough."

We hurried down the pedestrian walkway along the gray river. Reysalor held my hand and the five guards spread around us, two at the front, one on the side, and two bringing up the rear.

We seemed to be the only ones here at this hour. The mortals were probably cowering in their boxy houses and apartments, praying the gods' fire and lightning had forgotten their existence.

"Are we going to walk to the nightclub?" I asked, wanting to escape this terrible sight and get a drink in me as soon as possible. The fog had risen and concealed part of the wrecked city. "You can do this shift thing, Reys. Why don't you just poof and bring us there?"

"I thought you'd like taking a walk," Reys said. His teasing tone was back.

"We try not to use magic in the mortal realm," Hector said from beside me. "Unless it's necessary. We don't want to draw attention while we're at war with the gods. They're looking for any chance to infringe on our realm. They've already killed many of our kind."

Hector was observant and perceptive. Any mortal or immortal knew what was going on with the world and the gods, yet I was clueless. Though he'd never asked, he knew I hadn't been around for a long time. When I had thrown a fit in order to come to the human city, I'd mentioned the cage. He might have made a connection, but he showed no pity towards me.

"We try to travel between the two realms as rarely as possible," Rainer murmured behind me.

And they'd all come here because I wanted a cocktail. An unease rose in me. I darted my gaze around. The streets were eerily quiet, which screamed danger.

If a god was around, I might just get everyone killed. I chewed on my lip. Maybe I should ask Reys to take us back. I didn't want to be responsible for anyone's death. I was just starting to warm up to the five warriors.

"We have establishments in every human city," Reys said. "When we're in their territory, we use cars instead of shifting, to avoid leaving magical imprints the gods can trace."

I jogged quietly as I debated telling him we should go back. But I'd come so far. I'd fought Reys and won the right to have a drinking night in the mortal realm. All I wanted was a cocktail at Misery Twist, which I'd dreamed about for years. But, what if we encountered the psychopath gods?

I couldn't possibly have such bad luck. Or could I?

"Reys, I think maybe we should—" I said as Reysalor stopped me at the corner of a broad, tree-lined street.

I looked over and saw the place in my dream come to life.

"Misery Twist!" I cheered, completely forgetting what I had been about to say to Reysalor.

I strode straight toward the red door carved with the symbol of a black dragon biting its nail, not caring about the two, huge inhuman bouncers planted outside the door.

I was eager to go in and claim my cocktail. If they stopped me, I would cause a scene and let them have a taste of the ice I'd shoved down the vampire king's throat.

But someone else stopped me.

A strong arm sneaked out, lightning fast, and tugged me back against a hard chest. If the scent of autumn rain and the pure, intoxicating scent of man—all distinctly Reys—hadn't muddled my mind a little, I'd have stomped his toes.

"Not so fast, my fierce Cass," Reys purred, his warm breath trickling along my temple. "Remember the rules."

"Fine," I groaned. "What rules?"

Fuck all the rules.

Fuck all the cages, visible or invisible.

21

Reysalor nodded to his elite guards, and Rainer and Ambrosia beat me to the door. One of the bouncers stamped an inked rune on their wrists before swinging the door open to let them in.

As they disappeared into the club, Victor and Luke peeled themselves away from the group and blended into the shadows of the night. They wouldn't be coming in for a drink then. The poor guards would have to patrol in the frigid night.

"I seriously doubt any other patrons will make such a fuss," I bit out. "I understand that you want tight security since you're a control freak. But you gotta live a little, Reys. The whole point of going to a club is to relax and get drunk."

The bouncers tried not to laugh, so one of them coughed.

Hector smirked from his position next to me. He'd be glued to our asses for the entire night. "Is getting drunk your version of good time, Cass?"

"What else?" I retorted. This bunch didn't know how to have fun.

The bouncers bowed to Reysalor while I spoke. My eyes trained on them. I didn't trust strangers, especially not giant-sized ones.

"Do they know you?"

"Prince Reysalor is one of the owners of Misery Twist," said the bouncer whose hair was tied in a short ponytail. "He's the one who hired us."

Now I grinned. "Wicked, Reys! That means we can come here as often as we want! We can have the best drinks and we don't need to pay a penny." I turned to the bouncers. "Remember my face. I'm with Prince Reysalor. If I ever come alone, you'll let me in the door and you'll tell them put the bill on the house."

The ponytail bouncer winked at me. "What about tips? The bartenders live on the tips."

I blinked. "Huh?"

"We'll tip them," Hector said with a smile. "You don't need to worry, little Cass, and we won't let you come here all by yourself."

The other quiet bouncer pressed the wooden ink stamp on Hector's wrist. A black rune appeared on Hector's skin.

"Now it's your turn, Cass," the bouncer said, having picked up my name from the conversation.

"No," I said. "No fucking way. I'm not letting anyone stamp me like I'm fucking livestock."

After what Jezebel had done to me, I was done with spells. I would never allow any spell, runes, or symbols, to touch my skin again.

Both bouncers raised their eyebrows and looked to Reys for guidance.

"Cass," Reysalor said with a tolerant sigh. "Even I need the rune of permission to get into my own club. It's the rule of the place, for security. No one can enter that door without it, which serves as a barcode to the ward. Misery Twist is superiorly warded, to prevent any unwelcome being from stumbling into the only supernatural bar in the city. You want to get the famous house cocktail inside, don't you?"

I watched him warily.

He shrugged. "Or we can return to my house."

"Like hell we'll go back without a drink." I glared at him. "What would happen if someone tried a forced entry?"

"You wouldn't want to try that." The quiet bouncer shook his head. "The ward will repel the invader. Best-case scenario, the ward tosses the violator a few yards away after injuring them. Worst-case scenario, the ward kills the offender instantly, and we'll have to clean it up. And if any gods try to breach our perimeter, the alarm will go off."

Reys stretched his arm. The bouncer bowed to him again and pressed the stamp on the prince's wrist. An inked rune spread on Reys's skin. He was patiently showing me it was safe to be stamped.

I wasn't convinced.

I recalled the earth magic tugging at me at the riverside, longing for me to own it. I could use it now. At my summoning, it rippled under my feet like a blend of light and shadow. I pulled it into me, and it felt like second nature to do so, as if it was part of me.

I was careful not to take the vast amount of its power, for fear that it would devour me and shove Cass Saélihn to the sideline.

I had trust issues, even when it came to magic that hadn't been born with me.

I called, "All is mine—the land, the city, and the earth!"

A blast of black wind swirled around me, tearing everyone away from me.

The bouncers' eyes widened. Reys and Hector tried to reach me, fighting against the wind.

A Court of Blood and Void

"No fucking ward or door can stop me when all on it is *mine!*" I declared.

I marched toward the red door, my hands thrown out before me, my air current flinging the door wide open. I shot into the club like an arrow, not wanting the door to hit my face.

I grinned when it didn't.

I was in, and I was the first and only one getting in Misery Twist without bearing a fucking mark.

A wide smile stretched on my face when Reysalor and Hector charged in, followed by the bouncer with the ponytail. Their eyes were as round as saucers.

I regretted that I hadn't kicked the door open, which would have looked more badass. And I should have picked leather pants to wear, like Ambrosia, instead of letting Reysalor dominate me and select such lame clothing.

A hard lesson learned.

"Shit—." Ponytail glanced at the prince and swallowed his curse. He stared at me in awe. "What are you, Cass?"

Just then, the alarm went off in the club.

Everyone rose from their seats, and those who stood hurried toward the exit.

Panic spread through the air.

"The gods are here!" someone shouted.

The bouncers had mentioned that an alarm would sound if a god infiltrated the place. But I was not a god.

However, if the ward was sentient, I could scold it.

"Oh, stop!" I told it as I rolled my eyes.

The alarm stopped abruptly, as if it was ashamed. I felt it licking my skin to try to figure me out, but I shrugged it off.

Behave, I hissed.

"It's a glitch," Reysalor called. "Go back to what you were doing."

Everyone returned to their seats and unfinished drinks, but every head turned in our direction. Ambrosia and Rainer gathered round me, as if I needed protection. I really didn't appreciate their towering over me and crowding me.

I was powerful, but I was short, and their presence could seem overwhelming, even if it really wasn't.

"Some space?" I called.

They ignored me but reported to their prince.

"No usual suspects," Rainer said.

"Our spies brought back news, Your Highness," Ambrosia said.

Reysalor gave them a small nod and laced his fingers with mine again. He led me toward a secured table no doubt reserved for him.

Around the table, two fae males and an unknown female species with a pretty heart-shaped face waited for us. They were probably Reys's spies. Their gazes flicked over me curiously for a second. Reysalor was holding my hand as if I belonged to him.

I had no intention of joining them and getting into a serious discussion of this awful gods business. I wouldn't let them ruin my entire night.

"You guys go ahead and sit," I said, extracting my fingers from Reysalor's. "I want to strike out on my own and sit at the long bar."

Reysalor kissed the top of my head, scanning the room with a predatory look as he did. He was marking me to let everyone know not to mess with what was his. If I didn't like him so much, I would have kneed him in his nuts.

I didn't take kindly to anyone who tried to stake a claim on me.

But for the moment, I didn't fight him. I needed him to pay for my drinks. Plus, he'd given me an amazing orgasm earlier.

"Just don't go look for trouble, little Cass," Reys said.

I shrugged him off, and he chuckled and headed toward his table.

Hector hesitated for a heartbeat and followed me. I wheeled toward him with a hard stare. "Please show me you got the part about 'striking out on my own?'"

He darted a quick glance at Reysalor. "Our little Cass is declaring her independence, I see," he said. "Have fun. But don't go around hitting people."

I glared at him, but he simply laughed at me as he walked away.

These fae warriors were sly. They were the type who wouldn't hesitate to fight dirty. They'd be watching me like hawks. I only prayed their eyes wouldn't bore a hole into my back while I enjoyed my drink. Of course, that was the steep price of hanging out with the fae heir.

I moved to the long bar. There was a vacant seat in the corner, its angle blocking the full view from Reysalor's table.

Perfect.

I climbed onto the bar stool, and one of the three good-looking bartenders, glided to me immediately. They'd all seen me with Reysalor.

The bartender had a red hair and a ruby earring stubbed in one ear. A grin broke on his face. "Hello, little lady."

"Don't call me little," I said. "I'm full-figured, which is hardly little. Now, bring me five glasses of Devil's Love. Put

the bill on Reys's—Prince Reysalor's—tab. His minion
Hector will tip you, as he promised."

His eyes widened a little, and then he blinked.

Were five glasses too much to ask?

"Fine," I grunted. Must I always compromise? "Bring
me two glasses then. Make it quick. I've traveled a long way
and I'm thirsty."

"Lovely, I'm sorry," the redhead said. "Devil's Love
went out of fashion two years ago. It's no longer on the
menu."

I blinked before I growled.

A movement to my right sidetracked me. A demi-fae had
been nursing his drink in a sullen mood, but suddenly jumped
out of his seat and fled.

I grinned, pleased with myself. Even a growl from my
throat could scare a supernatural away. Perhaps I should tone
it down a little. If the bartenders fled, I'd get nothing to drink
for the night.

My bubble burst when another man took the seat next to
me. It wasn't my growl that had scared the demi-fae away;
he'd been afraid of this guy, and had given his seat up for
him.

Who the fuck was this scary-ass? If he thought he could
also take my seat, he was sorely mistaken. I was going

nowhere before I got my cocktail. I schooled my face into a sneer and turned to him.

Then I jumped out of my seat.

"What the fuck?" I shrieked.

He wore Reysalor's face, only he wasn't Reys.

The stranger's gorgeous turquoise eyes were two shades darker than Reysalor's, and he gazed at me with such intensity that my face flamed. This was the man who had suckled on my nipple in my dream and enjoyed the hell out of it.

Pyrder Iliathorr, Reysalor's twin, had come to my favorite club and taken the seat right beside me.

He wore a dark rose-colored t-shirt that stretched over his taut muscles. His gray-black jeans wrapped around what I suspected was a perfect, tight ass—just like Reysalor's. He was every bit as sexy and dashing as his twin.

But he had something Reys didn't have. A magnificent golden panther was etched on his muscled upper arm, disappearing under his shirtsleeve. I controlled the urge to trace my fingers over every line of the tattoo.

I wasn't the only one with such an itch. Every woman in the club turned her head and stared at him with heat, just as they'd looked at Reys's hot ass with blatant lust when he'd entered the club.

The females on the dance floor shook their bountiful boobs and rocked their hips invitingly, trying to catch Pyrder's eye. If he even wiggled a finger, any one of them would jump into his lap.

I wasn't pleased.

"Enjoying the view?" Pyrder asked, bringing my attention back to him.

"What view?" I asked huskily and roughly.

He seemed to like the sultriness in my voice because his sparkling eyes crinkled at the corners.

"The golden tattoo extends to half of my chest," he purred. "Pity you can't see it now, and I know you want to."

Reysalor's twin was cocky. I bet he knew that every female drooled over him and he took it for granted. He was what humans called a womanizer, a man whore. It was my job to represent other good women and put him in his place.

"Good for you," I said, letting indifference and disappointment into my voice. "But I was wondering why the panther on your arm looks sleepy. You got yourself a lazy cat."

He straightened his back, and with his height advantage, he looked down at me with a frown.

"You're mistaken," he said. "My panther looks magnificent, like me."

Unlike Reys, he was full of himself and didn't like criticism.

Ooh, I was going to have fun with this one.

I snickered but intended not to make any further comment.

He stared at me for a long beat before turning his gaze to his tattoo then back at me again. "You need to get your eyes checked, girl."

"My eyesight is better than yours, fae dude," I said. "My eyesight is better than any creature's, mortal and immortal alike. But since you just don't get it, I'm offering my professional opinion for free this one time. First, your panther be hunting instead of yawning."

"He isn't yawning," he said. "He's roaring."

"That looks like a big yawn to me, and his heavy eyelids are just about to drop for a good nap. And didn't you say this beast reflects his owner?" I gave him a measured once-over. "Hmm, I see." I turned to the redheaded bartender, no longer bothering to glance at the fae prince.

Everyone within the earshot became tensely quiet, and the bartenders gaped at me.

Was I the only one who had ever insulted and dismissed a fae prince in public? But he'd started it with his conquering attitude. He'd insulted me first.

His growl was neutralized by vicious, yet sensual laughter to my left.

Potent power rolled from that laughter across the space, and everyone felt the impact. All eyes homed in on the massive male leaning against a column to my left before quickly turning to other directions. Fear and fascination danced in every woman's eyes.

The man had been there all along, watching me, and I hadn't even spotted him until he wanted my attention. The stealthy bastard only now let me feel an iceberg of his power, part of which felt much like my own.

Ambrosia and Rainer hadn't done a good job when they'd told Reys that there were no usual suspects. We had two outstanding usual suspects right here, sandwiching me. Maybe these two were just fantastic at sneaking up on the innocent.

I immediately identified the demigod Alaric, who had fondled my perky breast like an expert in that dream that haunted my every waking moment. I met his honey-brown eyes promising no honey but glistened with amusement and cruelty under his perfect dark eyebrows.

Just one look, and I knew he was one of the most ruthless, dangerous males walking the earth.

The bartenders avoided direct eye contact with him to show their submissiveness, but Pyrder glared at him, obviously not happy that the demigod had just stolen his show.

As we appraised each other, I found that I liked what I saw. His sun-kissed skin went well with his golden-brown hair cut in military fashion. His lips could give off either sensuality or menace, or both, depending on his mood.

He flashed me a grin, trying to give me a false impression that he was harmless. And damn, when he did that, his dimple deepened. I blinked at him twice. How could such powerful ferocious being have such a disarming dimple?

I narrowed my eyes at him in irritation.

His fashion statement differed from the other patrons. He wore a plum scarf over his dressy shirt under an expensive leather jacket. His jeans fit him so well they showed every line of his sexy, muscled legs.

He looked like a warrior god clad in street fashion, menacing and hot as fuck.

How would it feel to have him pounding between my thighs? I'd rather have him down there than playing with my breast.

I blinked back, not liking my body's reaction to him. His smile broadened, as if he could feel the pulse of my purring body.

"Who the fuck are you?" I asked in exasperation to cover up my embarrassment.

The bartender gasped and shook his head subtly at me, trying to kick some self-preservation into me. His cautious, regretful expression told me that I'd be idiotic to make an enemy out of such a formidable being, even though I was under the protection of a powerful fae prince.

"You know who the fuck I am, Cass," the demigod said, "if you are it."

Reysalor had mentioned casually that Alaric was the king of all supernatural hybrids, who were part human and part something else, like him, and that the demigod ruled from Australia.

He'd heard Reys's endearment toward me. He'd been watching me all this time and I hadn't had a clue. He could have taken me out while I was ordering a drink.

I was supposed to keep my guard up, especially with Jezebel on the loose.

"Right, I know exactly what you are, Alaric Ash dick Desreaux," I said. "And I'm not *the* it."

I'd gotten his full name from the wet dream, though I'd creatively added dick as his middle name.

Surprise flitted over Alaric's face. It was gone so fast that no mortal eye could detect it. Then a sweet smile stretched his curvy lips. He was changing his tactics. He now aimed to seduce me instead of intimidating me.

Even though I knew what he was doing, my heart still fluttered like a pair of thin wings in the wind.

"How did you know the bastard's full name when you didn't even get my first name?" Pyrder demanded, tapping my arm twice with his fingers.

Tiny electric shocks rolled across my skin at his touch. It was so pleasant I wanted his hand on my skin again. Pyrder obviously felt the same. His eyes brightened with increased interest and desire. He looked like he wanted to hold me, but I gave him a warning glare.

His hand froze in the air.

"My twin Reysalor must have told you a lot about me," he said, beaming. Now he wanted to charm me.

"Uh, you think it's all about you," I said. "I hate to break the news though: Reys and I hardly had time to even mention you. But I do know he has a twin. I don't care much about this twin thing, to be honest. Who needs a copy when you have the original?"

Pyrder's face sank, and Alaric chuckled in delight.

"You've got it all wrong, Cass," Pyrder said. "Reys and I are as different as the North Pole and South Pole."

I stared at him blankly. I had no way of distinguishing the two poles from each other.

"Cass, sweetheart, a little bird told me that you have a fine taste for cuisine." Alaric said, standing closer to me than before. His body heat distracted me. He also smelled really nice, like a mix of pine, leather, and oil paintings. His male scent was strong and pure, despite his menacing vibe. "My realm has the most delicious food on this planet, and I'll personally cook the best wild boar for you."

"Cass baby," Pyrder cut in, "have you tried wine-tasting in wild country vineyards? It's spectacular. I'll take you—"

"Cass, sweetheart," the demigod called me again.

What were they doing? I turned my head left and right when they called me until I became fed up with the show. If I let them, these two, who were engaged in a pissing contest, would pull each of my arms in a different direction until I split in two.

I raised a finger in the air. "Hold your horses!" I turned to Alaric with a glare. "First, I'm not your sweetheart."

"I've never called another sweetheart, not even in the middle of the heat in the bedroom," Alaric said, and my heart jolted at the sex images his words brought to the forefront of my mind.

The dream I had about him rushed right back, and suddenly I was so turned on. This was stupid. My body was stupid. I resorted to intensifying my hard stare and let fire swirl in my eyes.

"Everyone is scared of me except you," Alaric said softly. "And that makes you my sweetheart. Consider it a compliment."

I would argue what was considered a compliment later. "Afraid of you?" I snorted. "Are you a comedian?"

Pyrder shook his head and laughed. "That's the best comeback I've ever heard."

I ignored him. I wasn't done with Alaric. "Second, there's no little bird telling you anything. Lorcan found you, didn't he? He won't appreciate you calling him a little bird. What he asked you to do no longer applies. Anyway, where's that vampire of the night?"

Pyrder chuckled louder. He really liked that I was ridiculing everyone except him.

I glanced around, waiting for Lorcan to jump out of the shadows—that was what the High Lord of Night was good at, right? I waited three seconds before sending my magical sense out to feel him—I'd been practicing sharpening my senses ever since I'd gotten out of the cage.

Lorcan wasn't here.

But I met an unexpected presence—a power stalking mine.

Before I could judge it, the sentient power boldly licked me with a smirk. It was delicious and familiar, but I didn't give a shit. No one licked Cass Saélihn without permission.

I formed a fist and punched the power right in the face, harder than necessary. The power blinked in shock and faded out with its tail between its mighty legs.

Alaric threw his head back and laughed in glee.

The bastard was testing me. I should have shoved my black fire up his ass as a welcome gift instead of only slamming him back with dignity.

"Our Cass doesn't like being pampered," he told Reysalor's twin.

He called that pampering? This demigod was really rough around the edges. And theirs? No way! I belonged to no one but myself. I narrowed my eyes.

Then they both sniffed, just like Reysalor and Lorcan had when they had first entered my presence.

Their eyes widened, their nostrils flaring, as if my funky scent slammed them right in their handsome faces.

I could understand Reysalor's and Lorcan's shock. As humiliating as it had been, when they'd first found me, I'd looked like filth and had smelled even worse.

But before I'd come to the club, I'd taken a long bath with good soap. These two shouldn't have reacted as if my scent threw them for a loop. Plus, if I'd smelled bad, Reys wouldn't have given me an oral pleasure. Thinking of Reys's wicked tongue and the way it had worked on me to my first orgasm had my blood heating. Would he do that for me again when we returned?

Wait a second!

Maybe these two assholes scented my arousal? I was constantly turned on, sitting between them with their delicious, pure male scent crushing me. Pyrder had a panther in him, so surely he could smell anything animalistic and base. And Alaric was a powerful demigod—I'd never asked Reys which god sired Alaric or if he was a bastard offspring.

My face reddened, my humiliation turning to anger.

"What the fuck are you two sniffing at?" I asked, my fist forming on the table. "Maybe you're the ones who need a long shower and scented soap!" I bared my teeth. "Get honey and vanilla."

They blinked, then roared with laughter.

I thought of letting out my black fire, but I'd promised
Reys I wouldn't draw any attention.

I'd said fuck the rules, but I didn't want to upset Reys
too much. I liked the food and bath he provided for me.

"Dicks," I said, shaking my head in pure disgust.

"You have no idea, do you, Cass baby?" Alaric said.
Now he was using Reys's endearment to provoke me. I liked
to challenge people too, to assure my dominance, but not
now. The demigod seemed to be the other side of the coin.
"You're what I hoped for, but I didn't expect you to be so
foul-mouthed. I kind of like it."

The best strategy was to ignore him, or deal with him
after I got my drink. Which was what I came here for, and I
wasn't going to let anyone, especially these two top-of-the-
range assholes, stop me from getting what I wanted.

The redheaded bartender had been darting his nervous
gaze between the three of us. I slammed a palm on the bar
and he jumped.

"Dude, where is my drink?" I asked. "I was rudely
interrupted, but you should have fixed me the Devil's Love
by now."

"I sincerely apologize, Cass." The redhead was able to
think on his feet after a quick recovery. "As I said, Devil's
Love went out of fashion a couple years ago. We no longer

make it." He eyed me with uncertainty. "You couldn't have had that drink a few years ago, could you? You'd have been underage then."

So, I'd come here for nothing. My eyes blazed with fire, not real fire, but the redhead stepped back in caution.

"Give Cass whatever she wants," Pyrder said sternly. "Just fix the drink for her."

"I–I don't know how, sir," the redheaded stuttered. "I only started working here three months ago. But they banished Devil's Love because it was bad luck. The rumor says every time they made the cursed cocktail, a fight broke out and someone died."

I snorted. "Because the devil—" I paused my retort. They did not fear the devil. The citizens of Earth were terrified of the Olympian gods. "—or the gods paid a visit every time you guys fixed a glass of cocktail that's named Devil's Love?"

"I can make you Rainbow-All-the-Way, our newest arrival," the redhead offered hopefully. "It's the most popular drink now."

I stared at him hard.

Pyrder sighed. "For fuck's sake, how hard is it to make a cocktail?"

He walked around the chair. With one hand pressed on the bar, he leapt and landed behind the bar with all the grace of a panther. The redhead moved himself to a corner to make room for Pyrder.

"I'll make DL or whatever shit for you, Cass baby," Pyrder said.

Which meant he was going to make shit instead of the Devil's Love.

"What's all the fuss?" a familiar voice asked to my right. It sounded nearly identical to Pyrder's, but an excellent ear could tell that Reys's was grittier while his twin's was on the silky side.

Reys wrapped his arm around my waist possessively.

He must have been watching us the entire time he'd been talking to his spies. My superior hearing caught their conversation now and then, and it was all boring shit about the gods and their moves. Even so, he'd never let me out of his sight, though he didn't have a good view of me. I could tell he was annoyed that he'd had to rely on his guards to keep track of me.

Yet he hadn't broken in because he was curious about how I would play with his twin and the demigod. I knew it, as if Reys and I already had some kind of bond. And I knew he'd been itching to come to me. Only his self-discipline had kept him in his seat.

I grinned. "Reys!" I was happy to have a backup, and Reys would always be in my corner. I leaned closer to him and pressed a hand on his broad, hard chest.

"They refused to make me the Devil's Love," I whimpered with a pout, ignoring the withering look the redhead flashed me. He seemed to want to protest but was too afraid to tick off the three alpha males around me. "And I'm not confident in your twin's skill. I think he's going to make shit and call it Devil's Love."

Even the other two bartenders chuckled. So, I was spot on—Pyrder Iliathorr was a fae prince who had no business tending a bar.

The only two who didn't laugh were Alaric and Pyrder. They both stared hard at Reysalor, and there was a sinister threat in Alaric's eyes as he watched Reys and I get cozy.

"Reysalor Iliathorr," the demigod drawled. "You know we have a pact."

"I didn't violate it," Reysalor snapped, his grip on me tightening. "I've been holding back, which is the hardest fucking thing to do!"

I narrowed my eyes. A pact? Reys had told me he couldn't fuck me because of the pact. Was this the pact he'd been talking about? What the fuck was going on?

"She isn't yours only, Reysalor," his twin said quietly, his turquoise eyes flashing darkly.

Had he meant me? What was I? A bone?

Terrible tension between the three males whipped through the air, and just when I was about to punch my way to get to the bottom of this pact, a cool-mannered, gorgeous bartender glided toward me with a large V-shaped glass full of dark red liquid.

The tiny hairs on the back of my neck stood up in alarm. I wasn't sure if it was because of this violet-eyed bartender, who seemed to carry a potent scent different from everyone here, or because I was finally getting my drink.

I dismissed the former idea, since the club was full of colorful supernatural characters and a variety of scents, even though Alaric also gave the new bartender a wary look before fixing his attention on me again.

Three cherries, a string of green leaves, and a few ice cubes floated on top of the glass. The drink fit the profile of what I had seen in my dream-visits. The color was also right. However, I had no way to tell if the taste was authentic. I could only hope that the bartender hadn't cheated me.

He placed the glass in front of me with a charming smile that somehow had teeth and claws. I blinked away the odd impression of him.

"I made an exception for you, Cass," he said. It was obvious that everyone here had good hearing, and now everyone knew I was Cass. "The Devil's Love is actually my design. I'm honored you insisted on having it."

I gave him a thumbs-up. "Good man!"

My three companions, who had the highest testosterone level in the room, growled at the bartender. He stepped back, raising his hands in the air in surrender. He didn't seem like a fae, and he was hiding a power I couldn't discern, as inexperienced as I was.

It didn't matter. He looked friendly.

"Hey, he fixed me a drink," I said. "Give the guy a break!"

Before I wrapped my fingers around the stem of the glass, Reysalor took it from me.

"Hey!" I glared at him. "That's my drink. That's what I came here for!"

"I need to make sure it's safe for you to drink, Cass baby," Reys said.

I sighed. His self-appointed role of my food taster was getting tiresome. He would only relax in his own house at the edge of the Academy.

Reysalor took a sip and frowned. "I don't see why it was ever that popular back then."

The violet-eyed bartender looked offended, but then he gazed at me expectantly, as if my judgment was all that mattered.

I snatched the glass from Reysalor's hand. "I was waiting for you to choke, Reys."

I picked up a cherry speared by a toothpick from the glass and popped it in my mouth. As I bit into the cherry, I took a big swig of the cocktail.

It tasted like sweet fire, then suddenly there was nothing but fire.

The intense liquid blaze rolled down my throat, burning a path to my stomach.

"Fuck!" I cried. "Devil's Love is inferno and mortal sin."

The men around me roared with laughter, the tension among them diffused.

A satisfied, inhuman, and malicious light shone in the bartender's eyes.

"Our Cass is fun," Pyrder said. "I'm keeping her."

Except it wasn't fun for me. My throat closed, and the fire in my belly exploded like fireworks in disarray.

I dropped the glass, and it shattered under my seat. I threw my head back, my hand stretching ahead and trying to grab something to support me, the other clutching at my throat. My eyes rolled to the back of my head, and I let out a shriek of pain.

My blurring vision caught Reysalor, Pyrder, and Alaric closing in on me in a protective formation, and my ringing ears heard them calling my name in panic. At the same time, the violet-eyed bartender punched Pyrder in the face, a sword suddenly appearing in his hand, and he lunged at me. The thick, oak wood bar didn't even pose a barrier for him. He went right through it.

Reysalor pushed me behind him, and then threw me to the floor to avoid the strike of the bartender's blade. Reys was incredibly fast, as was Alaric. Before I went down, I saw the demigod go for the bartender like a flash, his flaming sword that was just like Reys's crashing into the bartender's broadsword.

The magical alarm chose this moment to go off, joining the frightened shouts and chaos in the club. The front door banged open. Through the space of chair legs, I saw men wearing suits pouring in as the panicked patrons rushed toward the exit.

Vampires wore suits.

Among them, Lorcan's potent presence punched into me, even in my painful condition. It took me no time to realize that he was wounded, the tang of rustic blood, metal, and smoke coating his usual scent of faint pine and fine wine.

My worry for him only made my air passage lock tighter, and I couldn't breathe.

"The gods have infiltrated this place," the High Lord of Night shouted. "Where's Cass? We need to get her out. Now!"

22

I wanted to howl in pain, but I couldn't utter a sound. I scratched at my throat, needing to tear it open to have air.

Why did it feel like the déjà vu? Did Jezebel have a hand in this? This agony was different from the pain her spells had inflicted upon me.

Reysalor pulled me away from the fighting between the violet-eyed bartender and Alaric. Pyrder was battling a team of mages coming out of the shadows of the club. The long bar had shattered into splinters. Broken bottles and shards of glass littered the floor.

Everyone shouted over the sound of the blades clanging together. Lorcan's vampires and Reysalor's fae warriors all joined the fight.

We had been ambushed.

Things broke everywhere and bloody bodies and limbs piled up rapidly.

Misery Twist had turned to a slaughter house.

The poison that the bartender had delivered down my throat amplified my senses and sharpened my pain to extreme. Every tiny sound hurt my eardrums, and everyone was so fucking loud.

I tried to whimper and, again, I made no sound.

No air made its way into my lungs.

"Cass!" Reysalor called urgently, fear and panic storming in his darkened turquoise eyes. "Cass baby, breathe. Please, try to breathe, baby."

If only I could.

My eyes rolled back at the lack of oxygen. I clawed at my throat until I was sure I had torn my flesh from my body, but that pain still couldn't compare to the fire searing my lungs and throat.

I couldn't move my hands anymore, because Lorcan crouched beside me, pinning my hands to my sides, so I wouldn't tear my flesh off. His long trench coat was soaked with blood—his and his enemies'.

"Don't hurt yourself!" he ordered, as if I was his vampire soldier. "You need to fight, Cassandra Saélihn! Fight back and breathe! Survive this!"

I hated him calling me Cassandra. He'd done that intentionally to kick the fight into me.

It wasn't like I wasn't trying. I was fighting to death to get air! I would give up anything for just one mouthful of air. My lungs burst in pain.

I wouldn't last.

And I hadn't lived. I'd just had the Devil's Love, but it was the most lethal poison.

Painful thoughts swirled in my mind. Why hadn't the drink affected Reys? It had somehow bypassed his senses and immune system and aimed right at me.

The highlight of my short life.

If I had known this was my end, I'd have gotten Reys to fuck me properly. If this was how I had to die, I was glad at least it wasn't in that fucking cage. I'd had my first taste of fresh air. I'd gazed up at the sky, traveled to the Academy, and seen a burned city across the river. I'd had an orgasm and felt a powerful cock fill me, if only for a moment.

I had come to the club I'd dreamed about and demanded the Devil's Love, which had been my fatal mistake. It was a shame that I couldn't have a piece of that chocolate mousse cake Boone had promised me.

Reysalor was now doing mouth-to-mouth on me, trying to force air into my throat, but it wouldn't take.

"It's not working," Reys said in a tight voice, turning to Lorcan in desperation.

Lorcan cut his wrist and dripped his blood into my mouth. His blood of ancient power had once reduced my pain and partially healed me.

"My Lord," someone said beside us. "You can't bleed anymore. You've lost too much blood."

Lorcan snarled, and whoever had spoken backed off immediately.

His blood filled my mouth and I gagged. My throat was sealed. How could that even happen?

"It's not working," Reysalor shouted in rage and fear. "You're drowning her in your blood, vampire!"

"Whose fault is that?" Lorcan barked back. "You should never have exposed her before she was ready. If she dies, we lose everything. Every civilization will be wiped out. I'll kill you myself."

The fate of civilization had to do with me. But if Lorcan actually didn't need me in order to save the world, would he care about my death?

I would never know. The fuckers' hope of using me as a weapon against the gods had just been shattered. The bartender's poison had done me in.

Reysalor flipped me around and forced the vampire blood out of me.

My eyes turned glassy, their faces a blur of shadows in front of me. Their voices faded, passing like the wind in slow motion.

A loud explosion jerked me back to half-consciousness and made my every fiber hurt all over again. The club shook, threatening to collapse on us, but only one side of walls crumpled, and the roof was gone, a terrifying force blasting it away like snapping fingers.

Faint stars blinked in the night sky above me.

Harsh wind twirled with splinters of wood, concrete, dirt, and sand in the room. Reysalor and Lorcan shielded me as best they could, and their warriors fought to keep the mage from reaching their lord and prince, and possibly me.

If I could, I would tell them not to mind me. I was a dead woman walking anyway.

Why was I still here, staring, when I couldn't even breathe?

The stars faded into oblivion as lightning and fire raced across the sky. It was such a cruel, brutal, yet beautiful sight. Who could cause such destruction?

Part of me loved the glory of destruction, as if it was in my nature, even though I was blinking out of existence.

The spear of fire and lightning turned the direction and plunged down toward me, faster than a thought.

I prayed that it would leave my face alone.

I eyed Lorcan and Reysalor frantically, urging them to get away from the strike. They could still make it. They didn't have to burn with me.

Reysalor threw himself over me, and Lorcan shielded Reys and me with his massive body, throwing up his shield.

A pure lightning bolt crashed into the spear of fire and lightning from the sky, weakening its striking force, yet the spear still pierced through Lorcan.

The impact tossed both Lorcan and Reysalor away from me.

Today was not a good day, and the Devil's Love was indeed bad luck. I didn't even have the energy to blame myself for bringing death and misfortune to my companions. All because I was childish and wanted that goddamned cocktail.

In the wake of the destructive path were two mighty beings—a male and a female. They descended from the sky and landed in the center of the club littered with blood and broken bodies.

The female was a tall brunette with shining blue-green eyes and full lips. She was dressed in three pieces—armored bra and skirt down to her thighs. She pulled an arrow from her back quivers and nocked it—the arrow of lightning and fire. The former one had impaled Lorcan's chest.

I was going to kill this bitch!

In my imagination.

She scanned the room for her next target and found Alaric. If the demigod hadn't thrown the lightning bolt to diffuse her arrow, it would have impaled all three of us—Lorcan, Reysalor, and me.

"What took you so long, Ichnaea?" asked the violet-eyed bartender. His voice had a specific rich silkiness that I'd almost regarded as charming before I knew he was my killer. "Isn't tracking your specialty?"

The man who accompanied the brunette chuckled. "We were blowing up shit."

He was a giant male, with every inch of his muscles packed tightly on his massive, bare torso. He wore a plaid to cover his junk. His red cape flapped in the wind he'd brought with him.

A familiar yet otherworldly power rolled off them and whipped the air, and an ancient genetic memory clicked and unlocked in me.

These were the Olympian gods that Lorcan and Reysalor wanted me to kill, but the gods had beaten me to the punch. The violet-eyed bartender was one of them, but he'd used spells to disguise his essence and managed to pass Reys's ward.

All three of them, however, were minor gods. And now I could scent their powers. How ironic.

They'd known I would come here. How had they gotten the intel? This had been a set up and an ambush. The gods wanted me dead.

Now it seemed to make some sense that my mother had hidden me in a magical cage to keep anyone from detecting me—no, that was wrong. I wouldn't give her any excuse for mistreating a child.

"Did you get the net from Hephaestus, Enyalius?" the violet-eyed asshole god asked from across the room, still crossing blades with Alaric.

The fae warriors and the vampires were still engaged in fending off the gods' minions.

"Yes, yes, Phobos," Enyalius said. "It took us a while. The fucker hates you, and he's cheap as hell."

"Then what are you fucking waiting for?" Phobos called. "Cast the net! The demigod is growing stronger with desire to rescue the girl. I don't plan to stay in this shithole any longer. I've tended the fucking bar for a month waiting for her to turn up!"

Time slowed as a golden net materialized in a flash, cast in all directions. It spread over all who weren't on the gods' side and pinned them down.

"Get her out of here, Alaric!' Reysalor shouted, immobile as the net trapped him beside an unmoving Lorcan.

Alaric threw a sequence of his lightning bolts to neutralize the net and lunged toward me.

Even if Alaric succeeded in snatching me out of the claws of the gods, I wouldn't make it. I wanted to tell him to flee for his own life, and he might be the only one who could make it, but again, I couldn't mumble a word.

I couldn't breathe, yet I still lived. *Wait.* How could I still be tethered to this mortal world? I'd gone without oxygen for a while now. Shouldn't I have expired and crossed over to the great beyond, whatever it was?

The golden net fizzled at Alaric's lightning bolts before re-forming. It closed in on him, dragged him up, and hung him upside down. Alaric roared and kept throwing bolts at the grid to no avail. He slashed his flaming sword at the mesh, but that too failed.

The more he struggled, the tighter the net clutched him until it gagged him.

"The Blacksmith God enhanced the net since we last saw you," Phobos chuckled over Alaric's furious curses, fouler than mine. "Didn't recognize me this time, did you, little bastard cousin? I had a little makeover—courtesy of Hecate. She's all about experimenting with the darkest spells these days."

My heart skipped a beat. Had Jezebel gotten the spells from Hecate? If I lived through this, I would find this Hecate and terminate her, so no one could throw nasty spells at me or cage me again.

Phobos waved a hand and the glamour dropped off him. A terrifying power emitted from his every nasty pore. Those in the room gasped in unison, feeling his true essence.

"I'm the God of Terror," he said, his voice a cold blade.

He was over seven feet tall now in dark crimson armor, a silver spear appearing in his hand. He flexed his massive, muscled arms and thighs. This god was a narcissist.

His vicious violet eyes found me and he strode toward me, followed by the other two gods. The three of them towered over my lame body. Shards of glass, wood, and concrete chunks littered the floor, and some glass had cut into my flesh.

The trio stared down at me, as if I were a bug they hadn't expected to find.

But they'd been searching for me.

"Fuckers! Don't you touch her!" Alaric roared.

Reysalor and Pyrder roared with him, "Leave her alone! Pick someone your size."

"I know you hold a grudge against me, Phobos," Alaric shouted, cursing more, trying to distract the gods from me. "Take it to me like a man. I'll take any of your challenges. Let's duel, just you and me."

"I'm not a man, Alaric," Phobos said. "I'm a god. I don't duel anymore. It's boring. And you're even more annoying than before. You're in no position to challenge me. This isn't about you."

My protectors all snarled in fury, except Lorcan.

I couldn't see all of him from my vantage point, but judging from the angle of the arrow, I knew he was badly damaged. I could still feel him, which meant he was alive, but barely.

I'd brought all this to them on a whim, because I'd wanted a drink in a bar.

The poison burned me, choking me, and a teardrop rolled down my cheek.

23

Phobos squatted beside me while the other two gods stood
and watched with detachment.

"Look what we caught here, a little wounded bird," he
said with a chuckle. He thought he was funny.

I wanted to spit at him, but I couldn't. My brain churned,
and all I could do was to glare at him with pure hatred and
imagine knifing him in every possible way.

"The redhead warned you not to order the Devil's
Love," he continued, "but our little Cass is a stubborn hellion.
She had to have her way. She'd do anything to get what she
desired. That drink was made to test the bloodline of a major
god.

"You see, my seer friend foresaw your coming and that
you'd be a threat to us. Instead of telling every god of her
prophecy, I took the matter into my hands. I will be the one
who eliminates the threat and saves my race, and finally

ascend to become the thirteenth major god in Olympus. My father will be so proud, and my brother will be ever so jealous, but the glory will be mine and mine alone."

Enyalius cleared his throat, and Ichnaea shuffled the arrows in her quiver with annoyance.

Phobos barely gave them a glance. "Right, my god comrades have been assisting me on this critical business of capturing you. You were hidden from our senses. Even Ichnaea, the Goddess of Tracking, couldn't find a trace of you. Until recently, when you surfaced and glowed like a beacon. I wonder what transpired. And little Cass, you've just passed the test. Congratulations. The more potent the blood of the god, the worse the potion hurts you."

His cold knuckles grazed my burning cheek. His touch did nothing to cool the fire burning my flesh but sent a repulsive chill up my spine. I couldn't even shake the motherfucker off. My power wasn't working, which was a side effect of the poison. Or I would have set him ablaze.

Ferocious snarls from my trapped companions rose like waves in the club. They promised blood, murder, and worse, but none of the threats could materialize.

Their helplessness hurt me as much as my own, and I hated being helpless and powerless more than anything.

Phobos kept stroking me and his hand moved down to my neck.

"This hurts the worst, doesn't it?" the psychopath god gloated. "Your blood is powerful. I wonder who sired you, little Cass. You're full of complexities, and part of your essence is hidden."

"I can't scent her, either," Enyalius said. "She could be a hybrid, but there's no human in her, unlike the demigod."

"Her scent is unique yet obscure," Ichnaea said. "She might be from a different generation of gods. I'm slightly curious as to what kind of power she has since the seer believes this girl is a threat to us."

I eyed her directly, challenging her to give me the antidote so that I could show her my power.

"We won't release you," Ichnaea said with cold detachment. The bitch's empathy was like a corpse's. "We'll either kill you or take you to Olympus so we can experiment on you."

Violent growls from my companions rocked the walls. Fear charged the air, denser than butter. They did not fear for themselves, but for me. I was important to them, to all of them. Alaric and Pyrder had just met me, yet they'd put my life above theirs. I wasn't just a lethal weapon to them. They cared about me.

My heart fluttered as warmth melted the glacial walls that had surrounded me for a decade.

Phobos laughed. "We're their gods. But instead of worshiping us and begging us to permit them to breathe, Earth's supernatural army assumes they can take us down. And they just handed their last 'hope' to us so easily. What a joke! I'm almost disappointed. However, we did catch a prize here." His hand traced slowly and purposefully toward my breasts.

My stomached churned, and I felt my pupils dilate in cold fury.

They wouldn't just finish me off. They'd torture me, violate me, and experiment on me first. I thought of my decade of life in the cage.

From the moment I was born, I was abused, hunted, and now abused again. I'd never wronged or hurt anyone, except that I came into existence, which was not my fault.

Phobos slipped his silky hand into my blouse and plucked my left nipple between his fingers. At the stimulation from his kneading, another genetic memory flashed before my eyelids.

I suddenly knew who these minor gods were.

Phobos was the son of Ares, the notorious God of War. Ares cuckolded his ugly brother Hephaestus and fucked his sister-in-law Aphrodite. Their affairs produced a few offspring—the most notable were Phobos, God of Terror, and Deimos, God of Fear.

The God of Terror couldn't strike terror into my heart as he inflicted it on the others, but his slick touch angered and disgusted me like no other. My face morphed into a snarl, though no voice could come out. If I had been able to move, I would have puked before I tortured and killed this fucker.

The trapped warriors roared, struggling and cursing, but the golden net only cut deeper into their flesh.

I continued to live without air but with the alien fire burning in me.

"I regret that you hurt so much, little Cass," Phobos said. "For such a little pretty thing, you've got some strength in you. Even my touch can't evoke fear in you."

To my dismay, the god leaned down and pressed his plump lips against mine.

No, no, no. This wasn't happening. I didn't deserve to be molested before my death.

The fucker sniffed and inhaled deeply, trying to drink my energy.

Reysalor, Alaric, and Pyrder growled and urgently discussed among themselves how to break through the net. The gods ignored them.

When Phobos removed his red lips from me and raised his head, his violet eyes glowed with crimson light. "Your powers are layered, and some are latent," he said. "You have all five elements: earth, air, fire, water, and ether. Your fire is the oldest, as old as Earth's dirt, but you're so young. If I don't know that the first Dragon God had left this galaxy an eon ago, I'd say you could be his direct descendant. Beneath the old fire and everything, you also carried death."

"You mean she could be Hades' daughter?" Ichnaea asked, her cold eyes flicking down to me, showing interest for the first time.

Enyalius shook his head. "She can't be. Hades hasn't come out of his underground realm for decades. If he had offspring, Olympus would have sensed an energy flare from his realm. That's how it has worked every time when a god, a goddess, or a hybrid god is born. We'd have known."

I'd gleaned information from my deep genetic memory and known that Enyalius was Ares' follower, one of the minor war gods. If I wasn't beaten down by such agony, I'd be more intrigued in their conversation about my heritage.

"Are we leaving or not?" Ichnaea asked with irritation. "The show is over. And I have a date in an hour."

"Let's wrap it up," Phobos said with equal irritation. "We'll take her to my father. He'll break her and see what

she's made of." His fingers pinched my nipple so hard I
believed it might bleed or bruise. "But I won't give our little
Cass to him right away." He winked at me, extracting his
hand from my blouse and tracing my bottom lip. The fucker
just had to touch me, as if he was addicted to it. "I'll put you
in a cage as my little plaything. Only after—"

Red haze filled my head.

I would never go back to a cage.

The wrath in me was uncontrollable. Earth magic rippled
under me at my most desperate need and terrible rage. It
tugged at me like an invisible string. In my agony, I'd
forgotten that Earth was my kin and could aid me, as it had
helped me on the ShadesStar battlefield and broken Jezebel's
binding spells in me.

The Olympian gods are our enemies, I said to Earth.
They invade our land, trying to claim what isn't theirs.

I heard a rumble from the core of the earth. It agreed
with me. It was more than enraged, but somehow it couldn't
fight the gods. It needed a vessel.

Come to me! I commanded. *Merge with me. Purge my
poison.*

A power, with all the five elements—earth, fire, water,
wind, and void—surged into me. Earth had come to my aid

again. Its magic connected to mine, and our merged power coursed through me like a raging dark storm.

The void power quenched the alien fire, and water cleansed the last trace of poison in me.

Phobos rose to his feet and scanned the damage around him with a grin. His minions—the mega and some humans—looked up at him with fear and wonder.

"What about the others?" asked the minor war god.

"Kill them, except for the firstborn bastard son of Zeus," Phobos said. "I want to keep him as an audience when our little Cass entertains me. The despicable demigod has never taken a liking to anyone, but he can't take his eyes off our little Cass. This is going to be the best day of my life."

"You'll never take me, asshole!" I snarled, my voice breaking free and vibrating in the air.

A stream of fire, no longer all black but a blend of black and blue, spewed out of my mouth toward Phobos' face. I'd just unleashed one of my latent powers, though I had no clue of its origin. The fire blackened the god's cheek, peeled off his skin, and erased his depraved smile before he started regenerating.

"It's impossible!" Phobos shouted. "You can't have the divine fire, and no one has ever resisted the effect of the poison!"

I threw my hands up as I jumped to my feet, and a new power tore through the air and ripped the golden net apart.

Alaric flew in the air before the net completely released him, his flaming sword in hand. He sliced open his forearm, dipped his finger in his blood, and wrote an ancient rune on the blade.

Before Enyalius could raise his axe, Alaric thrust his flaming blade into the chest of the minor god of war. Enyalius widened his eyes in disbelief and dropped to his knees. A second later, he turned to a blackened statue before shattering into pieces.

Reysalor, Pyrder, the fae warriors, and vampires charged our foes with vengeful roars. The battle was even more brutal than before. Reysalor and Pyrder rounded up Ichnaea before she could fire another arrow of fire and lightning.

Alaric stepped in front of me, his flaming blade dripping with blood—his and the other god's.

I growled. "Fuck off, Alaric. The terror god's ass is mine."

Alaric ignored me. The alpha male wouldn't let me face battle no matter how pissed I was.

"Your blade tainted with your impure blood might kill a lesser god," Phobos said, meeting the wide swing of Alaric's sword with his silver spear, "but it won't work on me. None of you can take me down. No weapon on this planet can kill a god at my level and above. You've tried and failed again and again. Why don't you just give up already and beg us super beings to allow you to jump around a little longer?"

This god really liked to talk, as if the more he talked, the more terror he would rain down on the earthlings. But he was merely annoying.

The duo thrust, sliced, lunged, ducked, and lunged again, each desperate to put the other down.

Their blades crossed lethally from different arcs and angles. Both were excellent swordsman with super strength and speed. After a few rounds, they both had suffered their fair share of cuts and bruises. Phobos regenerated faster than Alaric.

Even though I wanted to tear Phobos apart piece by piece, limb to limb, I had to admit that I could believe he was the son of God of War.

"Pity." Phobos opened his mouth again. "I'll have to come back another day to claim my little Cass."

Had I mentioned how much I hated anyone calling me little?

Reysalor left his twin and Hector to take on the brunette goddess and strode toward me, pain, guilt, and relief flashing in his turquoise eyes.

"Cass baby," he called.

I wanted to throw myself into his arms and bury my face against his warm, solid chest, but now wasn't the time.

"Don't let any of them leave," Alaric shouted. "Kill the rest, and we'll figure out how to contain the gods. We can't let the rest of their kind learn about Cass." He wielded his sword in every direction to stop Phobos from vanishing.

He said what I was thinking. I wouldn't allow anyone to escape this club, either. This bunch had found me. If I let them go, they'd bring more to hunt me.

I dashed behind Phobos, taking advantage of his preoccupation with Alaric, and thrust my palm into his back. I was pleased that I was sneaky and super fast. Who didn't like to fight dirty?

His energy poured into me, rendering me drunk and giddy.

I was drinking him and draining him.

Phobos roared, trying to shake me off, but I didn't let go. I glued to him like a leech, sucking in his power greedily. And Alaric was keeping him busy to let me do my thing.

The energy of the God of Terror flowed into me like river, and I gave some to the land. It received the alien fertilizer with appreciation.

My hand glowed, and soon my whole body radiated with bright light, as the god grew duller, until he dropped to his knees, whimpering and weak.

And I had never felt so full, so energized, and so fucking good.

I threw my head back and cackled like a maniac.

Ichnaea caught a glimpse of her pal's condition and paled just as Pyrder, Hector, and a giant vampire pinned her down.

"What are you?" she hissed.

I smiled sweetly. "A monster." Then I nodded at Alaric. "Finish her, please?"

I'd learned that only a demigod could kill a lesser god with his flaming blade and blood.

"Anything you want, sweetheart," Alaric said.

He stalked to Ichnaea and plunged his sword into her heart as the fae and vampires cut down the rest of the minions.

I moved to stand before a kneeling Phobos. He barely had the energy to raise his head.

"You kissed me, didn't you, Phobos, your naughty boy?" I asked cheerfully. "Now I want to kiss you back. May I? You didn't ask permission when you touched me, but I have better manners. So, I'm now asking: may I kiss you back?"

Fear filled his eyes. The God of Terror knew exactly what terror was. He was worried that my kiss might be the death kind.

I was curious to test it.

"No, please," he rasped.

"You just hurt my feelings." I pouted. "I'm a girl, I'm sensitive, and I don't take rejection well."

"I didn't mean to hurt your feelings," he said trying to appease me.

"Who's the bitch now, little Phobos?" I cupped his face hard. "And you think I want to kiss you? Touching you disgusted me, except when I drank your energy." The next instant, I flashed him a sweetened smile. "Thanks for showing me the ropes."

Rage turned his violet eyes to dark purple.

"He's weakened," Reysalor said. "We can probably end him now. Alaric, your sword, please."

Everyone in the room darted awed glances between the god and me. There was fear in their eyes, too. None of them knew who I really was, and I didn't give a fuck that I didn't know either.

"No, don't end him," I said. "I've just found my free food source. I don't even need to ask for three meals a day anymore. Last time when I negotiated with Lorcan about the number of my meals and snacks, he frowned deeply at me."

"Did he put you on a diet?" Alaric asked in anger.

Pyrder also looked displeased. "And you let the vampire do it, Reys?"

Reysalor spread his arms. "Lorcan was thrown off balance when our Cass had to ask for a meal." Then he turned to me. "He didn't frown at you. He was furious with Jezebel. He was so angry that your own mother could do all those things to you, locking you in a cage and starving you, that he wanted to twist her head off. Which I should have done before she could hurt you again. We'll always provide for you, Cass baby. You don't need to ask for food or shelter or anything. The whole world can go hungry, but we'll make sure you won't lack anything."

That was touching, but I didn't do too well with emotions. I waved a hand dismissively at the men to show them I didn't want to dwell on the past.

"Our Cass makes a good point in keeping this asshole," Pyrder said. "We can also use him for information."

My smile turned predatory. "I'll drink from our little Phobos once a week and I'll never go hungry. And that's exactly the cocktail of the Devil's Love I've been looking for."

"You're the devil's daughter," Phobos cursed like a broken record. "I know that's part of what you are. Wherever you go, you'll leave chaos and destruction. The fools think you can help them overcome us but they should fear you more than anything."

24

The vampires guarded the High Lord of Night, but they let me, Reys, and Alaric through the ring of protection. Pyrder and the other fae warriors kept a close eye on Phobos, even though the god was too weak to move a finger.

The warriors' conversations drifted to me now and then. It was the first time the earthlings had ever brought down any gods, albeit minor ones.

They darted glances in my direction.

The vampires had kept one mage and one human alive. They had cut the mage's wrist open and fed their lord while I dealt with Phobos.

Lorcan was barely breathing, and his heart wasn't beating anymore, just like other vampires. Blood soaked him, and the wound in his chest wasn't healing.

My heart sank in icy fear.

"It's no use," a dark-haired vampire said in dismay, looking up at Reysalor. "This blood isn't potent enough to revive the High Lord."

Without a word, Reys cut his wrist and dripped his blood into Lorcan's mouth.

We waited for a miracle, but none came. Lorcan remained unmoving, and his wound didn't seal.

"Should we use Phobos?" I asked. "He's a god and his blood should be potent enough."

Phobos chuckled even in his feeble condition. "Try it. I welcome the results."

"According to the legend, the blood of gods will burn us to ashes," one of the elder vampires said.

"You're probably the only one who can drink from a god, Cass," Alaric said. "My blood isn't good for the vampires either." At my questioning look, he explained. "I fought side by side with Lorcan a millennium ago. He was wounded, and when I gave him blood, it only made his injury worse. I'm not surprised that Reysalor's magical fae blood can't help him, either."

"How did he recover back then?" I asked. "We could use the same method to cure him."

"He's the most powerful vampire," Alaric said. "He somehow survived. But I doubt he'll survive this. The god's bolt is lethal. If it were any other, except the four of us, they'd have been turned to ash right away."

"There must be a way," I said, my voice biting.

Then something hit home.

My blood might be the only thing that could save the High Lord of Night. My mother's blood was nectar to vampires. Her blood strengthened the vampire king a great deal, which was one reason he was addicted to her and would do anything to preserve her.

My blood was richer and more potent than hers.

But I'd sworn that I'd rather perish than offer my blood to a vampire. I'd vowed that they wouldn't even get it from my dead body.

I'd called Jezebel a blood whore.

But if I didn't give my blood to Lorcan, he would die.

I gazed down at him. His face was ashen, and the hole in his chest was grotesque. Even though his vampire warriors had bandaged it as best they could, blood still oozed out.

The High Lord of Night wouldn't last long.

A part of me withered as his pulse grew weaker, waiting for the ticking to stop altogether. An empty ache gnawed in my center, as if my soul knew that if he was gone, I'd forever miss a piece in me.

I didn't understand why and how I felt this way toward him. I'd hated and detested his kind since I was a child.

But I couldn't let Lorcan die.

If it weren't for him, both Reys and I would have been speared by Ichnaea's arrow. He'd put my life above his.

I let out a rasped breath. If I had to be a blood whore to save him, so be it.

"Fine, I'll let him have my blood. Just this once," I said to the vampires surrounding their lord. "My blood will save him, but I need all of you to stay away from me while I feed him."

My blood had sent the vampires into blood frenzy when Jade had cut me.

The vampires hesitated.

"Go!" I roared, ready to toss every kind of magic I possessed at them.

"Get the fuck away. Now!" Reysalor also roared.

"Let's roll," said the giant vampire who had helped Reys subdue the Goddess of Tracking.

The vampires zoomed away from us.

The fae warriors, led by Hector, immediately moved in and surrounded Lorcan and me in a protective ring, their backs to us, their fronts facing the vampires outside the open wall that the gods had blown away. All the warriors gripped their swords tightly, ready for any threat.

I conjured my fire, and the blue flame appeared instead of the black. It hesitated for a second, unwilling to cut me.

"Now!" I ordered.

The fire sliced open my vein.

I pressed my wrist onto Lorcan's lips and let my blood drip into his cold mouth.

As soon as my blood—rich, hot, and full of unknown power—hit his tongue and went down his throat, the hole in his chest started closing.

To my great relief, Lorcan was no longer bleeding out.

The vampires at the perimeter, guarding and patrolling, snapped their heads in my direction. All of them looked at me with intense craving, though they fought to control their urges.

I hissed at them. "Don't even think about it. Don't ever come near me!"

A few vampires snarled, wanting my blood more than their lives.

"Come near her, and you'll die, bloodsuckers!" Alaric snarled back, waving his flaming sword. "I don't give a fuck that your lord is like my brother. I'll personally kill you all should I deem you even the slightest threat to Cass Saélihn."

Pyrder added viciously beside the demigod. "And I'm Cass's ultimate shield."

The vampires faltered and stayed where they were.

"Stop inhaling the fucking air!" the giant vampire shouted at his brethren. "You can go for an hour without breathing."

His peers followed his order, and they quieted down. Some vampires with less control bolted into the distant shadow of night.

Lorcan snapped open his eyes and gazed up at me.

"Cass," he said, his gray eyes full of concern, pain, and relief. He raised his hand to touch my face, as if wanting to make sure I was real and safe. His fingers were cold, yet his touch still sent a shiver of pleasure over my skin.

"Foolish girl, you should not—" he said, and I scowled at him, not appreciating him calling me foolish after I'd just given him my blood.

Before I offered him scathing words, his hand dropped, and he blacked out again.

"Lorcan?" I called. "Don't fucking chicken out like that!"

He didn't respond.

I pressed a hand against his healed chest, and his heart started beating against my palm.

25

Instead of returning to Reysalor's mansion at the edge of Academy, we took Lorcan to his domain in Portland, Oregon, so he could enter the healing chamber there and recover faster. Reysalor's sunny mansion wasn't suitable for a wounded vampire and his horde.

The gods had crippled most of human technology, but some private planes still flew under the radar. We had to take a chance with a jet since though Reysalor and Pyrder could teleport us, we were too many for them to do that. Also, they didn't want to leave a strong magic imprint for the other gods to track us down. Furthermore, they weren't sure what teleporting would do to Lorcan in his injured state.

I was all for flying. It would be a new experience.

I was surprised that the High Lord of Night chose to set his center court—the Court of Blood and Void—in the mortal realm. All vampire courts in both mortal and immortal realms were a part of his court. That was why he could access ShadesStar and find me.

I'd never been to Portland, but I'd dream-visited the cloudy city a few times. Pyrder told me that a lot of supernatural beings who didn't dwell in the immortal realm chose to live in Portland.

It was more convenient for the vampires to stay near the mortals, their food sources. Fae and shifters were more elitist, so they preferred to remain on the other side of the veil. They didn't like other species, especially humans, finding out about their realms.

Fae were racists. Pyrder sent me a disapproving look after I gave him my conclusion.

"Pardon me. Don't expect me to see things through your panther's tunnel vision," I said to him as I gestured for the stewardess to bring me more drinks. It wasn't like I was thirsty again after I'd taken the energy drink from Phobos. But you gotta taste the world and everything in it. Mortals had the phrase *carpe diem*—seize the day, put very little trust in tomorrow. And Lorcan's private jet stashed some good stuff.

The pinkish cocktail with a string of three olives and a little umbrella on top was my favorite so far. It was called Hawaii Vacation. And boy, did I need a vacation.

But Pyrder the buzzkill told me the gods had tanked Hawaii. It was under the ocean now. California was gone too, reduced to rubble.

Even if he hadn't told me that, I'd begun hating gods after Phobos had served me the Devil's Love.

I darted a backward glance as I took another sip of my sweet, pungent booze. Poor Phobos was chained at the back of the plane, watched by Hector and his team. I didn't think they'd offer him a drink. I wondered if it was called inhumane treatment and torture.

The fae warriors guarded him like mean vultures, even though I already told them the God of Terror wouldn't bring down the plane since his energy level was super low, thanks to me. Phobos was napping now. It was good that he was sleeping. When he was awake, even in his low energy state, he carried a bad vibe of terror with him. It didn't affect me, but others—especially the lesser fae and vampires—could still feel every bite of his terror.

Lorcan was placed in a private room, as far away from Phobos as possible. The High Lord of Night was being guarded under extremely tight security. He hadn't opened his eyes again after touching my face and calling me foolish.

He'd bypassed a critical condition after I'd fed him my blood. When we reached his court, I might need to feed him again. But what if he still wouldn't wake up?

I refused to dwell on the dark thought. It only made my stomach and mind churn.

One step at a time.

"Where was I?" I asked Pyrder. I liked to talk to Reys's twin, even though I disagreed with him on almost everything.

"POV," he said, slanting me a glance. "You aren't at the age of forgetting things, are you?"

I punched his muscled upper arm and regretted it. It was like hitting a rock.

He grinned. "One more time."

I ignored him.

"C'mon, Cass," he called. He liked when I touched him.

Strangely, it was pleasant whenever our skin made contact, even a small gesture like our fingers brushing when he handed me a drink.

"Let me," Alaric said, and took the empty glass from me this time.

He'd fought with Reys for the right to sit on my other side.

"You and the vampire have spent a fair amount of time with Cass," Alaric had insisted, "which put me in an unfair competition."

In the end, Reysalor had backed off after making a few valid points. I'd say Alaric was lucky that Reys was easygoing at the moment.

As for me, I wasn't going to take a side if it didn't serve my interest. I knew how to look out for myself, and I liked the attention they showered on me. I'd been starved of it. For over a decade, it was just me and the cage.

Alaric gave my hand a playful, gentle squeeze, and it was just as pleasurable as Pyrder's touch. I had to control the urge to lay my head on his broad shoulder and purr. Maybe I could do that later if I pretended to fall asleep.

Alaric's scent of snow, hard ice, and sandalwood hadn't stopped caressing me, and I could get used to it. He carried harshness and menace with him as if they were his armor, but I didn't care, mainly because he was sexy as fuck. I could be shallow like that. Besides, he hadn't shown his vicious streak toward me. If he did or would, I'd put him in his place.

"Cass, sweetheart," Alaric called, as gently as he could, which surprised me since tenderness wasn't in his nature. I'd seen through him, but I didn't tell him that I didn't mind him being rough around the edges. Considering his demigod heritage, he might have had a bad childhood, like I'd had.

After the psychopath god had called me little Cass, my four male companions had ceased calling me that.

"Yes, Alaric, what do you want this time?" I asked teasingly, promising myself to enjoy every minute of their affection.

While I wrapped the boys around my little finger, I got them to tell me how they'd found me.

Jezebel had been thorough and meticulous in applying layers of most powerful spells to keep anyone from getting a whiff of me. Not even the vampires in her court, except the vampire king, knew that I'd been locked in the underground cage.

But Lorcan, Reysalor, Pyrder, and Alaric had all been given a vision about me at the same time, and they'd been assigned different tasks. Reysalor was to find Lorcan and get him to ShadesStar to search for me. Lorcan was gifted with runes that he would need to release me. Pyrder was sent to get Alaric to track me, and they were both led to Misery Twist.

"The bastard almost didn't come," Pyrder said. "But after I left, he followed me. Alaric is notoriously difficult, but he hasn't been too jaded to be curious. If he hadn't wasted my time, I'd have gotten to the club earlier. I'd have prevented the gods from hurting you, Cass."

"Careful, panther," Alaric said, staring hard at Pyrder. "I regret my actions, but I don't take kindly to you painting me badly in front of Cass. She's just getting to know me."

Pyrder shrugged. "Do I look like I give a fuck about what you take kindly to? Go intimidate someone else."

Alaric clenched his fists, and Pyrder tensed, ready to jump around me and take any challenge from the demigod.

Considering how mighty these alpha males were, if they got into a fight because of their high testosterone, they might punch a hole in the plane and we would all go down.

I raised a finger. "Hold your horses! And who the fuck is this person who sent you these ridiculous visions?"

Reysalor, Pyrder, and Alaric traded an uncertain look.

"We don't know who it is, Cass baby," Reys said. "We've been trying to figure it out."

Pyrder nodded. "Who has the power to send us all a vision at the same time except a god or a goddess? Who wants to kill the Olympian gods even more than us?"

"Can it be Gaea, the primal Earth Goddess?" Reysalor said.

"She faded when humans rose to a higher civilization millennia ago," Alaric said.

"The summons activated our pact," Pyrder said, his turquoise eyes an endless ocean under dark sky.

The pact again!

I narrowed my eyes. "What pact? I demand to know. You can't—"

Suddenly, the jet shook like a metal leaf in a violent wind.

"Buckle your seatbelts," someone called.

A few vampires and fae who hadn't been thrown to the floor clicked their seatbelts in place.

I grabbed the armrests just in time. Even if I hadn't, I wouldn't have been tossed out. Alaric had wrapped his arm around me, and he was a rock that didn't move an inch.

The co-pilot, who seemed to be a goblin, stumbled out of the cockpit. "There's a fucking storm ahead that wasn't there before," he said, looking at the alpha males.

The plane tilted at a steep angle, flinging a napping Phobos across the aisle and banging his forehead onto the metal wall. Phobos jerked awake, looked outside at the storm, and laughed hoarsely yet weakly.

Had some gods found us and caused the storm?

Those fuckers would tear the jet apart!

"Cass baby, let me help you secure your seatbelt," Pyrder said, reaching over to the belt. He wanted to take me out of Alaric's arms and buckle me in.

I pulled my lips back and snarled at him, and he was smart enough to let go with a sigh.

"Cass wants no restrictions of any kind," Reysalor said, rising to his feet and moving toward the pilot's cabin.

Alaric nodded at Pyrder, and Pyrder slid his arm around me when Alaric released me. The demigod followed Reysalor.

Zeus was the God of Sky, Storm, and Lightning. If anyone could stop the storm caused by a god, it was Alaric, the son of Zeus.

I swatted Pyrder's arm and threw it off me. Under other circumstance, I'd have relished being in his sexy arms. Instead, I jumped out of the seat and shot after Alaric and Reys.

"So wild," Pyrder murmured and chased after me. "Just my type."

Before I could squeeze into the pilot's cockpit after Alaric and Reys, the plane stabilized. The pilot stared at the sunlight glinting off the white clouds beneath. "The storm was gone in a blink of an eye."

Some dark force was playing with us.

But at least the storm had passed, even if temporarily.

26

We arrived at Lorcan's safe house several miles from his court in Portland.

I fed him one more time, and then they put him in the healing chamber.

A week passed, and the High Lord of Night still didn't wake up.

I visited him daily. Xihin, the giant vampire who had fought beside Reys, told me that whenever I entered the room, his lord's heart started beating, and when I left, it stopped.

Reysalor, Alaric, and Pyrder had tried everything in their power to bring Lorcan back to consciousness and failed. Fear seized me deeper every day when he didn't awake.

I lost my appetite, and not even chocolate cake interested me. Fortunately, I had Phobos to drink from. And whenever I sipped his godly energy, he sobbed like a baby, which made me feel like an asshole.

If I didn't constantly drain him to weaken him, he'd bring his terror around, which would be bad for everyone, except for him.

I told him that he had no one to blame but himself. He shouldn't have grown so ambitious and gone for a predator bigger than him.

"Don't be too softhearted, Cass sweetheart." Alaric stood at the doorway, watching the drama. "This is war. In war, we do whatever we can to survive. Think what he'd do to you if he caught you instead."

I shuddered at the image Phobos had mercilessly drawn for me in the club. He'd have tortured me, played with me, and even raped me, before he finally handed me to his father as a prize.

"When he fought me, I didn't feel bad kicking his ass," I said. "But I don't like kicking him when he's down and weeping."

"If you don't keep kicking him, he'll rise and go for your throat. That's what he is. That's what the gods are. They're all fucking rattlesnakes."

"That isn't a correct metaphor," Phobos said between his weak sobs. "I wouldn't hurt Cass. Earlier, I was only teasing her, because I felt I'd finally met my equal. Let me go, please.

I swear on my father's life that I won't tell a soul. I'll do whatever you ask me to do. Just name your price."

"You'll never be her equal, douchebag. None of you gods will," Alaric snarled. "Quit sniveling. You're the fucking God of Terror. Act like it!"

He pulled me to him and slammed the door behind us.

Phobos wouldn't be able to break out while he was weak and the demigod's force field warded the house.

"Come, sweetheart," Alaric said, lifting me into his arms. "They're all waiting. We need to talk."

His embrace comforted me. I rested my head on the crook of his shoulder and neck as I let him carry me wherever he wanted. To get even closer to him, I wrapped my arms around his massive, hard torso and the pleasure of his touch rocked me.

He chuckled. "That's my girl."

His large hand held my butt; the other ran through my hair to make me purr.

Ferrying me effortlessly, he exited the reinforced side house and strode toward the even more security-enhanced main house, his gait showing his powerful legs.

"Lorcan's safe house isn't as fancy and sunny like Reysalor's," I told him. "But it's bigger."

The High Lord's safe house was like a military compound, warded and heavily patrolled. Its three domed structures had been planted in the middle of a cloudy desert. There was no lush greenery around. Even so, I felt pure, potent magic beneath me. It felt me, too.

"When Loran gets on his feet, I'm taking you to my home in Sydney. You'll love the city, and I'll give whatever you want in the world."

"I need to think about it," I said.

I'd love to visit Sydney, but I wasn't ready to leave Reys, Lorcan, and Pyrder.

Alaric pulled my face closer to his with his large hand. Just as I was thinking how easily his big hands could crush my skull, he kissed the tip of my nose.

"Take all the time you need, sweetheart," he said, a sly smile dancing in his dark bronze eyes, before he returned my face to rest upon the hollow of his neck, which was really a good place to rest.

His power enveloped me like the winter sun, distant, yet full of immeasurable strength.

The Olympian gods, like the ones I'd encountered, had no magic but pure alien power. Alaric, however, had both power and earth magic. I nudged my nose against his skin to inhale him, drawn by his pure male scent and magic.

"Can't get enough of me?" He laughed, pleased with himself.

That suddenly reminded me of my independence. What had made me lose my mind and let him ferry me like a doll when I had my own strong legs? What happened to the Cass Saélihn who had declared that she'd never be tamed? And now it was too late to save my carefully maintained public image. A few guards, both fae and vampires, had seen Alaric carrying me.

I lifted my face from his neck and wiggled to get on my feet.

"I like you snuggling against me, sweet bug," Alaric said. "Stop fighting me. We're here."

I was now degraded from sweetheart to a bug? I dared not picture the next devolution I'd hear from him.

Alaric stepped into the outer suite of the most secured chamber, where Lorcan lay in deep slumber. The twins, who sat on the vast white couch, snapped their heads in my direction, two sets of turquoise eyes now blazing golden, one pair a shade darker.

"Let me down," I demanded.

"Let her down!" Pyrder also demanded, rising from the comfortable couch and clenching his fists.

Reys appeared more relaxed, and here I thought he would have been more possessive, since he and I had half-mated. But I wasn't fooled by his calm exterior. I'd glimpsed the panther peeking out of his fiery eyes.

"Easy, tiger," Alaric said, and helped me glide down.

I looked around. For the first time, there were no guards, either vampires or fae, anywhere near the perimeter of the suite. And judging from the identical expression on the twins' faces, I'd say there was some serious shit brewing.

My pulse raced with anticipation. It felt like the tension before the storm, but I kept my face blank and my manner cool.

"Come sit beside me, Cass baby," Reysalor said.

I stalked toward him.

"Cass can sit with me," Alaric said. "Since you two have occupied the other sofa. We want some balance."

"Are you really going to keep pushing the button and have Cass all for yourself?" Reysalor grated. "I didn't fight you on the plane when I could have. If you want balance, Pyrder can sit with you."

"Give me a fucking break!" Pyrder said before Alaric could object. "Why should I sit with the insufferable demigod? Cass can sit between us. And that'll be good balance as well."

I braced my hands on my hips and stood between them. "Really? Now you're going to fight over the seating arrangement while Lorcan is still out cold?"

They all looked ashamed for a second, and Reysalor sighed. "We're acting like adolescents around our Cass. For fuck's sake, we're ancient, superior males."

Instead of sitting beside any of them, I summoned a chair with my wind magic. The chair slid toward me until it found the proper place at the head of the coffee table between the two large couches, where the twins and Alaric lounged, facing each other in a glare match.

I sat down, spine straight, my hands planted on my hips to show the boys my determination to get to the bottom of this, though I didn't know what this was about.

"Cass baby," Pyrder said, using his bedroom eyes on me, and my heart stuttered. "We're about to tell you of the pact."

Right, the pact. I hadn't revisited the unfinished topic. I had been too distraught over Lorcan's unimproved condition.

Pyrder raised his eyebrow at his twin, urging Reys to open the box.

"Millennia ago," Reys began, his intense gaze never leaving my face, "the four of us led our species to fight the dragon race when they flooded Earth and burned everything in their wake. We won the war at great cost, and the dragons fled to another galaxy. During the war, the four of us formed the brotherhood. We were bonded, and for it to last forever, we swore that we wouldn't take any mate for us alone unless we found the same mate for all of us. With her holding our bodies, souls, and hearts, we'll always be united. But we've never found the one true mate. Until now. Until you came along."

My hand left my hip and waved in the air. "Fuck," I said. "You didn't have women for millennia?"

Alaric grinned wickedly. "We had numerous women, just not the right one. And none of us agreed on the same woman."

"None of them were our equal," Pyrder said. "And gradually our brotherhood broke and we drifted apart. We haven't seen each other for over a thousand years, except Reysalor and I, because we stay together in our realm. Even when the Olympian gods returned and made Earth their hunting ground, we fought our own wars and didn't want to cross paths due to our shame in breaking our bond. We're proud males. The last we want to see is our own weakness. Until our visions called us to you."

"I had to admit that, for the first time, I wasn't disappointed when I laid my eyes on you in the club," Alaric said, his honey-brown eyes softening.

But my own eyes hardened. My fingers flicked my hair. "What's to be disappointed about?"

"Indeed," Alaric's eyes sparkled. "At first sight of you, I felt a jerk and a tear in my heart. I felt emotions, which had never happened before. At the moment, all I wanted was to make you mine alone. I mulled over the idea of kidnapping you and taking you to my kingdom."

Reys and Pyrder turned their hard glare on Alaric, and the demigod flicked a regretful glance at them. "But I couldn't do it. I felt our bond kicking in with my next heartbeat. It was truly activated, and I knew Cass was our fated mate."

Reysalor nodded. "Both Lorcan and I scented Cass as our true mate when she stalked toward us like a lioness in that cage, even in her unwashed state."

I remembered his shocked expression when he'd sniffed at me. And now my dumbfounded look must have matched his as my mouth formed an O.

"And the primordial vampire's heart started beating for his mate," Reysalor said, his ocean blue eyes roving over me with equal hunger and tenderness. "That's why I couldn't claim you back then, Cass baby, no matter how much I wanted to. I had to wait until the four of us were together with you. You're the woman for all of us."

"Your brought us together, Cass baby," Pyrder said tenderly. "We won't separate again and won't feel so lost with you anchoring us and binding us to you. And when we all claim you—"

I shot to my feet with a shout. "Slow the fuck down!" My hands returned to my hips. "No one is claiming me! The pact between you four was during the age of dinosaurs. I wasn't even born then. Why does it have anything to do with me?"

Alaric had the nerve to quirk a long eyebrow at me. "It wasn't made in the age of dinosaurs, sweetheart. It was the age of the dragons—fire-breathing, nasty creatures."

I glared at him at the correction, my face flaming.

Reysalor sent the demigod a scolding look while Pyrder glared daggers at him before turning to smile at me. Pyrder's gorgeous long lashes batted a couple times. I bet he turned this charm on all females to make their knees weak and get whatever the fuck he wanted.

I stood on my ground, my legs planted wide apart.

"It has everything to do with you, Cass baby," Pyrder said in a honeyed tone. "You're our destined mate, the only female we've ever chosen for all of us."

"You're attracted to us, too," Alaric said almost like an accusation. "Whenever one of us touches you, you feel the

pleasure, don't you? When I carried you all the way here,
you nearly melted. You inhaled my scent deeply because you
couldn't resist your true mate's pheromones."

That was utterly outrageous!

"That's because that cunt Jezebel locked me up in a
fucking cage and I didn't get to touch anyone for over a
decade!" I yelled at him.

Alaric raised an eyebrow again at the c-word no lady
would ever dare say, but I was no lady.

"We'll deal with Jezebel soon," Alaric said with all the
menace in the world.

"When Phobos touched you," Pyrder offered quietly,
"you were so revolted that you nearly gagged."

Each of the four had booted the God of Terror in the face
in the dungeon because of what he'd done to me. The kicks
couldn't do much physical damage to the god but served to
vent their rage and humiliate our captive.

"Really?" I said. "You use Phobos to counter me? He's a
psychopath."

"We're all psychopaths to a degree," Alaric said.

I glared at him. "That's why you don't get to claim me."

"You're not helping, Alaric," Pyrder said through
clenched teeth. "You'll only scare our Cass away. Maybe

you need more practice in talking to members of the fair sex. You seem rusty."

"I never bothered to please anyone until I met my woman, who is in front of me now. I'd do anything to please and pleasure my Cass."

My face flamed furiously.

"You don't want the vampires' touch, either," Reysalor said.

"Are you kidding me? They're fucking bloodsuckers!" I said.

Reysalor smiled at me with patience. "Yet you have feelings for the lord of them. You vowed never to let anyone have your blood, but you feed Lorcan every day."

He had me trapped right there. The heir to Sihde was a most cunning being.

"Because you won't let any of your mates die," Reysalor continued. "And now the vampire beast in him won't wake up unless his true mate calls."

"I called him," I said, fighting back tears. "I talked to him every day. I even sang to him, but he still didn't wake up. I can't be this mate you're talking about."

The thought that someone else could be his—their—mate sent an intense jolt of jealousy and pain to my chest. Before I forced out a rasped breath, I suddenly realized a horrible mistake I'd made. I'd sung Lorcan a lullaby, which might have kicked him into deeper slumber. I should have sung a battle song to get his blood boiling and wake him up. But the lullaby was the only song I knew. I'd often sung myself to sleep when I'd felt unbearably lonely and hopeless in my cage, when there hadn't been a sliver of light in my life.

I darted a sheepish glance at the three powerful males, and their focus homed in on me—not on my guilt but on my response to their revelation.

"Talking about your favorite cake, soap, or threatening him to wake up isn't enticing enough to bring him back," Reysalor said. Evidently, he'd been eavesdropping on me when I'd been with Lorcan, but then all supernatural had superior hearing. I just kept forgetting it.

"Cass baby," Reys continued, his voice beautiful and masculine, "you'll need to call him from the depth of your need."

"I can try again, now that you shared some useful information," I said. I desperately wanted Lorcan to wake the hell up.

"You must call him from your soul, as his true mate," Alaric said.

My eyes flashed darkly. Uncertainty swirled in me. What if I wasn't their mate?

"If and when he wakes up, he'll have to feed from you again," Reysalor said softly.

"Fine." I shrugged. "As long as he opens his eyes."

"It won't be the same way you've been feeding him," Reysalor said cautiously, and all of them watched me carefully as if I might bolt at his next words. So far none of what I'd heard was excellent news, but how much worse could it get? "He'll take control from feeding on you. His fangs will come out and pierce your skin."

I shuddered.

"He won't be able to help it," Reys said. "The primordial vampire in him needs to claim you as his forever mate. He'll be the first of us who bonds with you, under the unfortunate circumstances."

Pyrder growled. Alaric scowled, and Reysalor's eyes flashed darkly. They all looked like they wanted to kill someone.

"What if I fight him when tries to do this caveman claim thing?" I asked, contemplating my exit.

As I drilled it down to the root, the whole claiming mate thing was about him drinking from me and then fucking me.

You give a man an inch and he takes a mile.

"He won't force you," Reysalor said with a sigh. "None of us will ever force ourselves on you, no matter how much we want you, no matter how desperate we want to claim your every inch every second of the day."

Their eyes all brightened with longing, hunger, and lust.

If I weren't Cass Saélihn, I'd go up in flames from the heat in their gazes.

"If he doesn't claim you, he'll withdraw to himself and never be the High Lord of Night, believing his mate rejects him because he's failed to provide for her and protect her," Pyrder said. "Or he'll go mad with self-loathing at being unable to win you."

So, in a nutshell, if I didn't call him to me as a promised mate, he'd be in a coma forever and fade off sometime in the future. If I got him to wake up, he'd feed on me with his sharp fangs piercing my skin and then fuck me. And if I didn't let him screw me, he'd become a nutcase.

Just great.

"I'm still a virgin." I blurted out.

I should still count as a virgin, right? Even though I'd had Reys's big cock in me for half a minute, and Reys had given me a couple of solid orgasms with his wicked tongue and skillful fingers. I darted a quick glance at Reys, and the scorching lust in his eyes heated my blood in an instant.

The males shared a quick grin, as if it was the best thing they'd ever heard.

"We'll all be there to help and guide you," Alaric said gently. "We'll never hurt our one and only mate."

Pyrder nodded. "We'll make sure all the mating is pleasurable and amazing for you."

Reys smiled at me with warmth and assurance. He didn't need to say anything. I knew he'd always protect me above anyone and anything else. All of them had proved that they'd put my life above theirs without hesitation.

"We want to wait until you're ready, Cass baby," Reysalor said. "But Lorcan is running out of time. We're afraid if we don't act soon, we'll lose him forever."

"The four of us shared our bond of brotherhood," Alaric said. "We can feel each other's needs, emotions, and thoughts if we don't put up our mental block. Lorcan has no mental shield now while he's defenseless."

It broke my heart to hear that the once most-feared, formidable High Lord of Night had become so powerless, but he'd fallen to save Reys and me.

"He needs you desperately," Reys said, "but he doesn't know where to seek you. He can't find the surface under the deep water, so you'll have to show him the light."

"I don't get to choose, do I?" I asked softly, yet bitterness tinged my voice.

"The choice is always yours, Cass," Alaric said. "You can deny him. You can deny any of us. But none of us are capable of walking away from you, and we aren't weak-willed males. You're our fated mate, no matter whether you feel it or not. We'll always want you. And now we live and breathe to protect you."

"You all have to choose me because you believe we're fated," I said, somehow feeling unsatisfied and hurt.

"If we don't want you by our own will, no fate can make us want you," Alaric said, his eyes tender and hard at the same time.

"You were forced to live in a cage all your life until we found you, yet you weren't broken," Reysalor said. "When you gazed up at the night sky and laughed, I fell for you right there. Nothing can break you, Cass baby."

"You refused to put up with my crap from the moment I sat next to you," Pyrder said with a grin. "You're the only woman who can resist me and put me in my place. I'm glad fate chose you for me."

"You were caged, starved, and abused," Alaric snarled, "yet you still possess compassion that I'm utterly lacking. Despite your foul mouth and hard exterior, you're a kind,

bright soul. My Cass will make a cold bastard like me a
better man. Though I'm certain most of the time you'll still
be the great pain in the butt."

All they had said were the sweetest, kindest things I'd
ever heard in my life, except the "great pain in the butt."

I fought back tears and a choke as warmth came up to
my throat in waves. My hands still braced on my hips in a
gesture of challenge, but now they shook slightly.

"Don't you want me, Cass baby? Don't you want us?"
Reysalor asked nervously.

Panic marred their handsome faces as they waited for my
answer hardly breathing.

I felt connected to each of them. I'd spent more time
with Lorcan and Reys, especially Reys. But this week I also
spent a lot of time with Alaric and Pyrder, getting to know
them, and getting pulled to them like a pin to a magnet.

The idea of walking away from any of them turned the
warmth in my chest to acid burn.

True mates or not, when Lorcan and Reys had freed me,
when Reys had saved me from Jezebel and the vampire
horde, and when Pyrder and Alaric had put themselves
between the sadistic gods and me, my future had been tied to
these four men.

I studied each male in return, and my pulse soared. Fuck, they were all smoldering hot. My heart pounded at the impossible prospect of having four mates. Could I handle all of them—the hottest, most powerful males walking the earth?

A shift in the wind, and my males' needs, wants, and lust slammed into me. A mystic song started humming in my veins, bringing out heat and desire this world couldn't contain.

Fire lashed at my molten core, stripping off my every pretense and showing me how much I truly wanted them— every one of them.

A premonition played through my mind.

My mates' masculine scent of pine, fire, wine, steel, and ice caressed my senses, delighting me beyond words.

Then Lorcan's sensual mouth traced along the column of my neck and halted beneath my artery. His fangs pierced my skin. I gasped harshly at the pain, but then a hot flood of ecstasy washed over it.

Lorcan drank only a mouthful from me. As I urged him to keep going, liquid fire pooling between my thighs, he shook his head. He gazed upon me as if I was, not his food, but the most precious being to him in the entire universe.

I was his mate.

I writhed against him, rocking my hips against his crotch. His huge bulge made my throat dry and my lips moist.

I wanted his cock inside me now. The fire was too hot in me, only he could cool it down before it burned me to stardust.

Mating fever soared mercilessly in me.

Lorcan growled. His large, powerful hand lifted me and gathered me onto his lap. He heaved up my bare ass, aiming the thick head of his shaft between my plump folds.

Then he plunged me down, and at the same time thrust into my depths.

As his cock thrust wildly in my tight pussy, an assault of earth-shattering pleasure erupted in me.

He thrust and thrust, fucking me with abandon.

I blinked back as the images of mating with Lorcan swirled away. Alaric, Reys, and Pyrder all surrounded me, wrapping me in their arms. I had a hard time telling which arm belonged to whom, but they all had piece of me.

I knew they were all incredibly fast, but I'd been so entranced that I hadn't noticed them moving.

My lust and need for them fused with theirs, endlessly into the blackest night.

I shivered, wet heat soaking my panties.

I turned to look at the oak door—on the other side one of my prospective mates slumbered deeply, and only I could wake him up. Once I turned the knob and entered, everything would change.

I would be different when I came out.

Was I brave enough for that?

My heart beat erratically. I was eager. I was nervous. I was in heat. But I wouldn't know if I was ready until I walked through the door.

- Continue on book 2: A Court of Fire and Metal –

Coming in Oct 2018

Author's Notes

Dear Readers,

I know a lot of you hate cliffhangers, and I've just ended this book at a major one. After a long, heated debate with myself, and after taking into account the structures of the coming books, I decided this was still the right place to end for the first book. However, I plan to publish A Court of Fire and Metal as soon as I can, so there'll be no long wait between book one and two. For the love of Cass and her four smoking-hot mates, forgive my sin?

~ Meg

THE EMPRESS OF MYSTH

Forbidden. Sworn Enemy. Wicked Seduction.

Savage Angels have turned Earth into their hunting ground. To save all earthborn, the Fey princess Rose cedes to the marriage demands of the King of Angels, knowing she won't survive the wedding night. When she comes to Atlantis to find a secret weapon to banish Angels from our planet, she awakens the darkest lust in the king's lethal brother.

The most formidable Archangel comes across the universe and finds her. He will stop at nothing to possess her, even if he must fall.

The High Prince offers Rose an indecent proposal: sleep with him once and he'll protect her from the Angel King. Rose will turn his urge against him and destroy the Angels' house. While unbridled lust burns the prince, it also torments her.

SNEAK PREVIEW

PRINCESS ROSE

I lounged on Seth's enormous bed. His male scent lingered on the pillow, and I pressed my nose against it and inhaled.

His bedroom was more like a luxury hotel than a cherished home. He hadn't planned on staying on Earth anyway. And a valued penthouse wouldn't have so many punched holes on the walls. Such anger. Such power.

The prince was approaching. As soon as I smelled him, I leaned on my side with my head on my elbow and picked up a book.

Seth halted at door, eyes widening at the sight of me. My heart pounded hard, but I kept a cool mask in place and sent him a careless glance.

He lunged at me. Before I knew it, I was on his lap, my sex against his hard erection. It felt delicious already.

I threw my arms around his neck and moved my hips up and down against its impressive length. Just a little fun. The prince let out a low groan, which only made the fire in me leap higher and my blood race faster.

"I noticed a lot holes on the walls." I gestured casually to calm my nerves. "Is that a new trend for angels?"

"I got frustrated," he breathed, his hungry mouth on my neck, tracing down.

I grew breathless at his kiss. He seemed to know my every sensitive spot. "Because?"

"I couldn't have you. You wouldn't let me. I thought I could never get a relief."

I wanted to laugh.

But his mouth was on mine in a second, raw and demanding, as if avenging me for denying him for so long.

At his urging, I opened my mouth to him. I didn't come to resist him today.

His tongue swept over and tangled with mine, holding me captive.

His familiar scent of pine and wine and male musk wrapped around me, telling me that I was forever safe with him. He also smelt of sky and wind and mist. Obviously, he had been flying.

The High Prince of Angels was everything I wasn't.

His lips, hands, and teeth roamed all over my mouth, neck, breasts, inner thighs, and sex. His heartbeat thumped against my palm, then against my breasts. Our limbs were all over each other, exploring and claiming.

I grazed my teeth over his throat, his most vulnerable spot. He hesitated for a heartbeat, then allowed me to keep at it.

Angels didn't trust anyone. They were taught to never show

any weakness.

Having my teeth lingering on his throat was a test. I knew that he had never showed anyone his neck and wouldn't let anyone touch his wings. But he had let me do all those things to him. I had to admit that he treated me better than I'd ever treated him.

The reputed heartless angel had been patient with me. He had protected me and saved me. When he could have claimed his rights to have me, he had let me go.

So today I came to offer myself to him willingly.

My teeth left his throat and traced his strong jaw and nipped his skin.

He liked it.

But I wanted to venture into a more challenging area.

His wings arched behind him, golden with blue dust at the feather tips. Wings allowed the angels to ride the wild wind and soar free in the open sky.

I reached for his left wing, gliding my fingers over its ridge. Wouldn't it be nice if I had a pair? Seth sucked in a sharp breath, a shocked pleasure twisting his once perfect marble face.

As our bodies tangled and our limbs explored each other and our tongues locked, the heat level rocketed higher and higher, and the prince was on the verge of losing control.

He attempted to aim his cock at my entrance and glide in, but I blocked his each try even when I needed it inside me more than anything.

A translucent bead rose from the slit in his crown, and he contemplated it with an amazed expression. I hadn't a clue why he was awed. He had bedded countless females before—this shouldn't be anything new for him.

Unlike me.

When I kneed up, my feet pushing his chest to prevent him for the third time from entering me, he was trembling. He looked like he wanted to shake me, or to strangle me, but he compensated with letting out a half-snarl, which would be scary to others but not to me. A lustful storm and extreme frustration brewed in his grey eyes, darkening them further and further.

I would finally let him enjoy a release, but not just yet.

I knew I was treading on a minefield, and the prince would go off any second now, judging from the wild, savage look in his eyes.

Even so, my instinct bet that he would not force me. Never force me. Despite his seducing, blackmailing, and threatening.

The ache between my thighs was also undoing me, yet I held onto a thin thread of control that could break at any time.

I stalled him for a reason.

I was a virgin. I had never been with a male before. I didn't want to disappoint him, while his lust burned like a firestorm. Before I gave myself to him, I wanted to give him more.

I was going to gift him the fantasy every male dreamt of.

He had earned it. He had put his future in jeopardy to save me again and again.

My elite courtiers entered the prince's quarters and joined us. Their masks made them even sexier, besides gorgeous and mysterious.

They were the most skilled females in the bedroom. I would watch and learn. And today, they weren't my weapons. They were my reward to the High Prince of All Angels. Of course, I'd asked their permission first.

Seth had to be enthralled as breasts bumped and rubbed all around him. The most striking fey females surrounded him, aiming to please.

While he was distracted by a dozen naked, masked courtiers, I had withdrawn to blend in and hide among them.

And I watched.

PRINCE SETH

The masked females closed in on me.

Perfumes filled the room.

They joined me and Rose in bed.

Someone's hands were on my ass, grabbing it, massaging it, and pinching it.

The courtier who wore a green peacock mask had moved to my front, curving an arm around my neck and leaning for a kiss. Her other hand grabbed my hardness.

Another female's hand also held my length. Two soft hands of a different temperature and feel pumped my cock, which was supposed to increase the degree of pleasure.

"It's huge," a female gasped.

"A steel rod," another said.

And then the hands were gone, but full lips wrapped around my shaft and moved down.

I didn't feel any pleasure at their touch despite my cock aching with the urgent need for release.

I cupped the female's cheeks, hard enough for her to stop

sucking me. I yanked my cock out of her mouth, then grabbed the hand that held my heavy balls and removed it from my male member.

I shoved away the two courtiers facing me and looked for Rose.

My wings fanned out and covered my front, so no one would come to grab my cock again. For added security, I let black lightning spark on every inch of my wings. It would stun whoever dared touch me. I had to protect myself from being molested.

The courtiers moved away from me like ebbing waves, respectfully and fearfully giving me a wide berth.

Except for Rose.

She was right in front of me, leaning on the high pillows. She opened her legs, her sex glistening and enticing, waiting for my cock to charge in and enjoy.

"You want me?" She crooked a finger at me. "Come and get me."

This time she wouldn't pull the plug, the eager look in her whiskey-colored eyes promised the pleasure of the world and more.

All I had to do was to drive my cock into her heated channel, and I could finally have her. I could finally fuck her.

But there was one problem.

She might look like Rose; she didn't smell of Rose.

Because she wasn't Rose.

One of the courtiers had the magic of illusion. So clearly, this one waiting for me to fuck her was an imposter.

The courtier with the gift of glamour had disguised Rose and hid her among others.

Rose had brought them in; she'd given me the permission to have any and every female I wanted in the room.

"Will you put out your magnificent lightning please, my prince?" the Rose imposter requested.

Totally not Rose. My Rose didn't beg. She demanded and commanded and ridiculed. She had no fear for my lightning. And she would never call it magnificent. She would use the word "unholy" or "obnoxious" to describe it when she wasn't in a good mood.

I leapt off the bed, my eyes surveying the courtiers for the real princess.

The courtiers sensed my intention and came toward me. A bold one touched my feathers and immediately jumped back, yelping in pain.

Yeah, babes, come touch me again.

Black lightning sparkled brightly on my feather tips.

"If it weren't for your princess's sake," I said, "a touch without my permission would get you killed."

Someone hissed back. It was the real Rose. Panic left me. I'd been worried sick that she had slipped out of the room and that my lamb had gotten away again when I'd been distracted by these crazy, crafty Mysthian females.

I whipped my head in the direction, but the courtiers had all moved like annoying waves. Other than the fake princess in my bed, all others, Rose among them, wore masks.

"You," I said, my chin jerking toward the phony, "get out. You're not the princess. I've seen through your glamour."

The courtiers froze for a beat.

I sniffed. Rose's scent was fresh and vivid. I calmed. "Other males might be fooled by your tricks," I said. "But I am the High Prince of All Angels. So stop your prank."

The fake princess rolled off bed and padded toward me, swaying her hips. She wouldn't give up, would she?

"Come and grab my dick," I warned, "and I'll hurt you."

She halted and studied me, a real interest forming in her eyes. "You can have every one of us, including the princess. You can start with me as an appetizer."

"Thanks, but I'm afraid I have to decline," I said. My arms folding across my chest and my wings enfolding myself for protection, I scanned all the pretty masked faces. "Now, the party is over. Everyone leaves, except your princess. I want only the one who's mine!"

"Good luck then, Prince," the fake princess said acidly. She walked back into the courtiers' ranks and blended in with the rest.

And now there were thirteen masked females in my quarters.

"Find her, then you'll have your true lust," someone

challenged.

I sneered. Like that could stop me.

"You'll have only one chance," another masked courtier said. "Once you choose, you'll stick with the one you pick, and the rest of us will leave."

These damned Mysthians loved to play games!

"You really want to play this game, Rose?" I gritted.

The masked females stared back at me collectively.

I dropped my lightning and grabbed a courtier with a white lace venetian mask and sniffed. "Definitely not the princess." I shoved her toward the door. "One out. Eleven to go."

Before I snatched another to kick her out of the game, a courtier, who had the same sunset-auburn hair as Rose, stepped up and said, "This is not how we play, High Prince. You can't just pick us one by one and sniff us like we are—"

"Yeah, yeah, you're not bones," I cut in. "You're flowers. Yet none of you are that delicate when it comes to ambushing, manipulating, and tricking me."

"High Prince, restrain yourself," the one with Rose's hair said. "Her Highness won't be pleased if you're so rude to her courtiers."

She even mimicked Rose's tone and hit every pitch. I narrowed my eyes. These females were not what they appeared to be under the disguises. I trained my eyes on the bold one and sniffed, then another courtier called, "One chance means you'll get only one pick among us to find the real princess."

"If you blow it, you'll never have her, or me," the sunset-auburn haired female added, drawing attention to herself. She might be the head of the courtiers, or the one who glamoured them all.

I frowned. "Are all fey females this annoying and opinionated?" Then I pointed at her and thumbed toward the door. "You sound like Princess Rose and even have her hair color, but you're definitely not her. Out."

She shrugged. "Are you sure, Seth? Your next pick will be your final."

My nostrils flared.

Her scent, jasmine of night sky and her unique arousing female pheromones sang to me. No other scent could cover hers. No other scent could top hers. Even if I was blind, I would still single her out amid millions. I also smelled my own scent on her. It gratified me that my scent had already marked her as mine.

I followed our joined scent to a quiet female who wore a jeweled mask with blue diamonds. She stared back at me blankly.

I strode toward her. She didn't back off, but she was holding her breath.

All of the courtiers stood very still. No hush, no laughter, and no mocking. The complete silence was bliss. They just watched.

Rose's scent sang loudly and joyfully, beckoning me forward.

I couldn't see her expression beneath her mask, but I heard

her erratic heartbeat.

That was my Rose. She was waiting for me. I had passed the test. This fucking, frustrating game was over.

My black lightning flared on my wings in victory, reaching for the true princess.

The courtiers lunged to me. "Don't hurt her!" they called.

"Step back, wenches," I snarled. "I won't hurt her."

The courtiers stopped short as my wings came around and cocooned Rose; my lightning trailed along her face, neck, and arms, caressing and adoring her.

I trapped her inside. I wouldn't give her a chance to vanish into the thin air. Who knew what those crazy females would do next. "Only the real princess can touch my lightning unharmed," I declared, grabbing her waist and pulling her against my hard body.

Rose, who wore the blue jeweled mask, clasped her hands behind my neck, not protesting my hardness sticking against her belly. She gave me a sly look. "Are you sure I'm the one you want, High Prince?" she purred. "Careful of what you choose. Once you pick, there's no turning back."

"I can sniff you out even if they hide you among an army of millions on the bloody battlefield," I scowled. "Even if you flee to Earth's farthest corner, I'll still find you. And Princess, don't forget my scent is all over you."

She smiled, but I didn't feel even slightly amused.

I'd been sure that I finally got to fuck her, and then all this drama wheeled in and hit me in the face. I grew weary.

My cock was steely hard and ached so much. I was going to explode if she pulled out another stunt.

Rose snapped her fingers behind my neck, and I jumped. Until I saw that she wasn't going to trick me but instead, her glamour fell off.

She wore no mask but a white gown.

"You found me, Seth," she whispered in delight.

"Of course," I snorted. "Why should it be a surprise?"

"I thought you'd appreciate my generous gesture," she said. "I was offering you the best females who know every trick in bed. And you can have all of us. Isn't that every male's fantasy?"

"Been there, done that. The fantasy sucked." I barked a dark laugh. "And I'm not every male. My deal is with you. You can't just shift the package at the last minute!"

She rolled her eyes. "I remember that you said you wouldn't hold me to my part of the bargain anymore. You gave up your rights to claim me. You said I was free."

"I said all those things and meant them," I said. "But then you had to come back to seek me out and toy with me more, as if my past torture wasn't enough. And then you decided to dump me to your courtiers as if I meant nothing to you. One does not taunt me like that—" I swallowed the rest "—still got to live to see the light."

"I wasn't teasing or taunting you, Seth," she said. "As I said, I was offering you the fantasy every male dreamed of. You can have me. You can have us all."

My wing swept toward a courtier and brought her to our circle. "You want me to fuck her before you?" I cupped the female's breast, my eyes never leaving Rose. I wanted to see her reaction. "You want me to fuck all of them?"

A dark light flashed by her eyes before she put on an emotionless mask. How I wanted to tear her mask off and grind it to dust with my bare hands.

"As you wish," she said, her arms loosening from my neck. She stepped back to put distance between us.

"When did you start to care what I want?" I asked, letting go of the female courtier. I didn't even pay attention to which one I'd grabbed.

Rose placed her hands on her enticing hips. "Are we going to stand here and quarrel for the rest of the day? Decide, Prince. I have better things to do."

"Fine," I said with anger. "I'll fuck every one of them except you!"

I was beyond fury that she would share me. Then I squinted in puzzlement. I had never had an exclusive sexual relationship with any female before. Why was I so upset that the princess didn't want exclusiveness? If any angel heard about this, they would laugh to tears, supposing they could believe it.

"Fine!" the princess said. "Enjoy yourself."

She turned to leave, but I lunged, grabbing her shoulders, and my wings formed walls around us again. "You're not going anywhere, Princess!" I said. "I'm not done with you."

The courtiers closed in on us, ready to defend their princess; some of them produced daggers that could cut into an angel's flesh. I could kill them all with one strike. They knew that, yet it didn't stop them.

Those seductresses had shifted to warriors, no longer soft and sexy. Menace and hatred rolled off them. The days with my brother had taken a toll on them. Rose sensed that too.

"I'll be fine," she called. "The High Prince won't hurt me." She turned to me. "Are you going to force me, Seth?"

"You still ask me that after all this time with me?" I asked.

"Then let me go," she said.

I withdrew my hands and wings. I had never felt so deflated and defeated in my long existence. The universe really hated me. "Go as you desire." I sighed. "Send the word when you're ready and I'll deliver you to safety. The wedding is in three days, so you'd better decide tonight."

Instead of walking away, the fey princess stepped toward me and pressed her palm against my face. "Seth, you're too frustrated to think straight. You misunderstood my intention. I wouldn't taunt you after you put your own future in jeopardy to save me." She swallowed. "I thought this is what you wanted. You have a reputation. You once had over a hundred females in one night. You broke the record of all males."

I had been drunk with the strongest angel brew that night, for I had long since lost a sense of myself and all dreams and visions. I had fucked non stop to rip out that unbearable cold abyss inside me. I'd known then that soon I would turn to unfeeling, so I'd fucked every female and everything that moved in the room to feel something. That night I had turned into the living dead when I'd been inside the females.

After that night, I hadn't been able to feel anything, not even the ripple of time, until Rose came to my life.

"That was before I met you," I said. "I'm now even more doomed than I'd ever been. You just broadcasted my secret that I can only have a hard-on for you, but you'll never let me have you. I'm cursed through and through. This unbridled lust boils in me like poison and it will never leave my veins."

Rose winced, and I noticed that my hands on her arms had tightened to an iron grip. I at once released her. "Sorry, Rose. I didn't mean to hurt you. I'll never hurt you. But I don't want to share you, and I hate it when you don't care and want to throw me away like I'm yesterday's meat."

"Such temper," Rose said.

The courtiers watched quietly. I'd shown my weakness and vulnerability in front of them all. Look what Rose could make me do.

"Is it so wrong that I want only you?" I asked quietly.

"No, Seth," she said, brushing her thumb over my mouth.

The pleasure from her tender touch expelled some of my dark anger and angst.

It pained me that I still wanted her so much. I still wanted her more than anything in the whole universe.

Rose tilted her chin toward her courtiers. They bowed and filed out of the room.

No one spared me a second look, but one of them closed the door behind them.

Her hand laced in my hair, and Rose pressed her lips against mine. As I demanded she open her mouth, she obliged and let her tongue dance with mine.

"No more games?" I rasped against her lips.

"A favor then?"

"Please, no more fancy ideas."

I wanted her. I needed her. I had to have her now, or I would go supernova.

I moved her gown up to her waist, and she wrapped a leg around my thigh.

Her pink, plump petals parted for me.

I exhaled.

Wasting no time, I held the crown of my hard cock, placed it against her entrance, and shoved into her tight sheath.

Finally!

She gasped. Her eyes widened.

Mine! My primal male instinct roared as I drove home with my first thrust.

Mine!

More Books by Meg Xuemei X

EMPRESS OF MYSTH SERIES

Angel's Forbidden Lust
Angel's Indecent Proposal
Angel's Fated Mate
Angel's Storm Magic

THE WAR OF GODS SERIES

A Court of Blood and Void
A Court of Fire and Metal
A Court of Ice and Wind
A Court of Earth and Ether

THE FIRST WITCH SERIES

The Dragonian's Witch
The Witch's Consort

TRUE MATE SERIES

Claim the Wolf King
Claim the Leopard Princess
Claim the Vampire Consort

THE CURSED DRAGON QUEEN & HER MATES

The Fury Queen's Harem
The Dragon Queen's Harem
The Fae Queen's Harem

DARK CHEMISTRY SERIES

The Siren
The Prince
The Red Queen

THE WICKEDEST WITCH SERIES

Wicked Witch
Dark Vampire
Fallen Angel

The Girl Next Door: A Small Town Romance

Claim the Wolf King received the
2017 SFR Galaxy Best Dare award

"The story is a fun combination of supernatural and science fiction with strong characters and a wicked love story. This book packs a punch." - Recognizing the Standout Books in Science Fiction Romance - SFR Galaxy Award. ★★★★★

About the Author

Meg Xuemei X is a USA Today bestselling author. She writes steamy paranormal and sci-fi romance. She finds it dreamingly delightful to be around drop-dead gorgeous alpha males who are forever tormented by her feisty heroines, formidable alien angels, wild shifters, haughty fey, dark vampires, and cunning witches.

She's visited the universe of The Empress of Mysth, The First Witch, and Dark Chemistry. Next she'll boldly go to the badland of The Wickedest Witch. At this moment, in her southern California abode, she's packing as many forbidden weapons as she can carry. Her favorite one is a magical whip.

She is always happy to hear from readers and welcome new friends on Facebook.
Email: megxuemei@gmail.com

She'll be giddy if you sign up to her mailing list to hear about her new release, discounts, giveaways and fun stuff!